WEBTOON

THE OFFICIAL

CURSED PRINCESS CLUB

COLORING BOOK

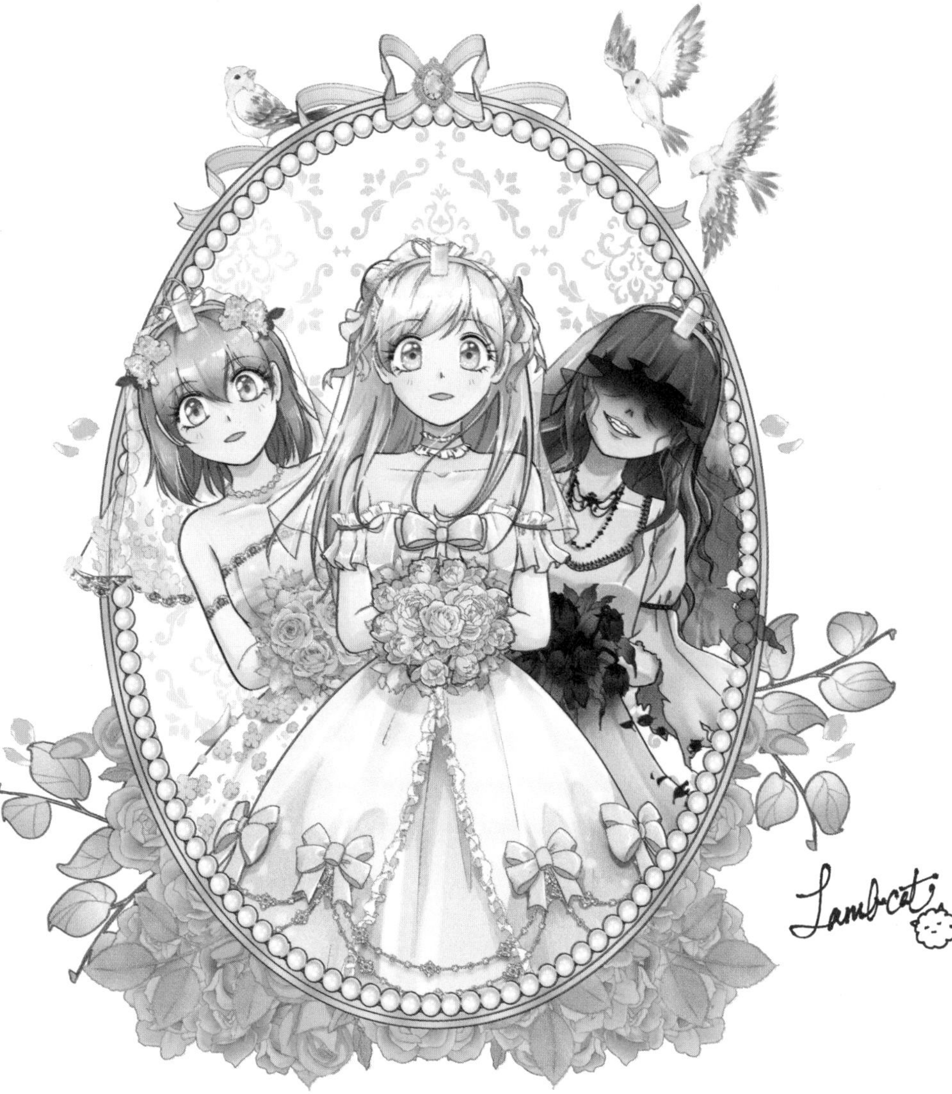

Lamb-cat

Walter Foster

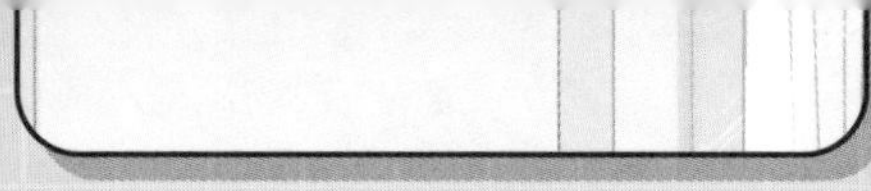

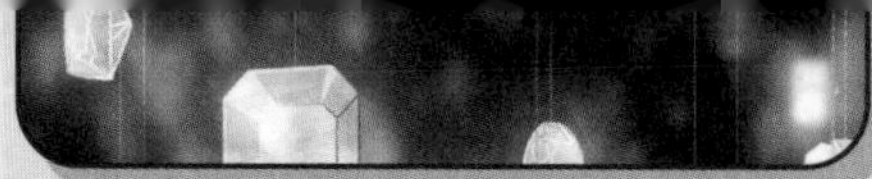

INTRODUCTION

Just because you're cursed doesn't mean you're not special!

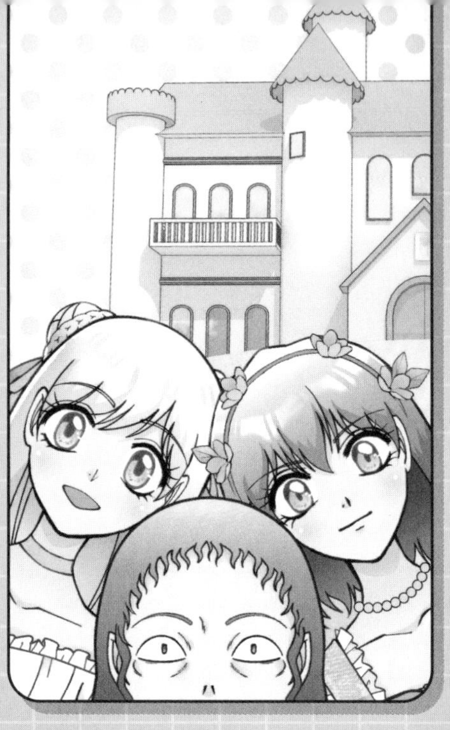

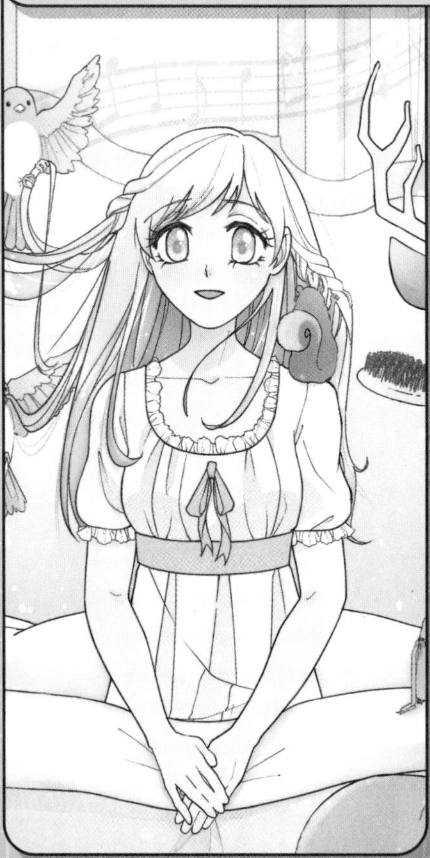

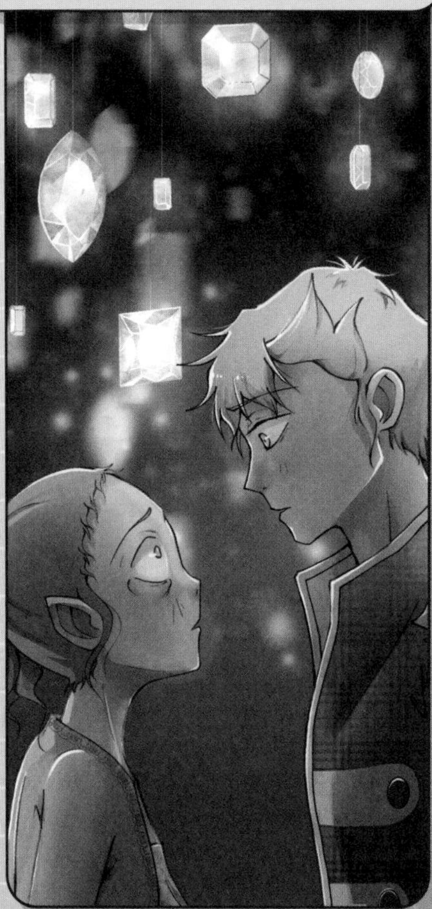

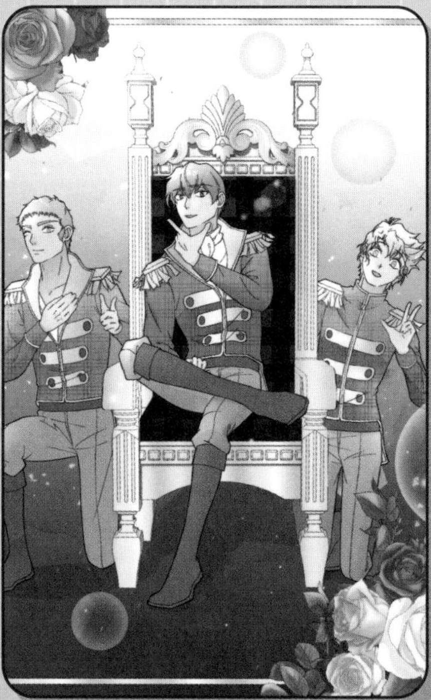

Get ready to immerse yourself in the hilarious world of the WEBTOON Originals series Cursed Princess Club, a webcomic about a young unconventional princess, her journey of self-exploration, and how she stumbles upon a secret club she never knew she needed.

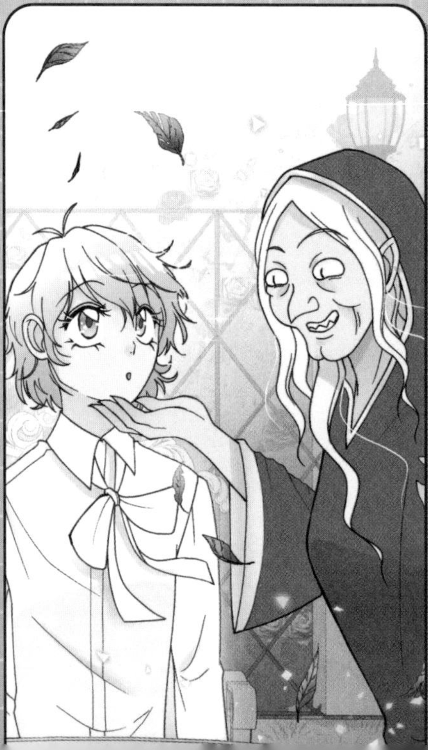

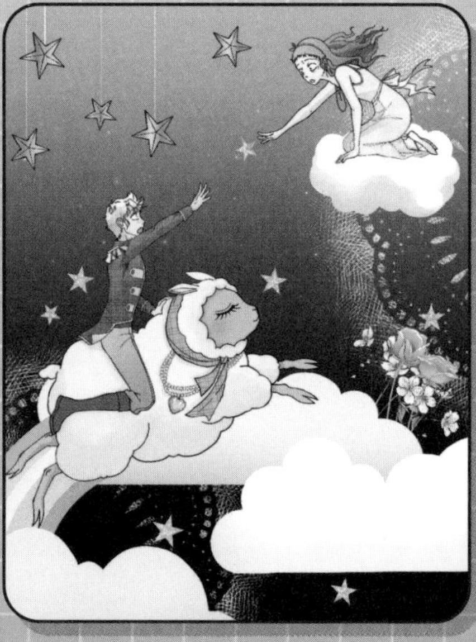

What Is Cursed Princess Club?

The Cursed Princess Club series follows the story of Gwendolyn, an unconventional fairy-tale princess who accidentally stumbles upon the twisted world of the Cursed Princess Club, where she meets other princesses who have been hexed and cast out of their kingdoms. Gwendolyn is living proof that princesses don't always have it all!

Check out the latest episode of the hit WEBTOON series!

SYNOPSIS

The beautiful Pastel Kingdom is home to an equally beautiful royal family. Princess Lorena is so gorgeous that flowers bloom around her. Princess Maria is always surrounded by helpful woodland creatures. Prince Jamie's popularity and heart have made him a royal treasure. And then, there's Gwen. With her sickly green skin and her fanglike teeth, to say she doesn't quite fit the mold of her family would be an understatement.

Despite this, Gwen's family has always been loving and protective of her. It's not until the sisters are betrothed to princes from a neighboring kingdom that Gwen begins to understand just how different she really is. Thankfully, she's not without help. Gwen soon discovers the secret CPC—the Cursed Princess Club—a group of outcast royalty who might be exactly what she needs to learn that not fitting the mold doesn't make her any less of a princess.

Note from the Creator

I've always loved coloring books since I was little, so I'm over the moon for you to color this and make it your own!

There are many ruffles, bows, and other intricate details, so you may want to sharpen your pencils and crayons. But as you might expect, the Cursed Princess Club is all for coloring outside the lines!

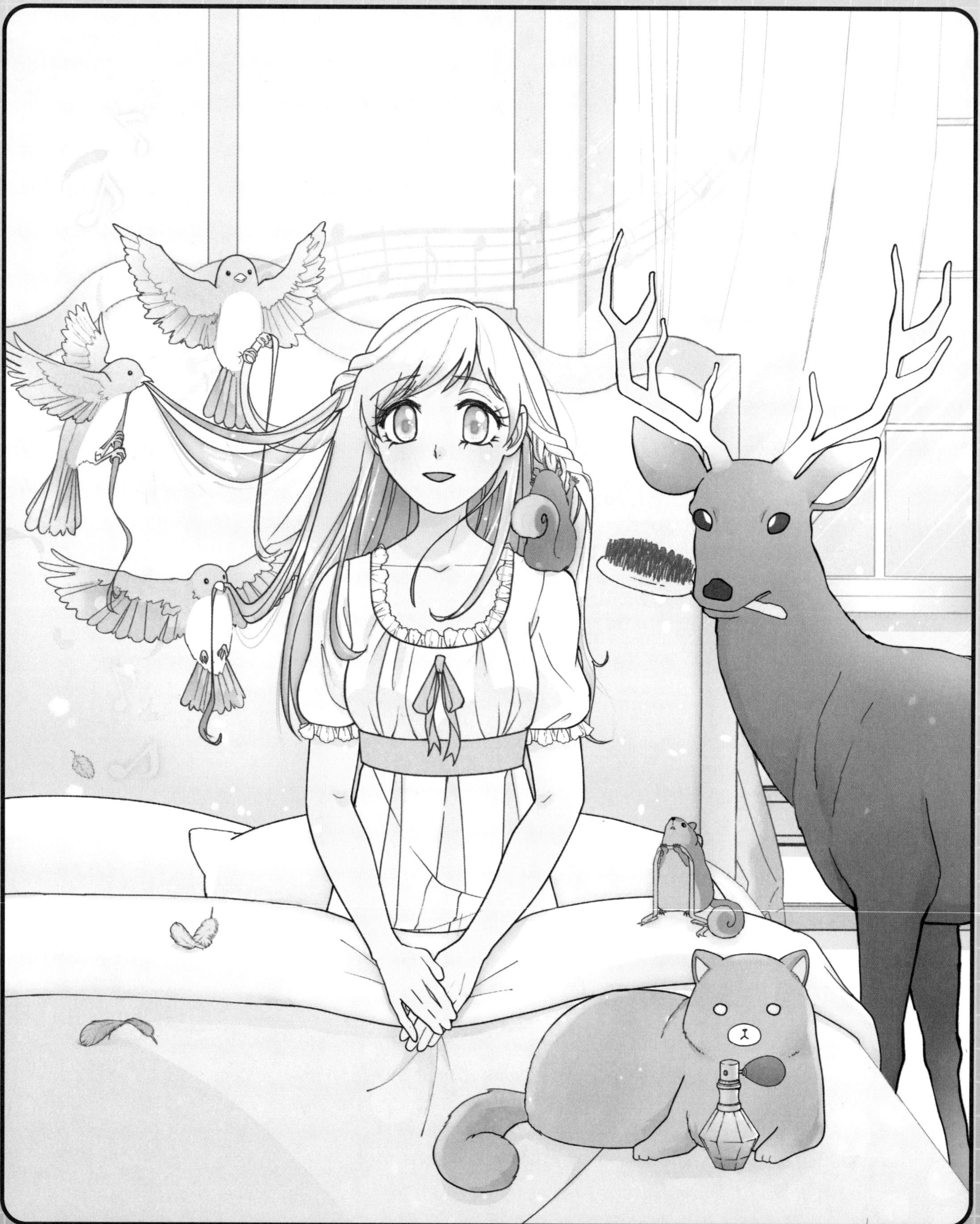

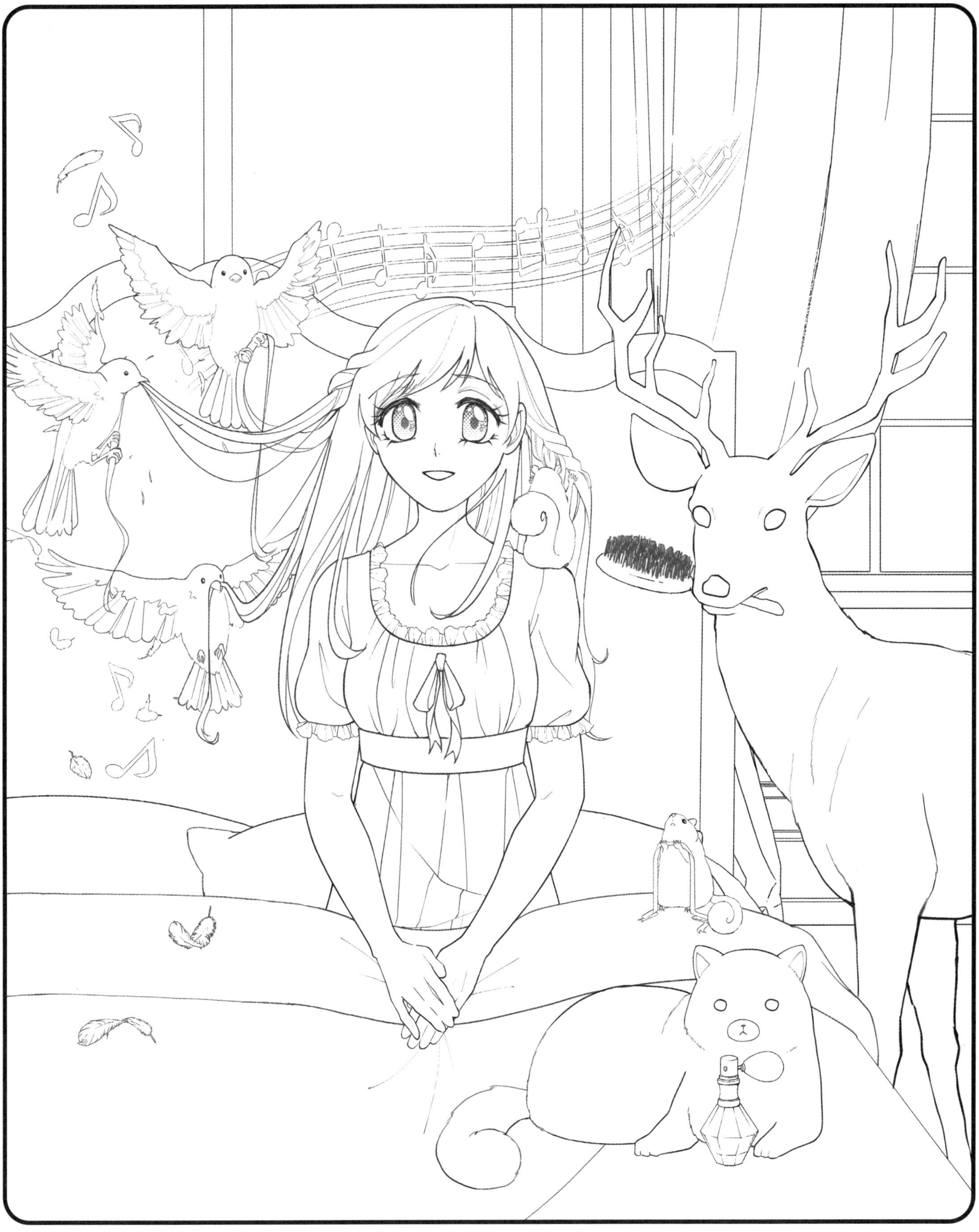

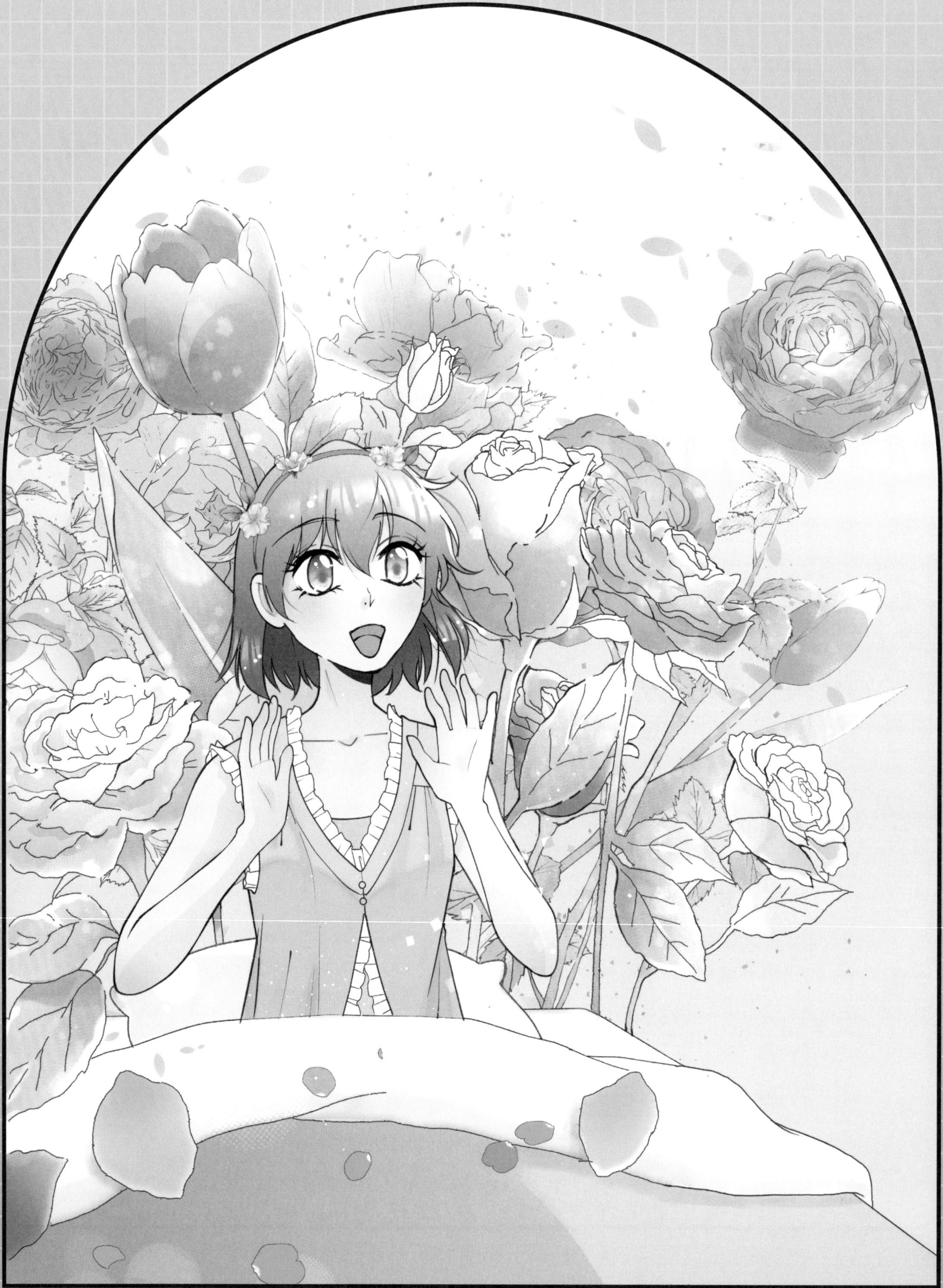

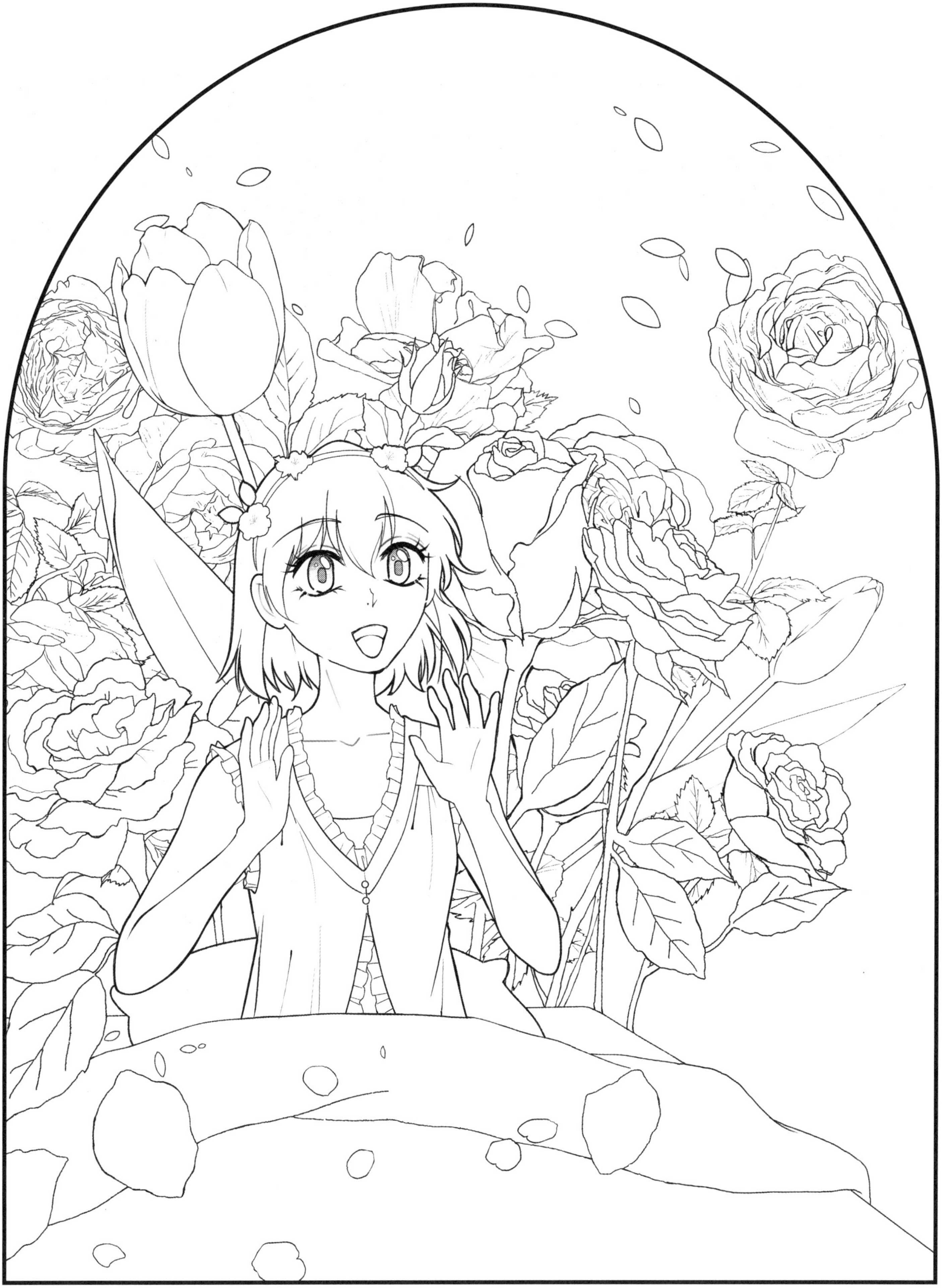

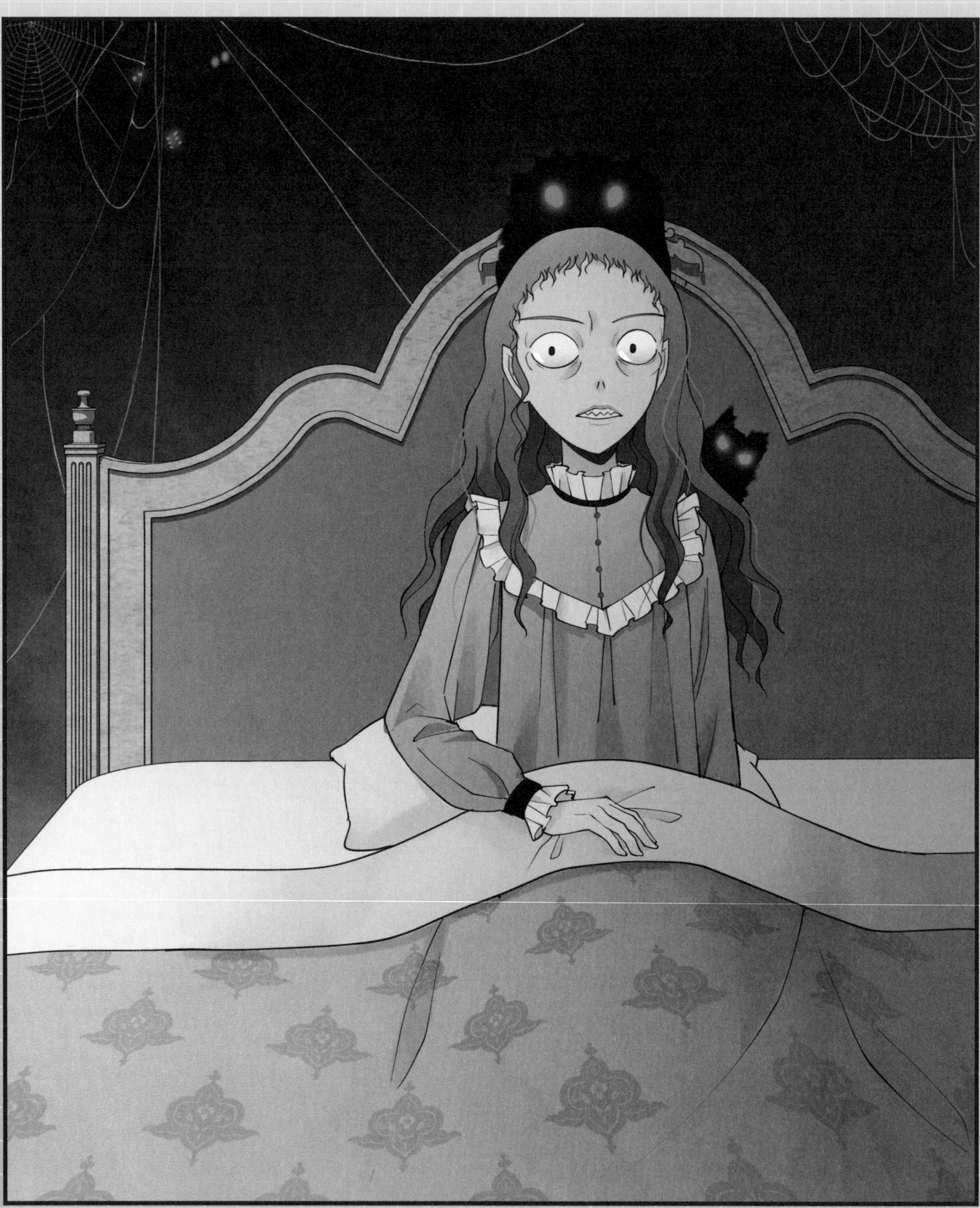

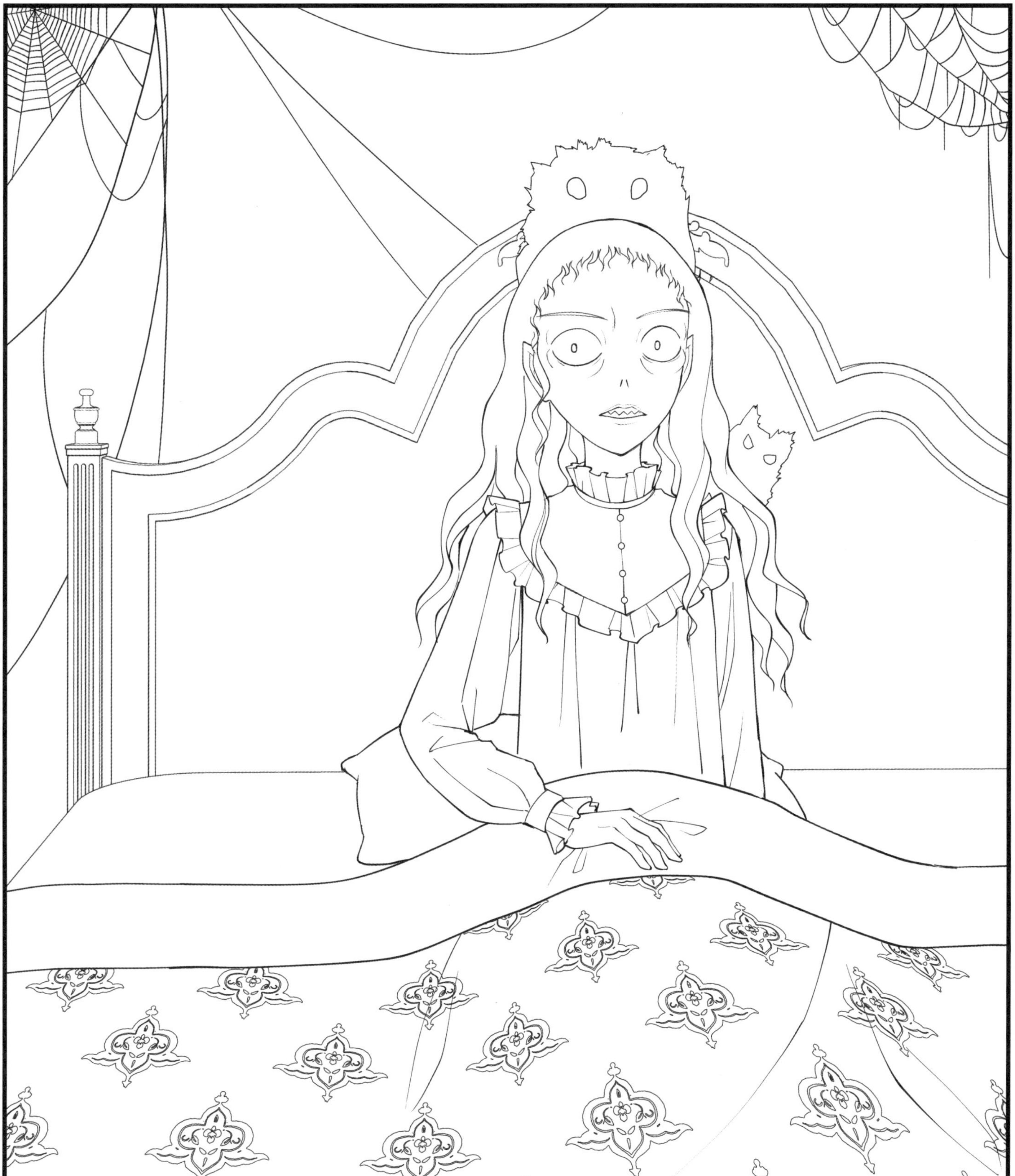

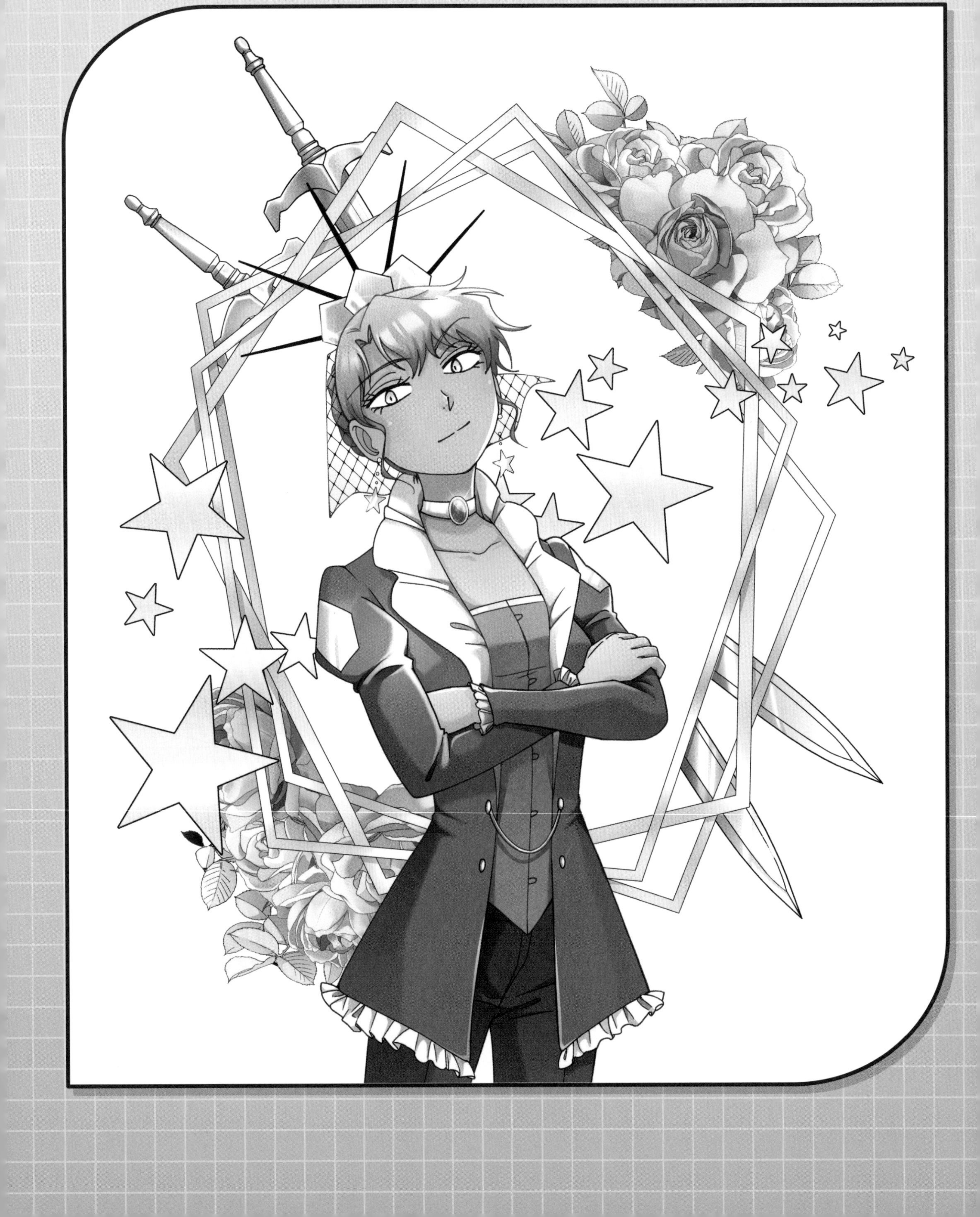

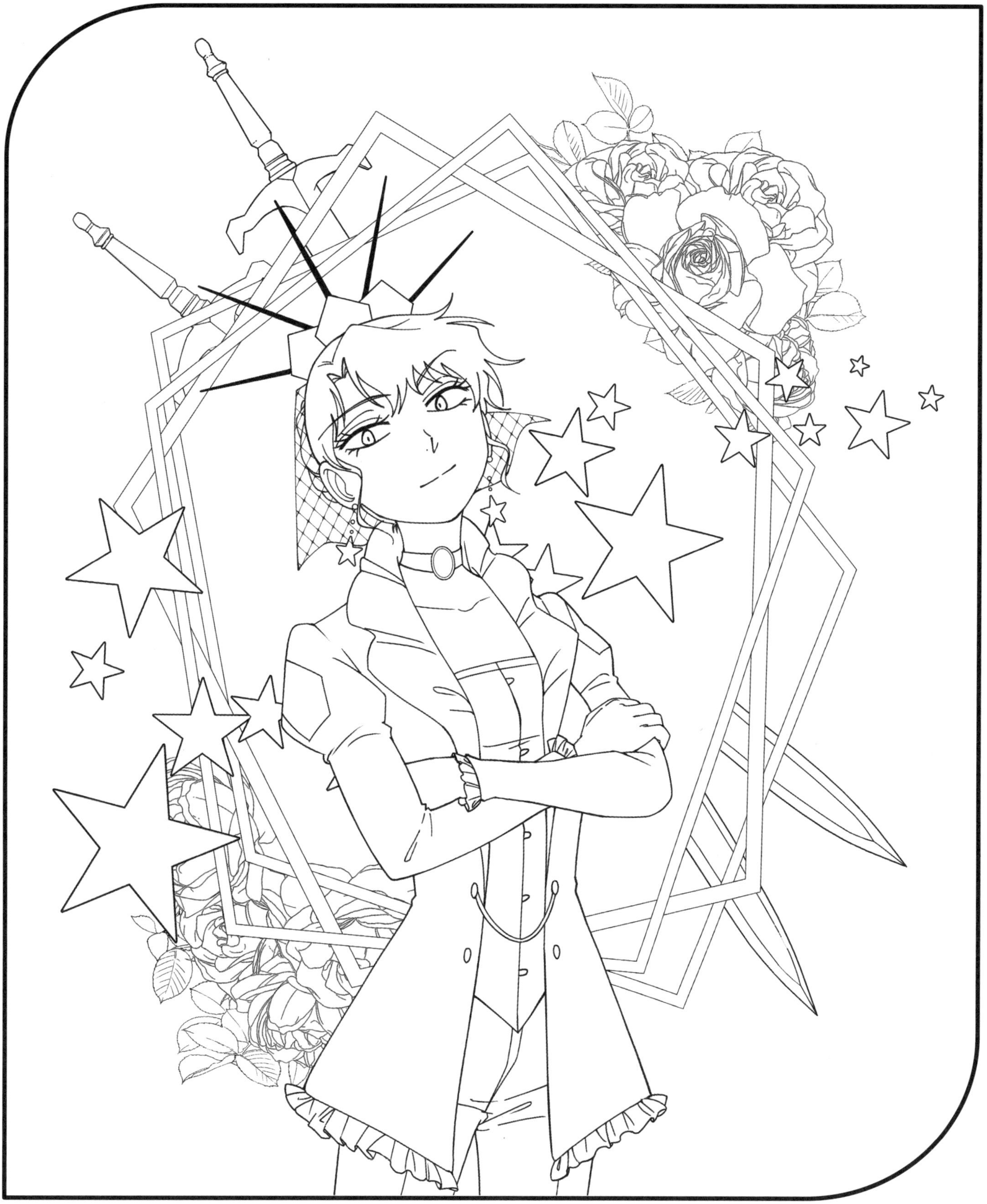

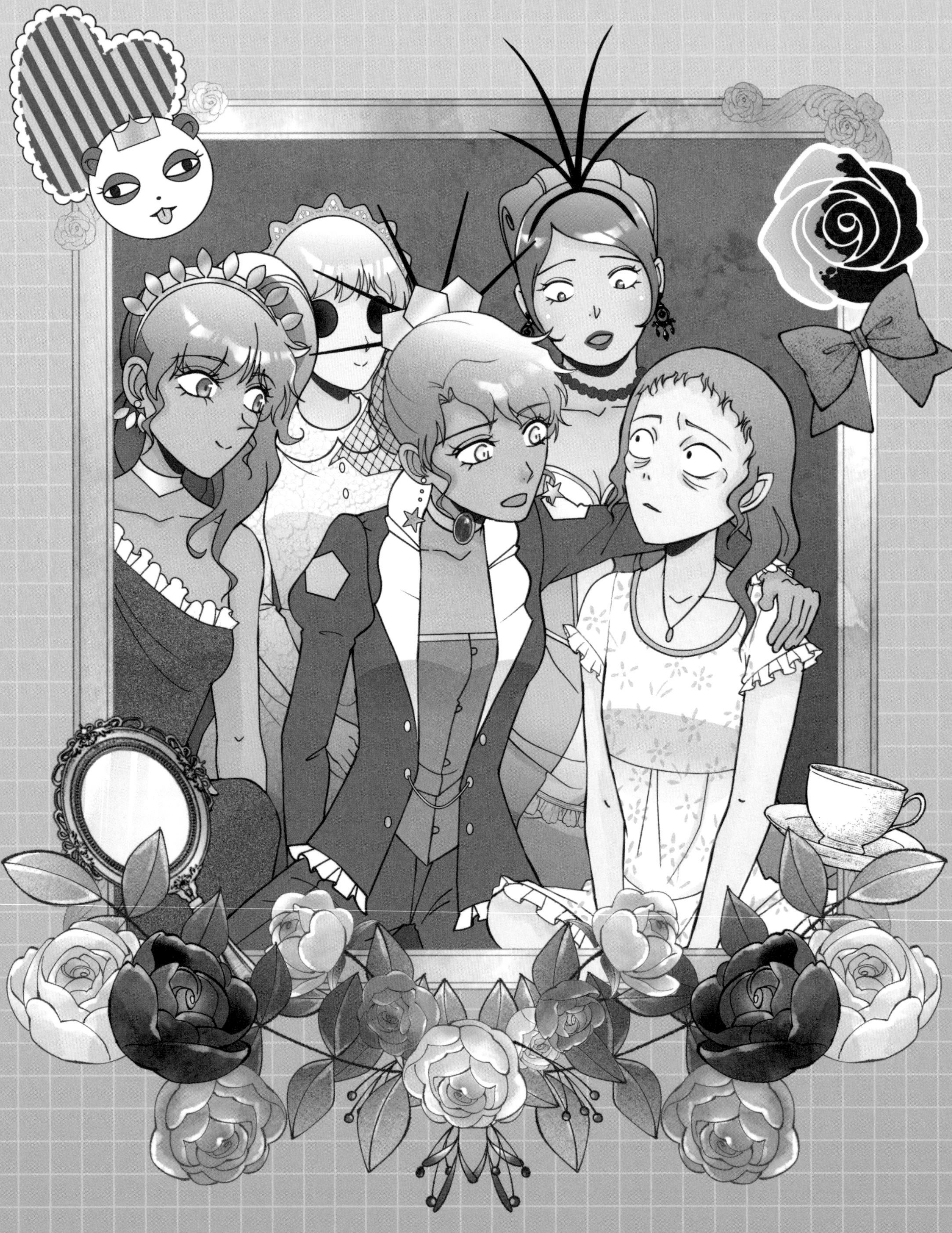

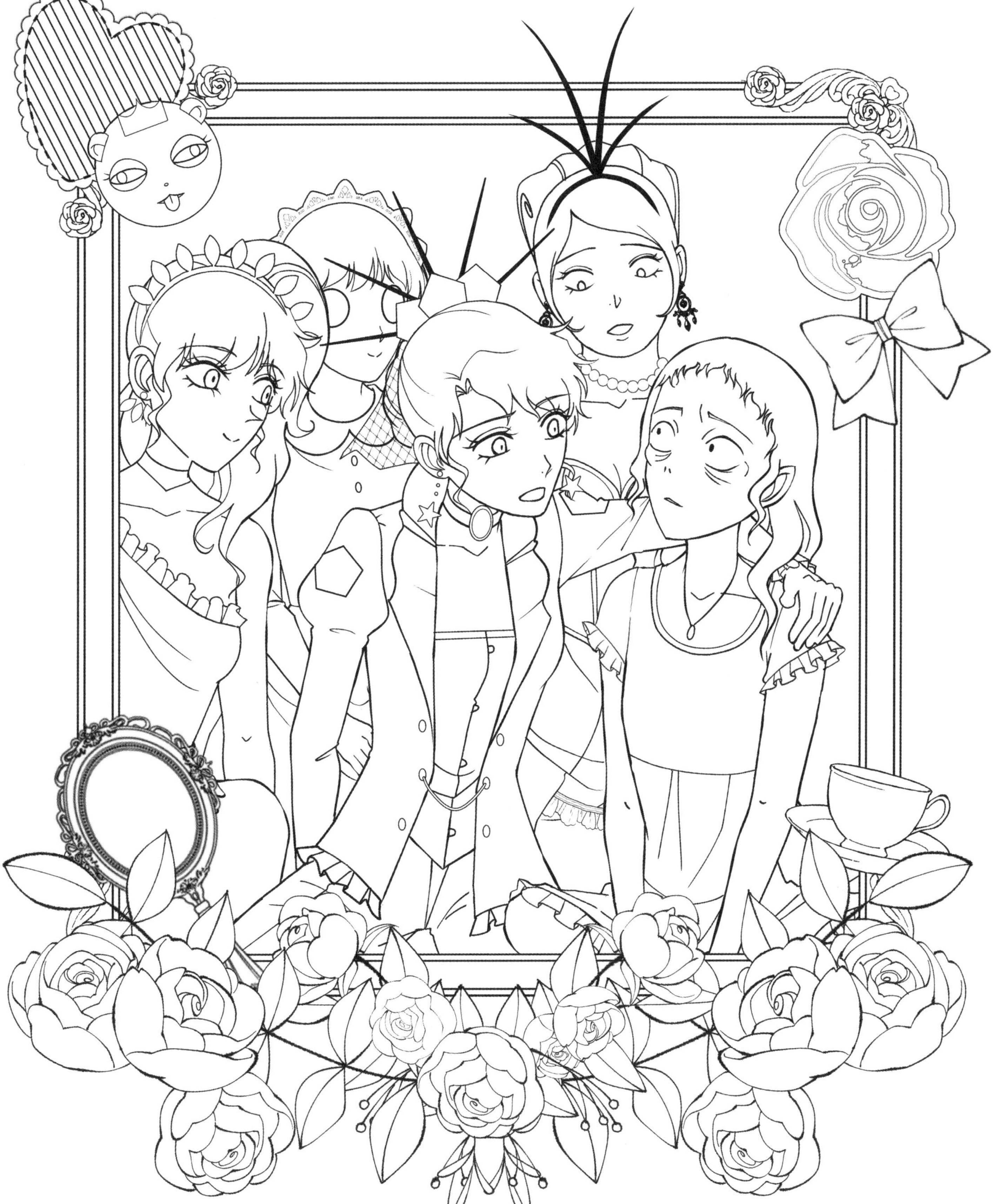

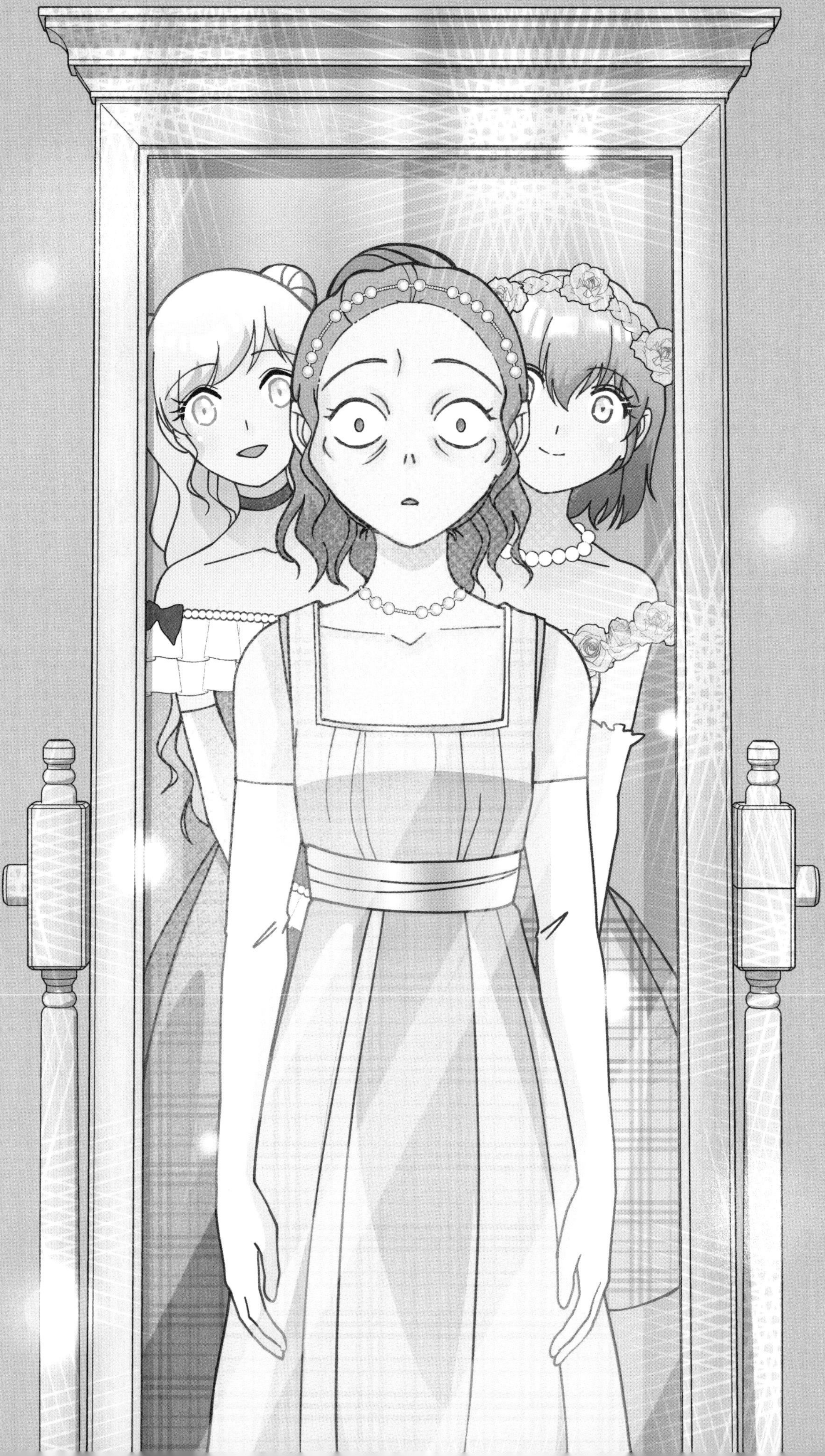

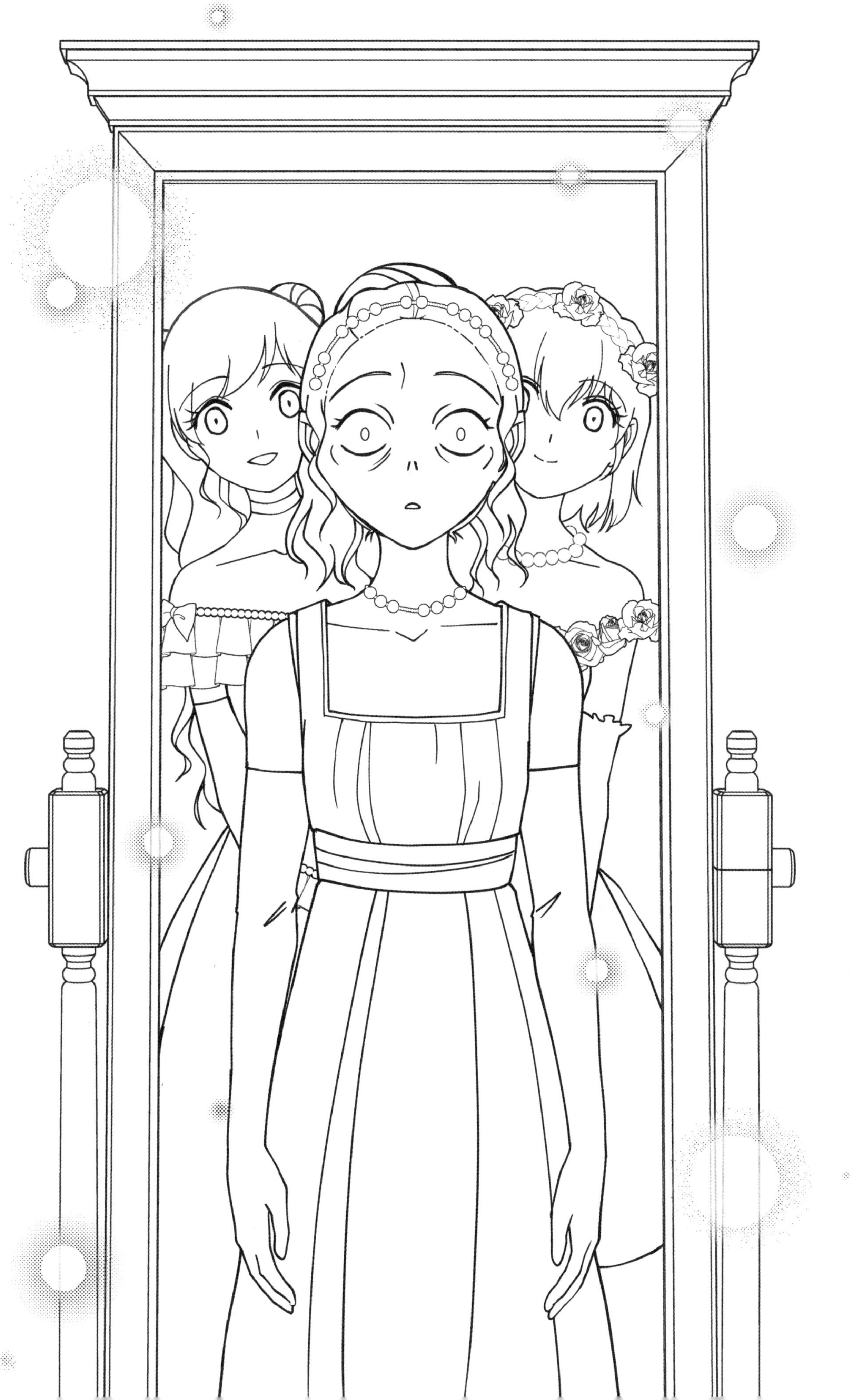

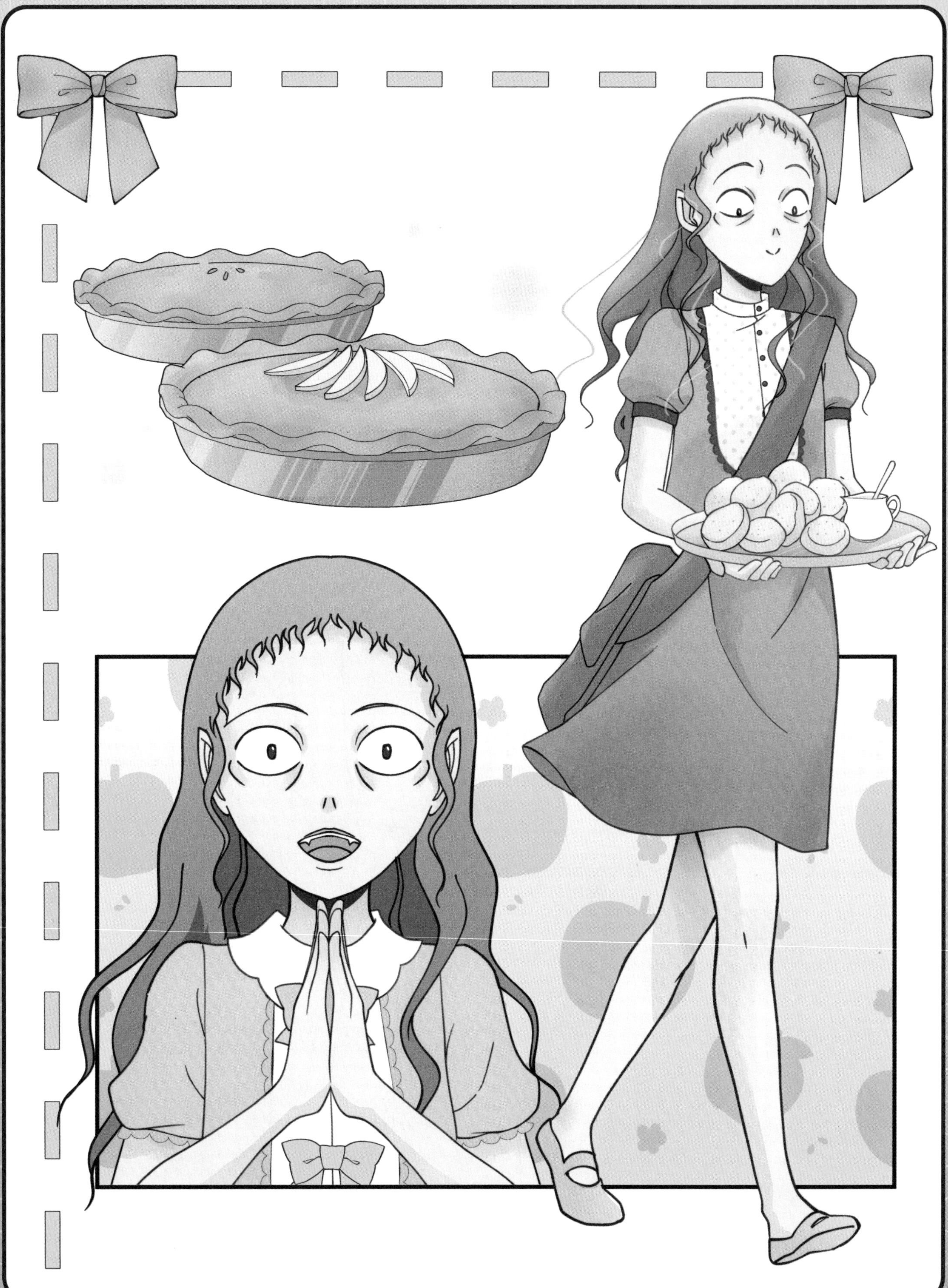

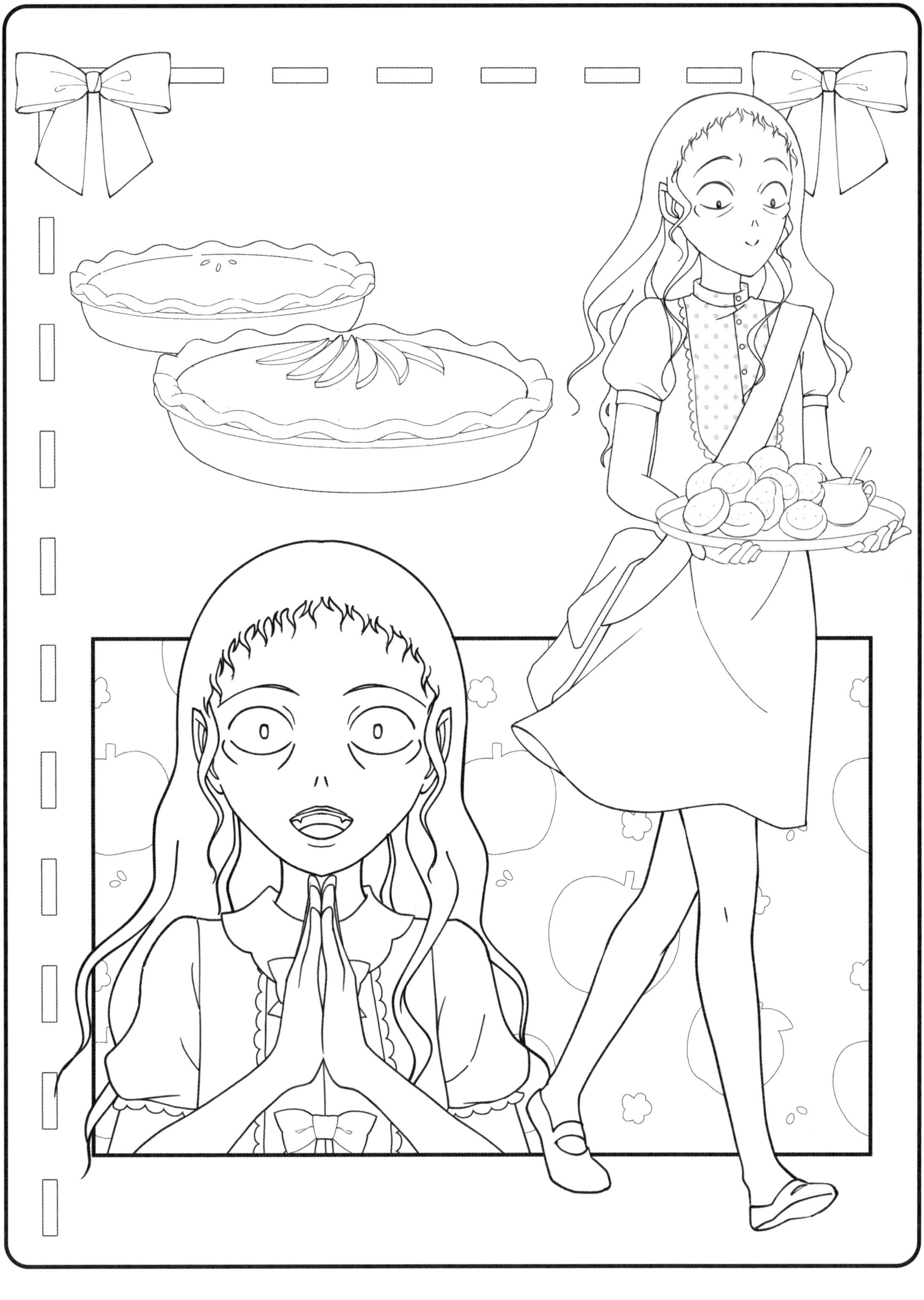

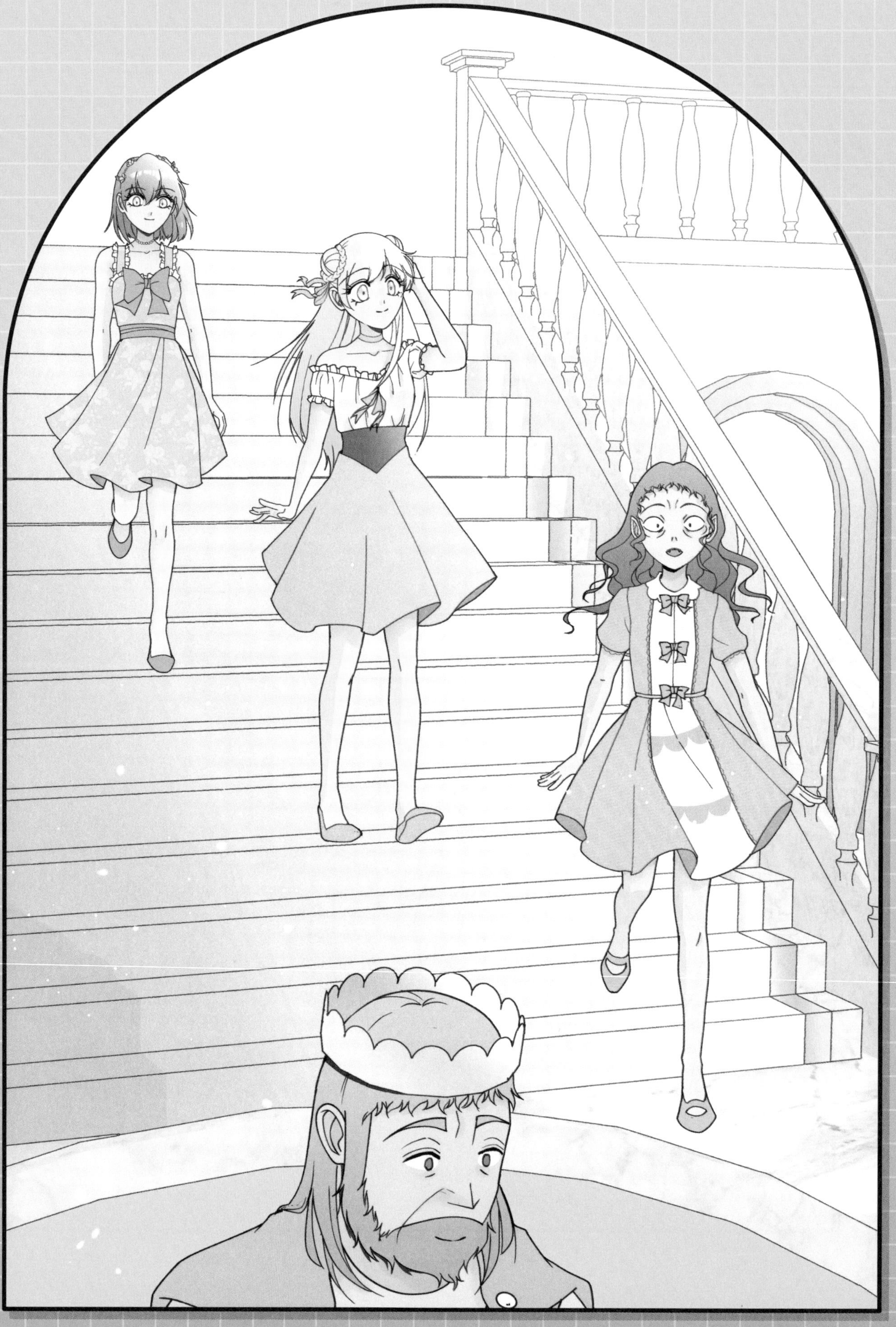

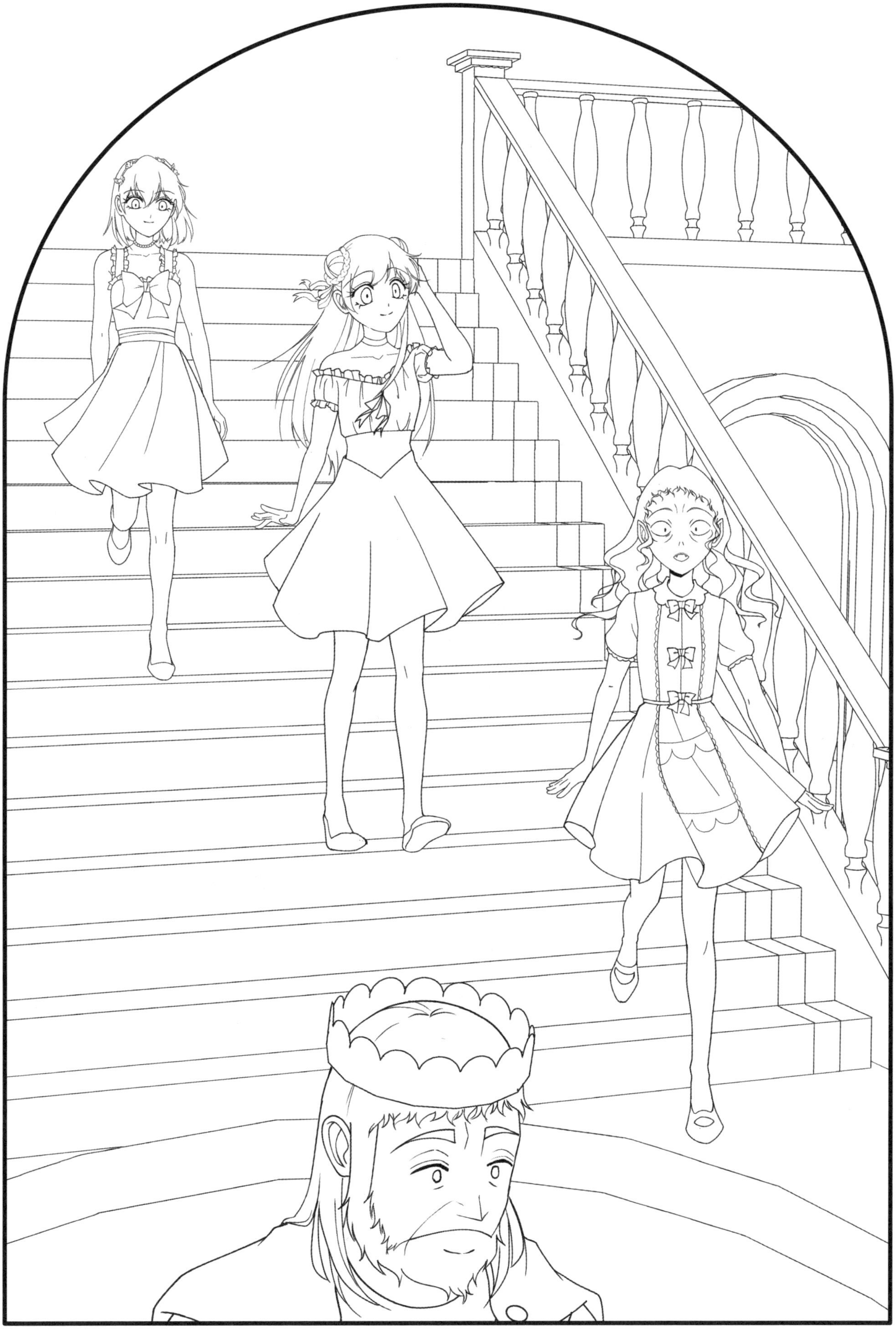

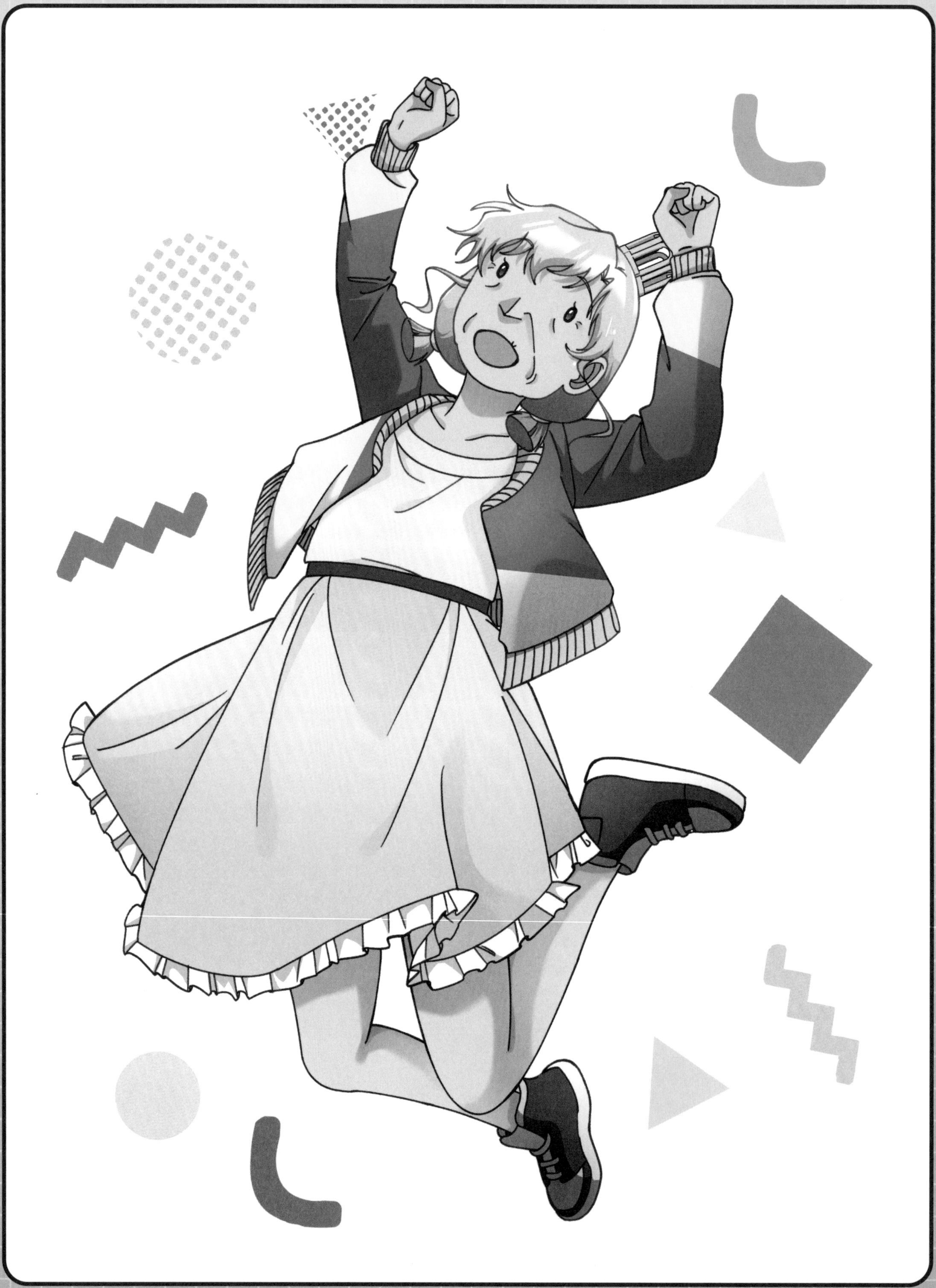

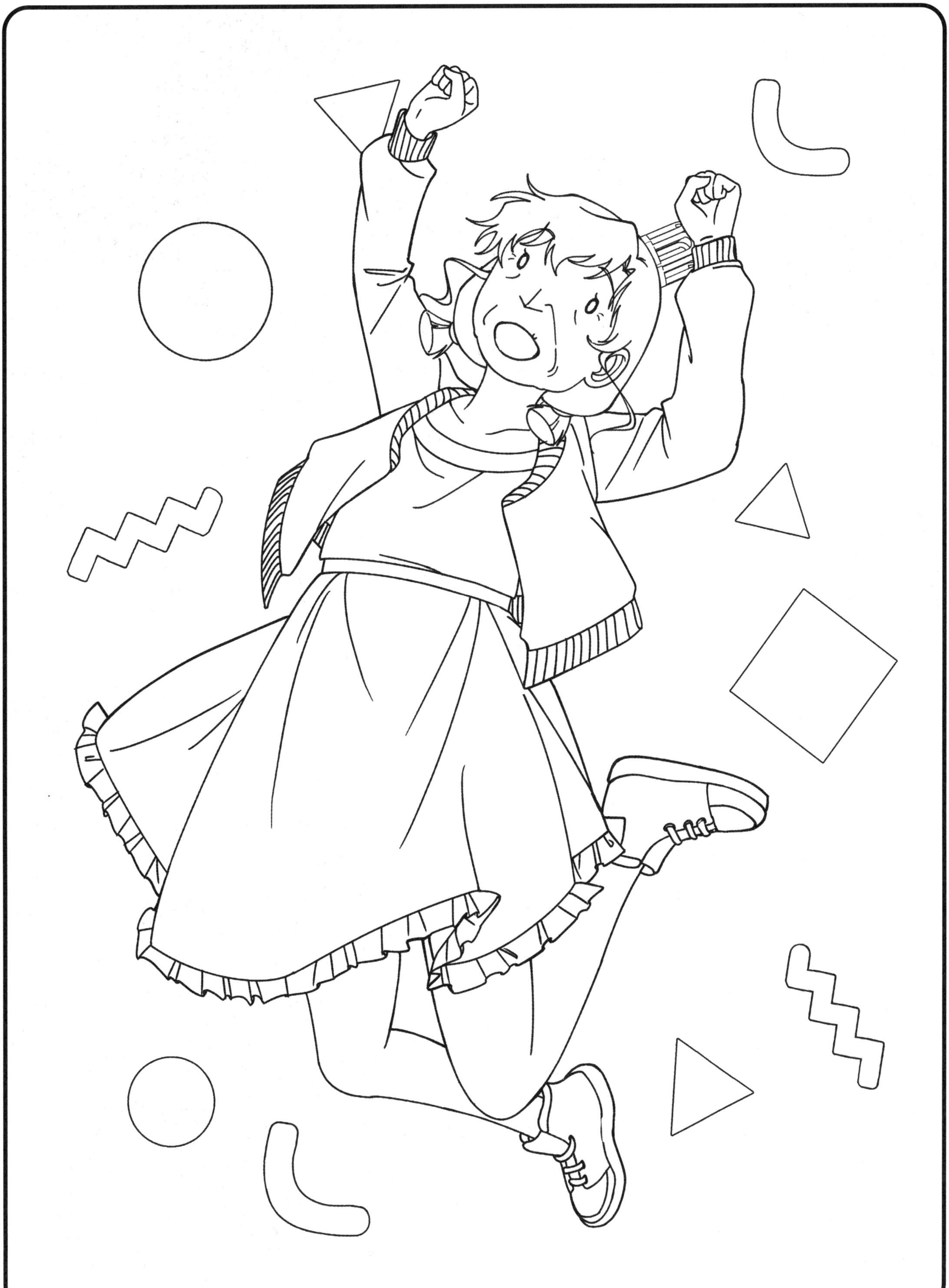

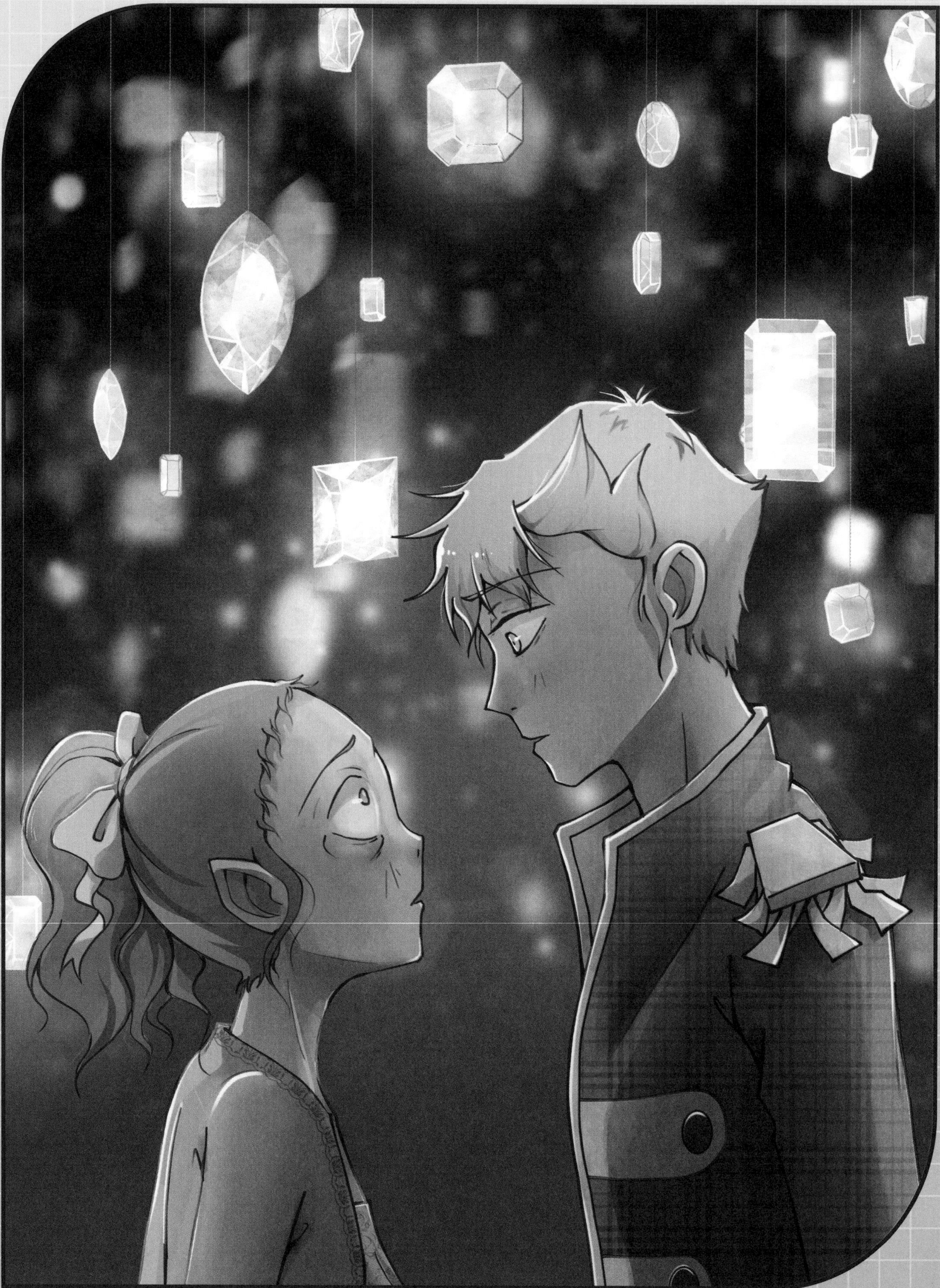

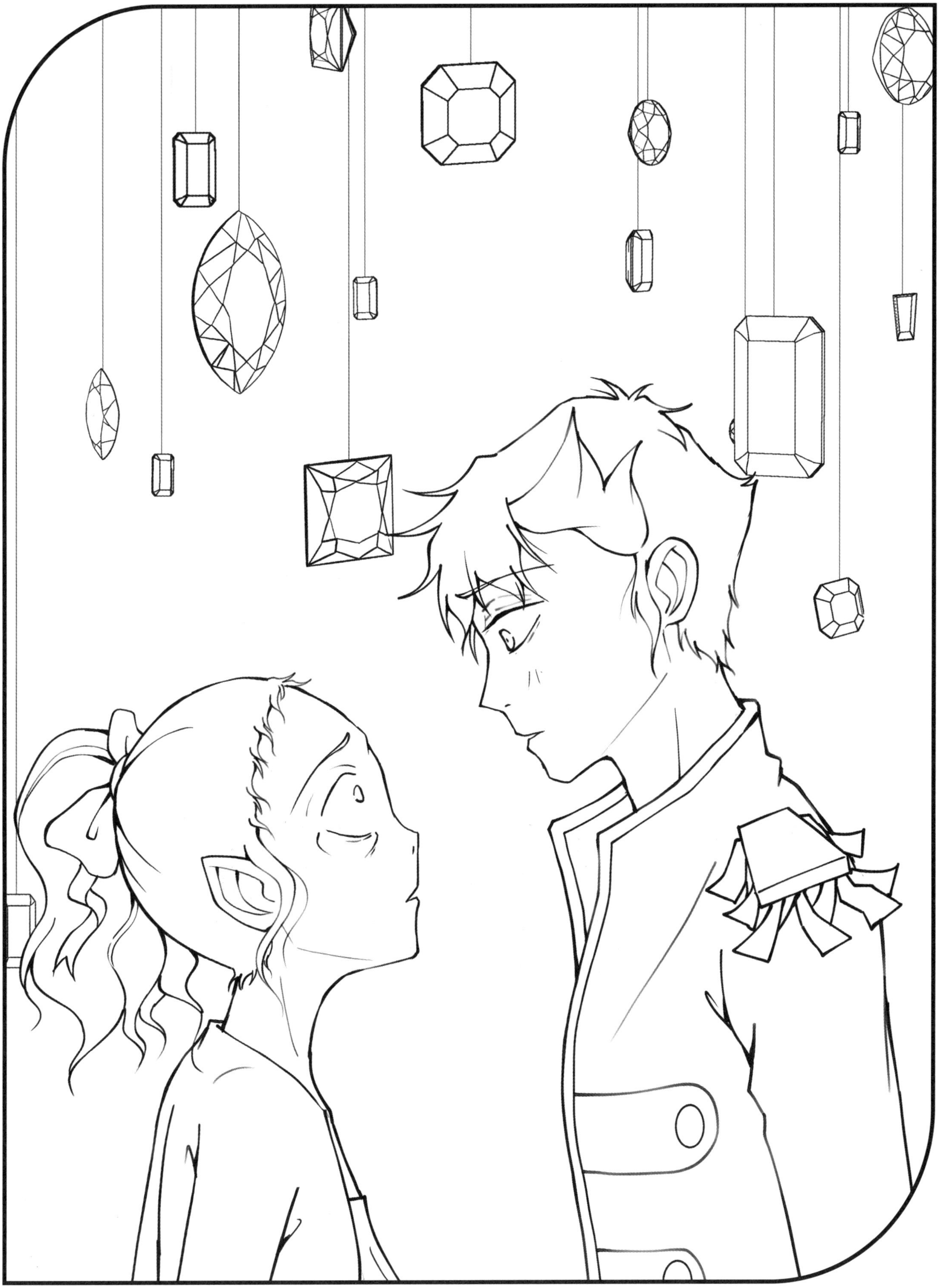

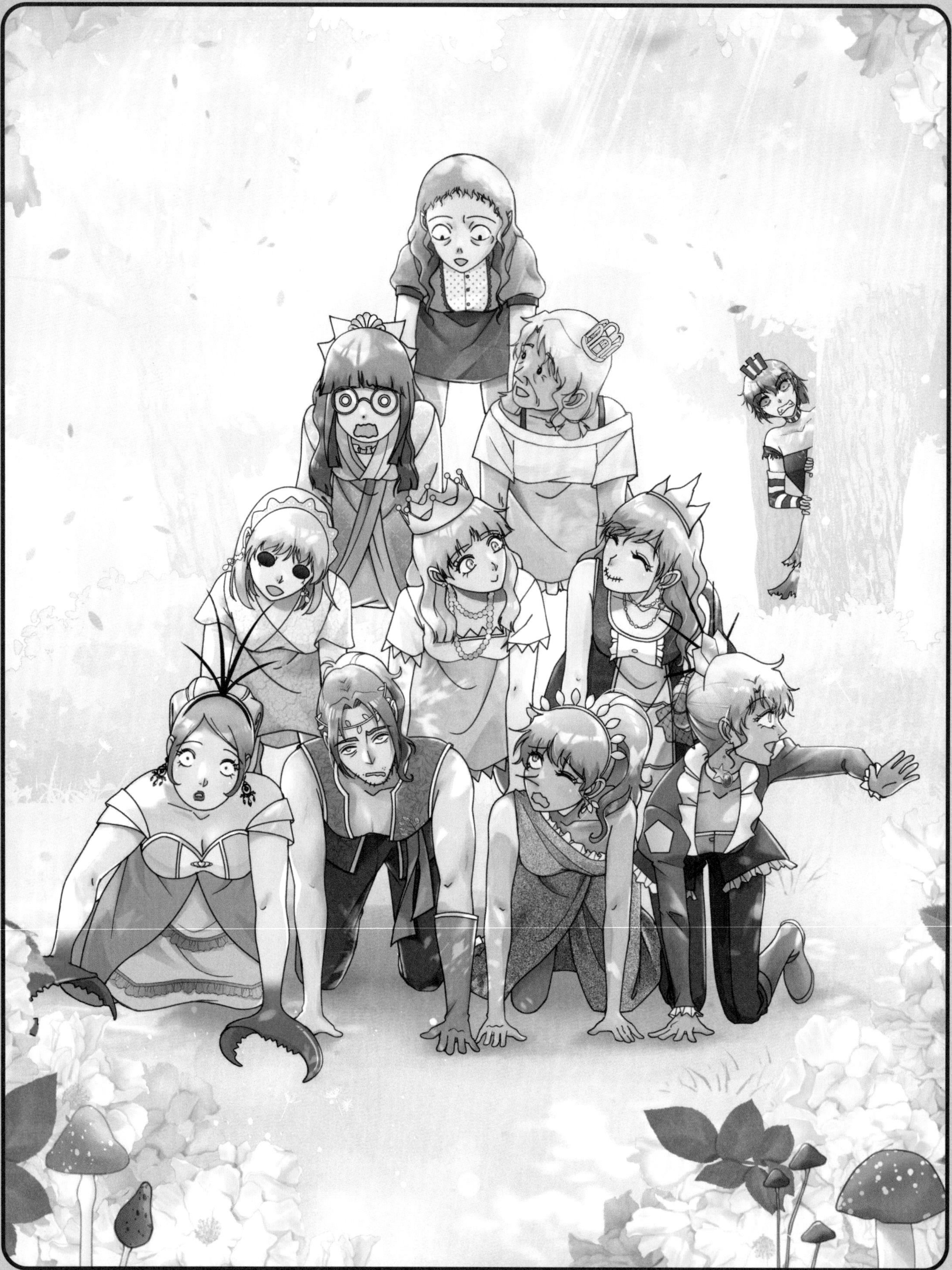

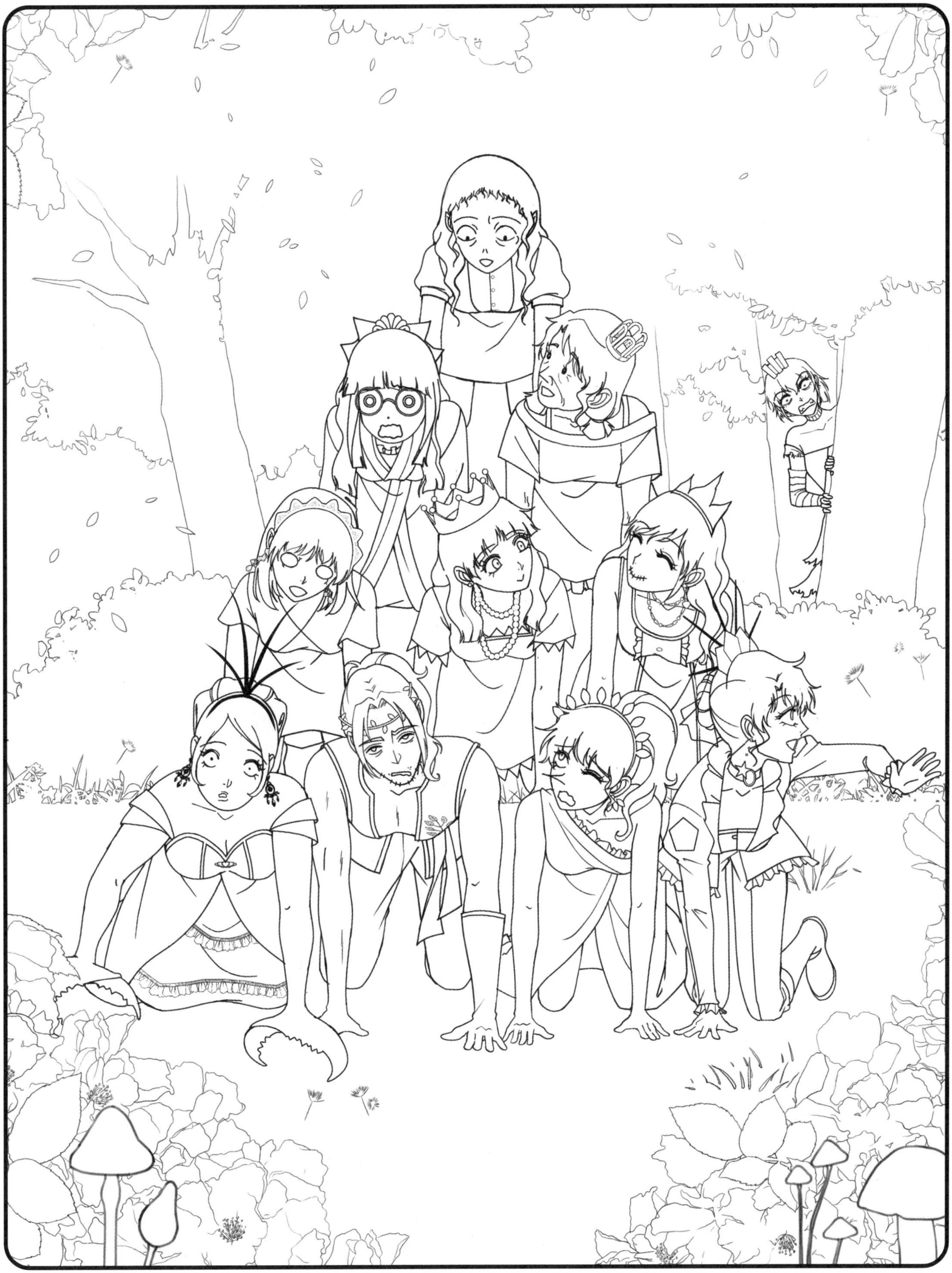

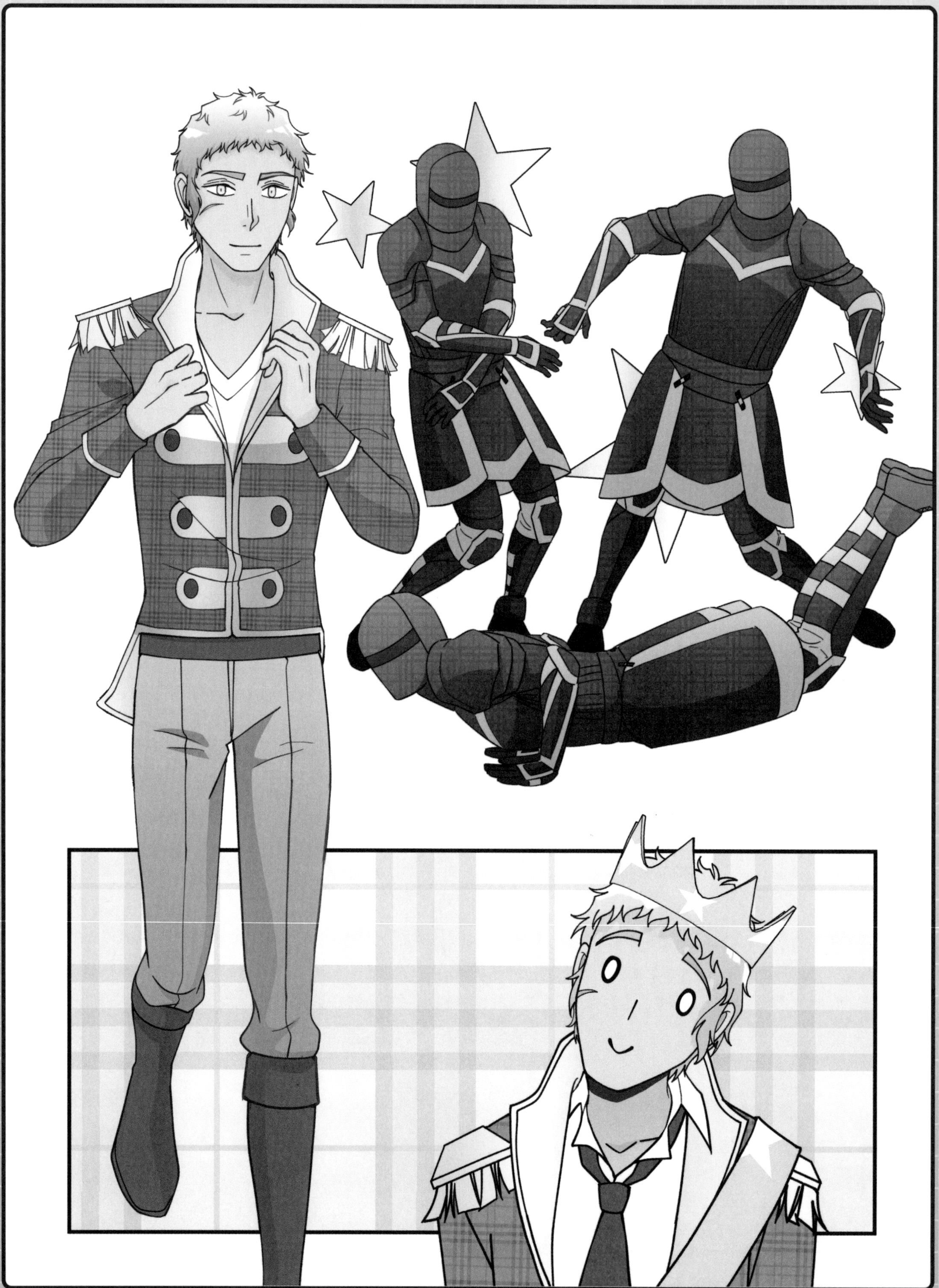

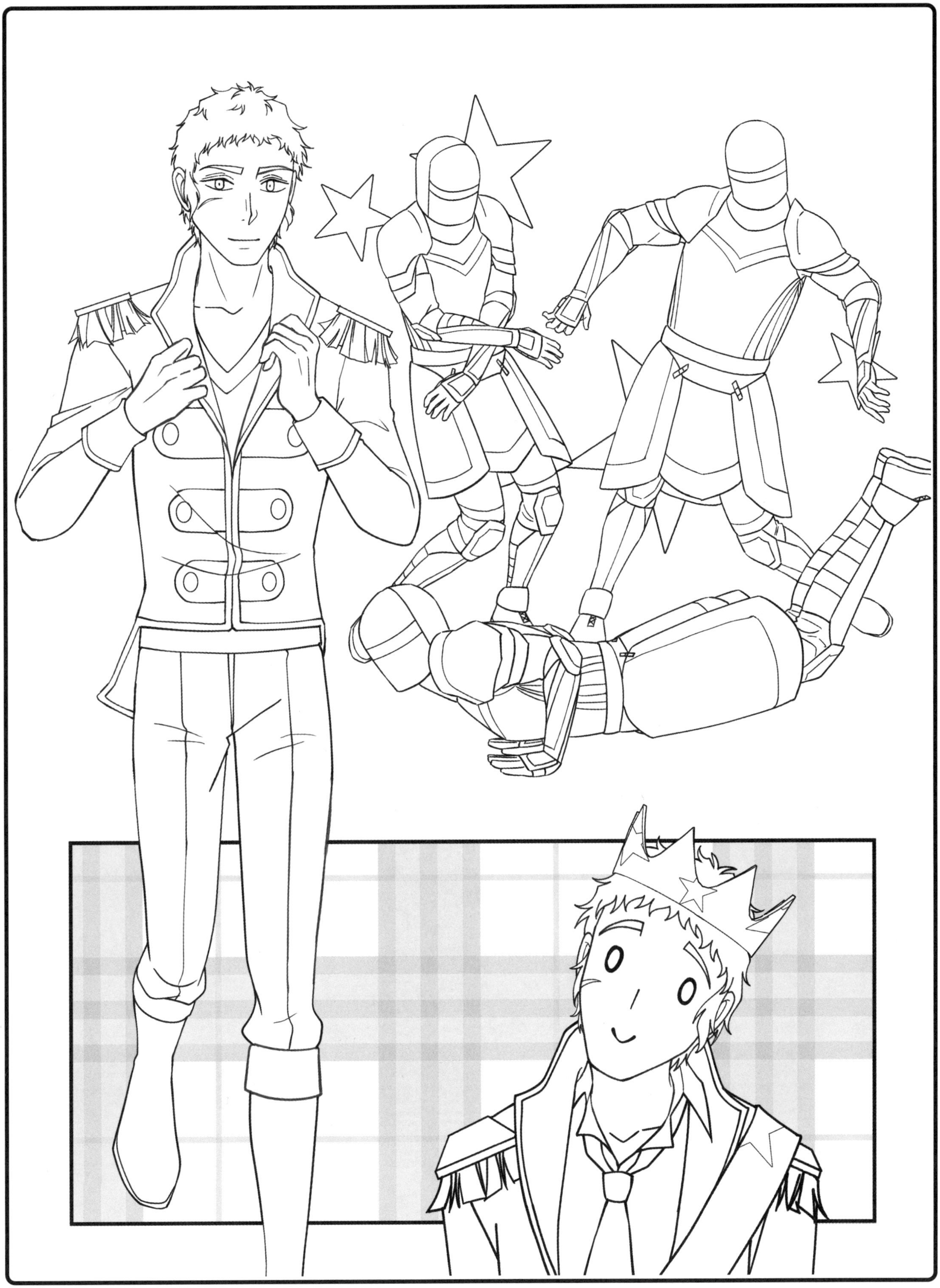

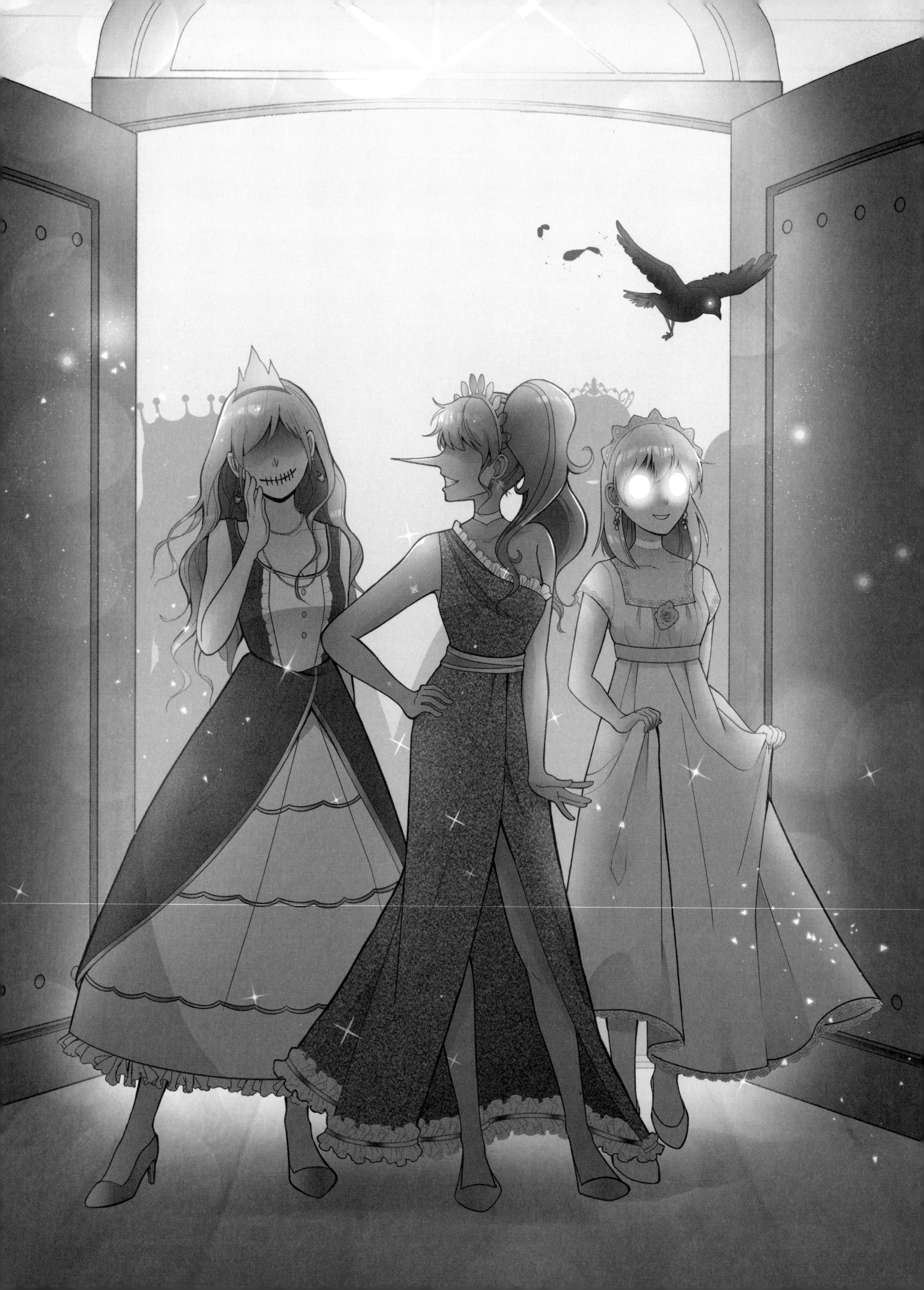

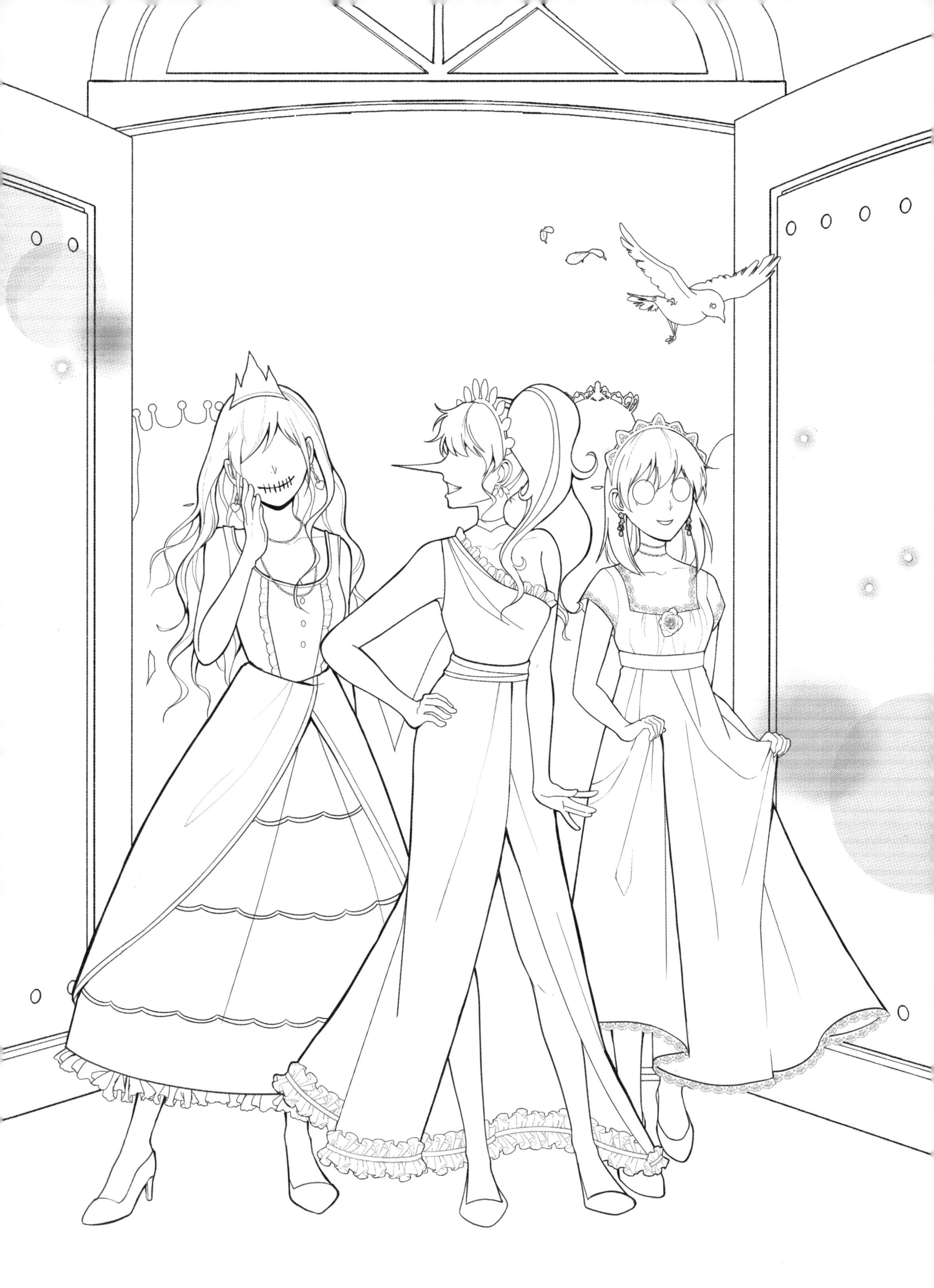

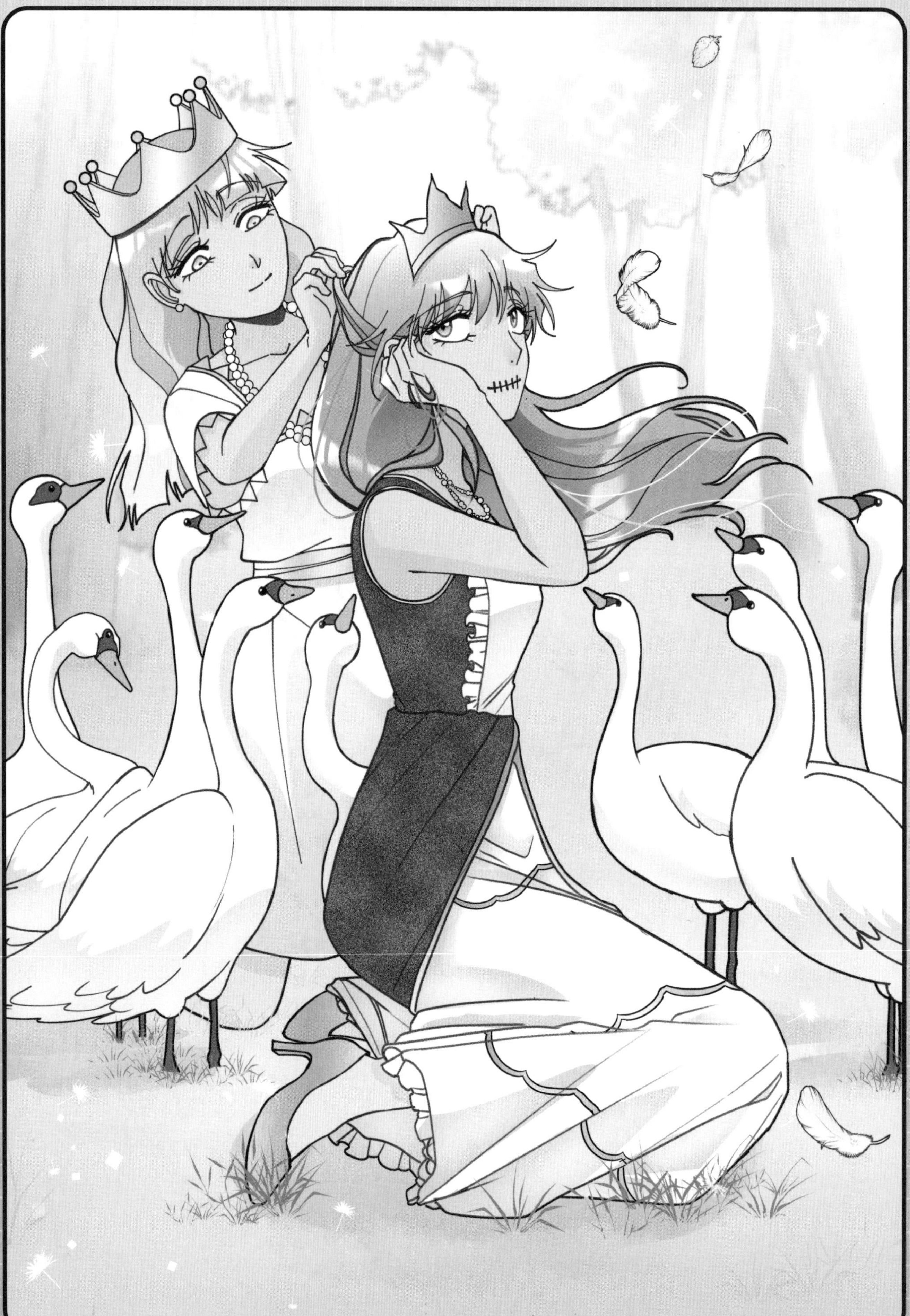

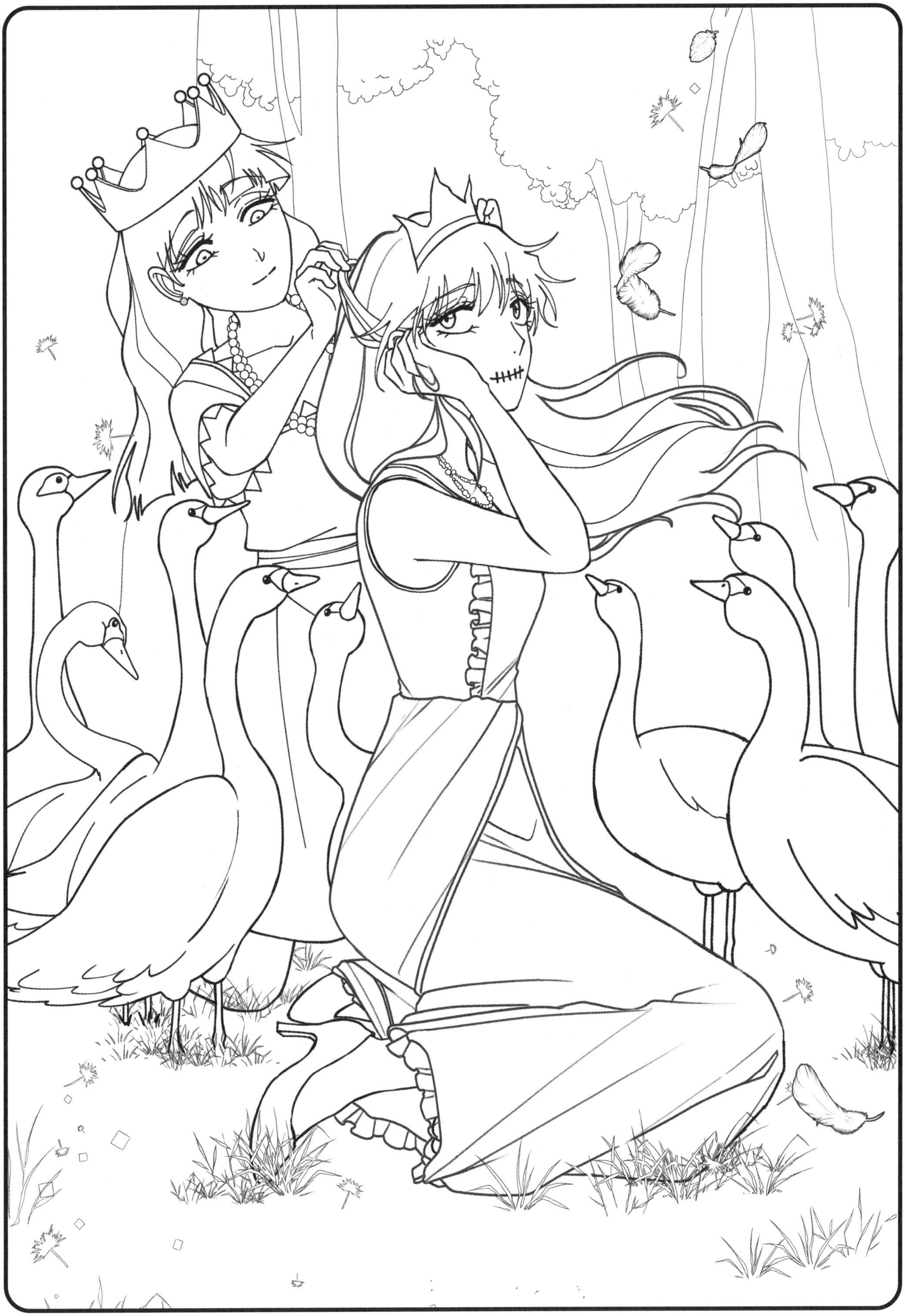

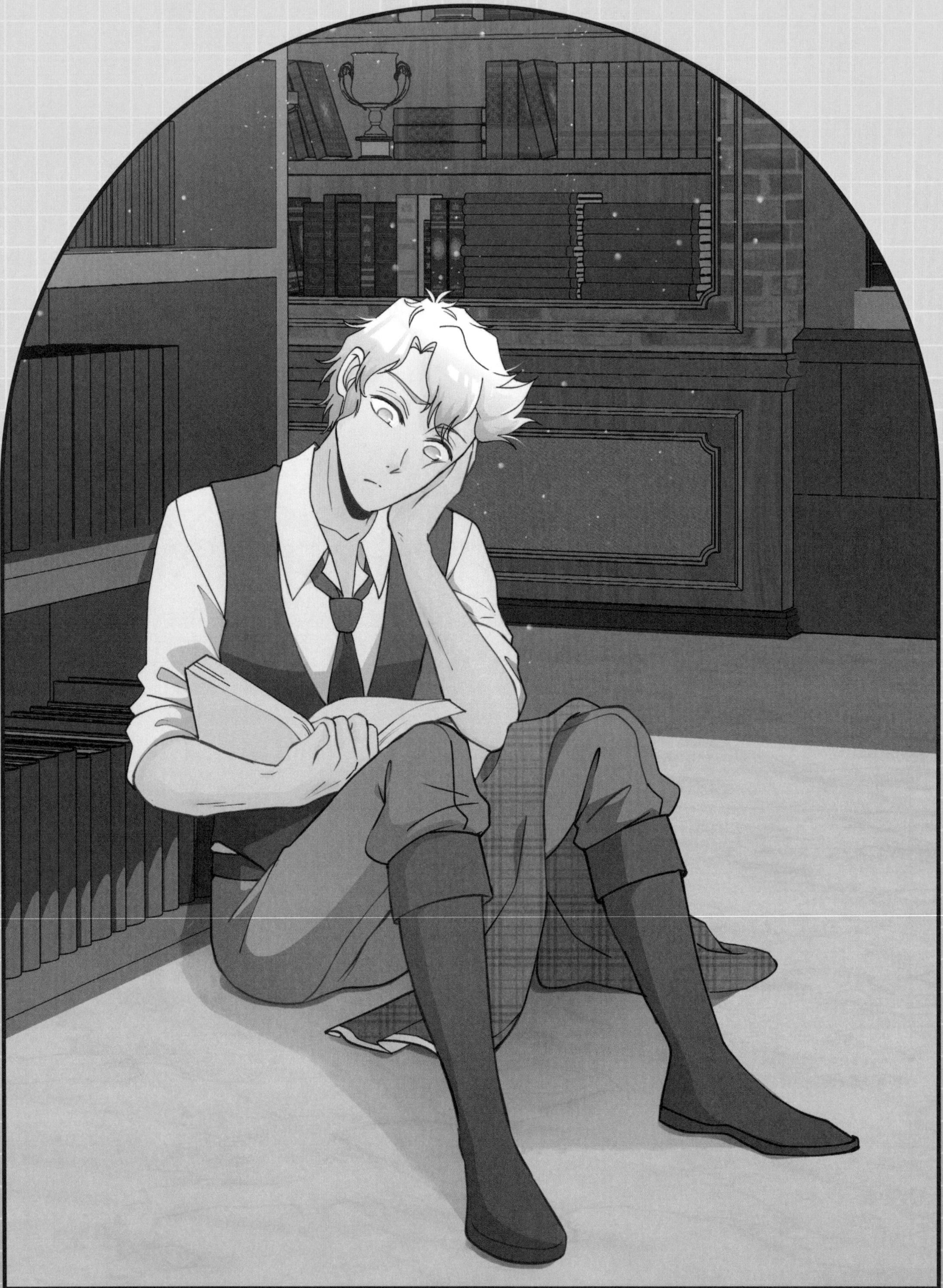

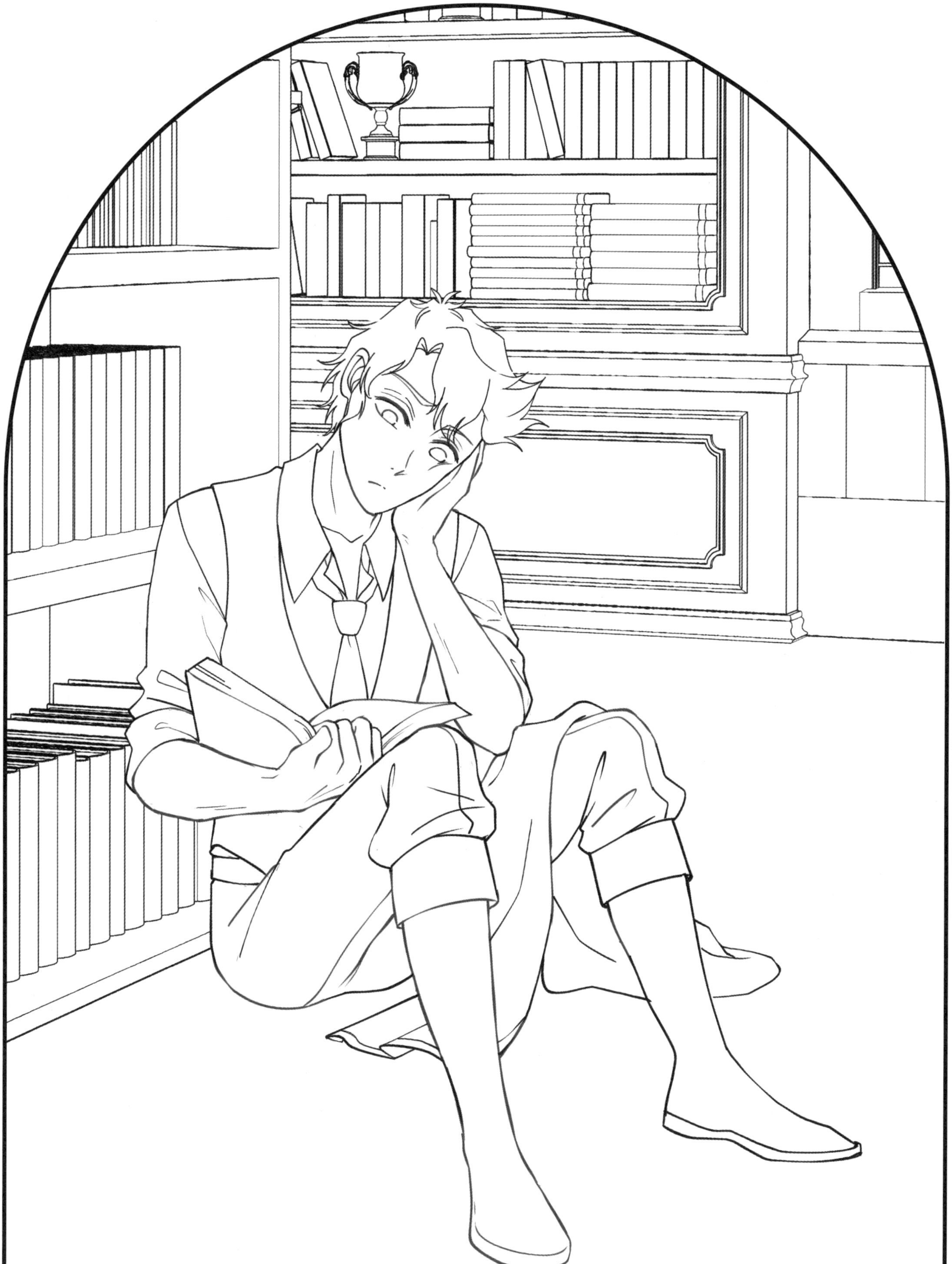

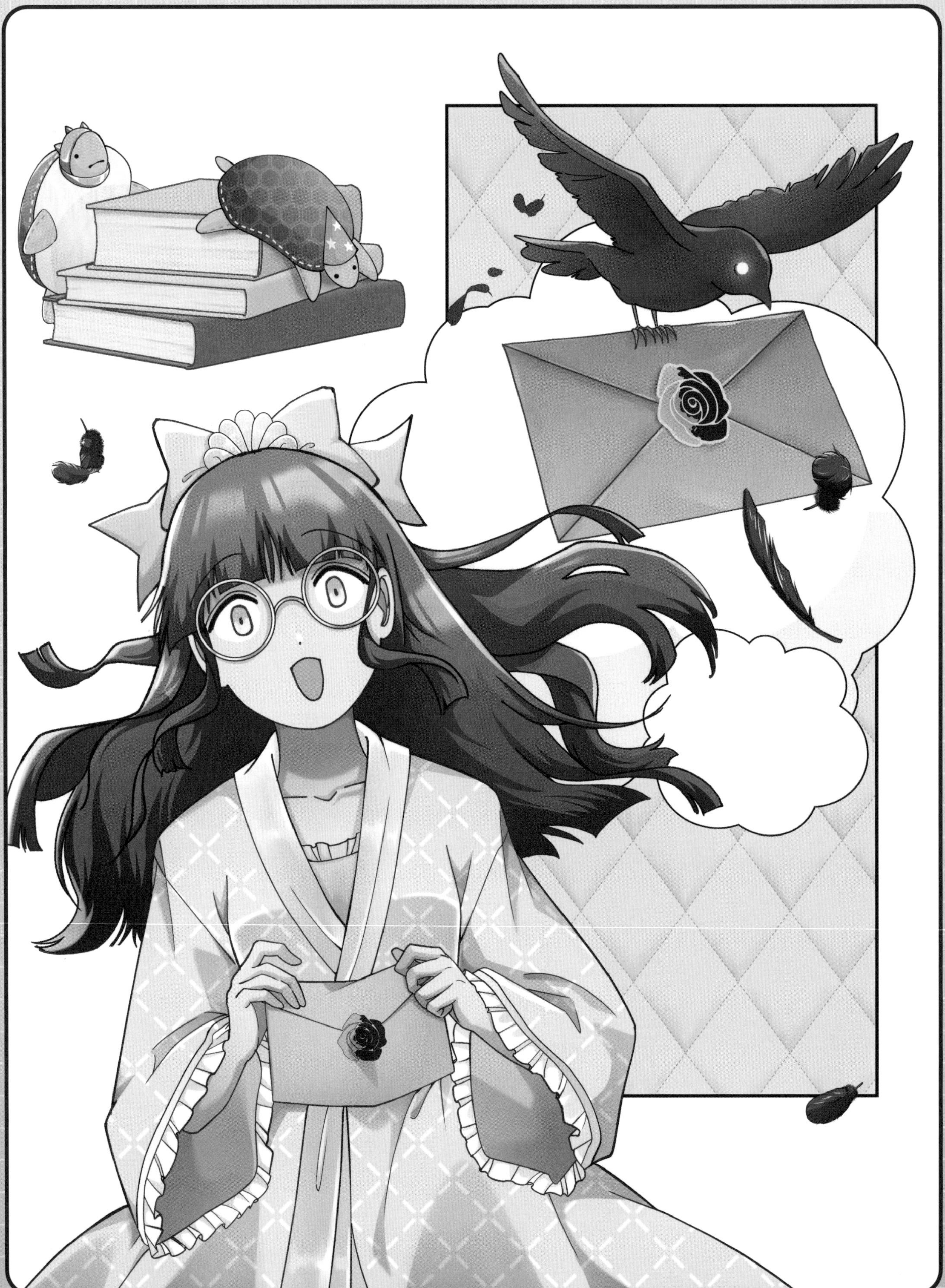

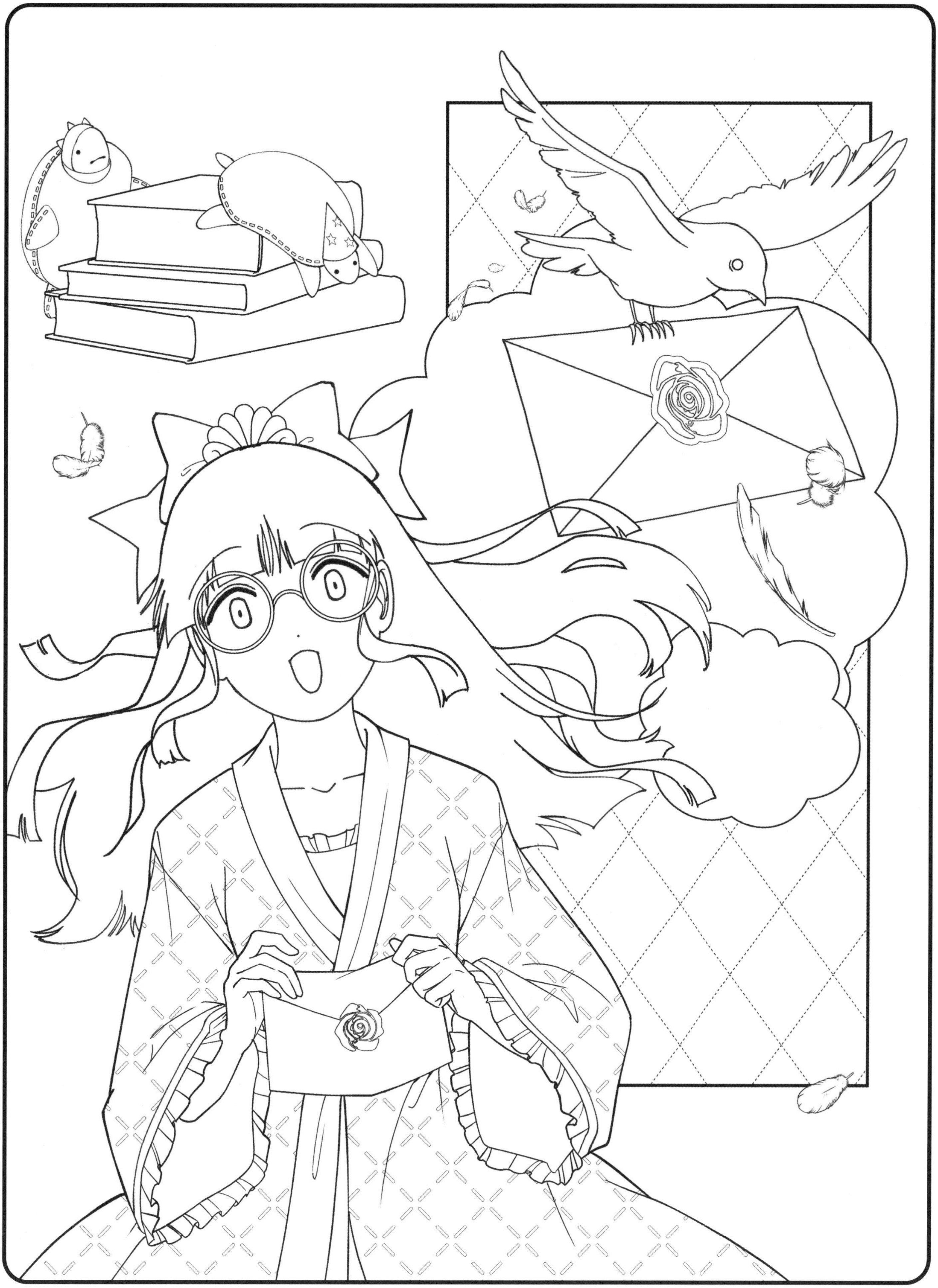

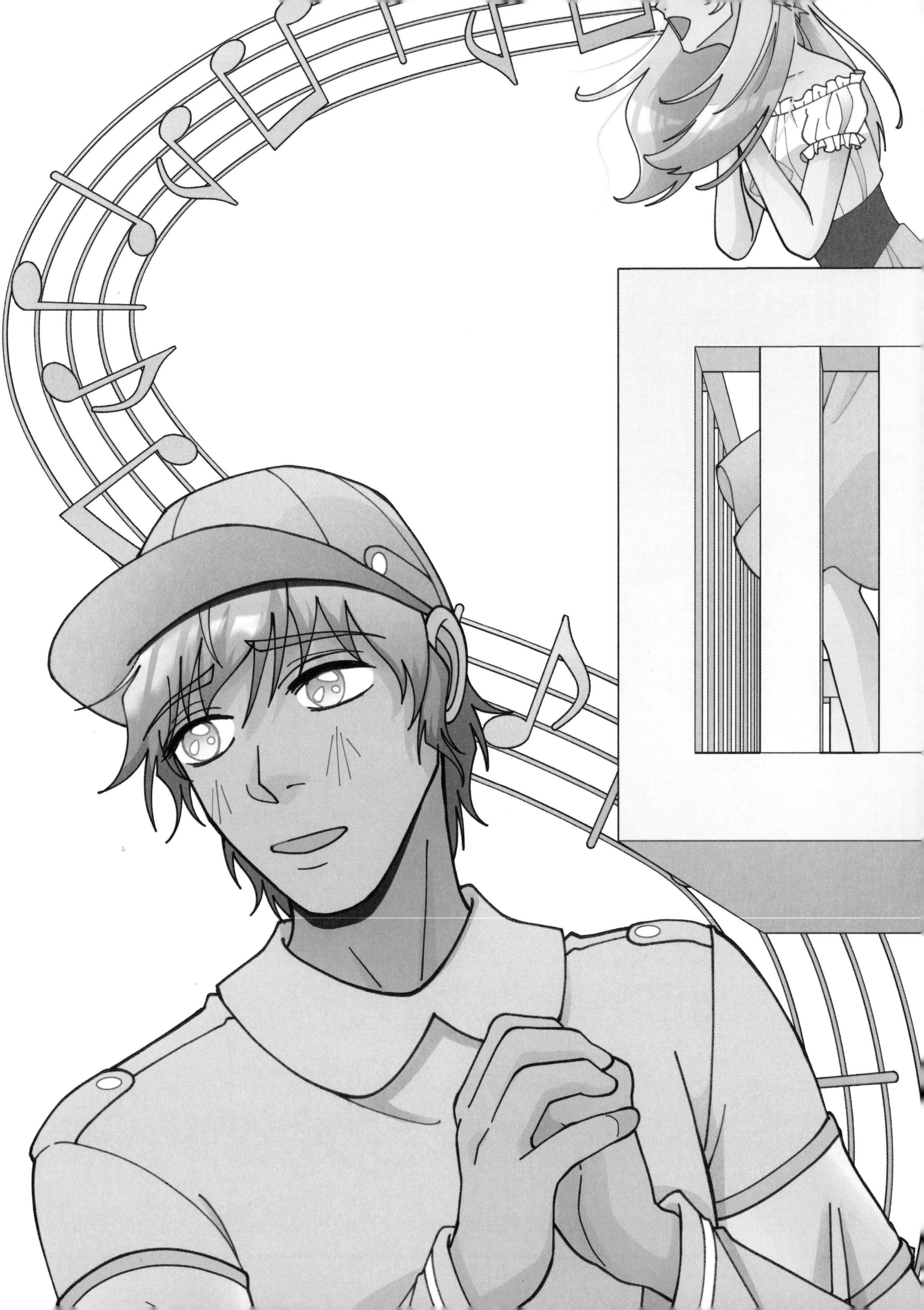

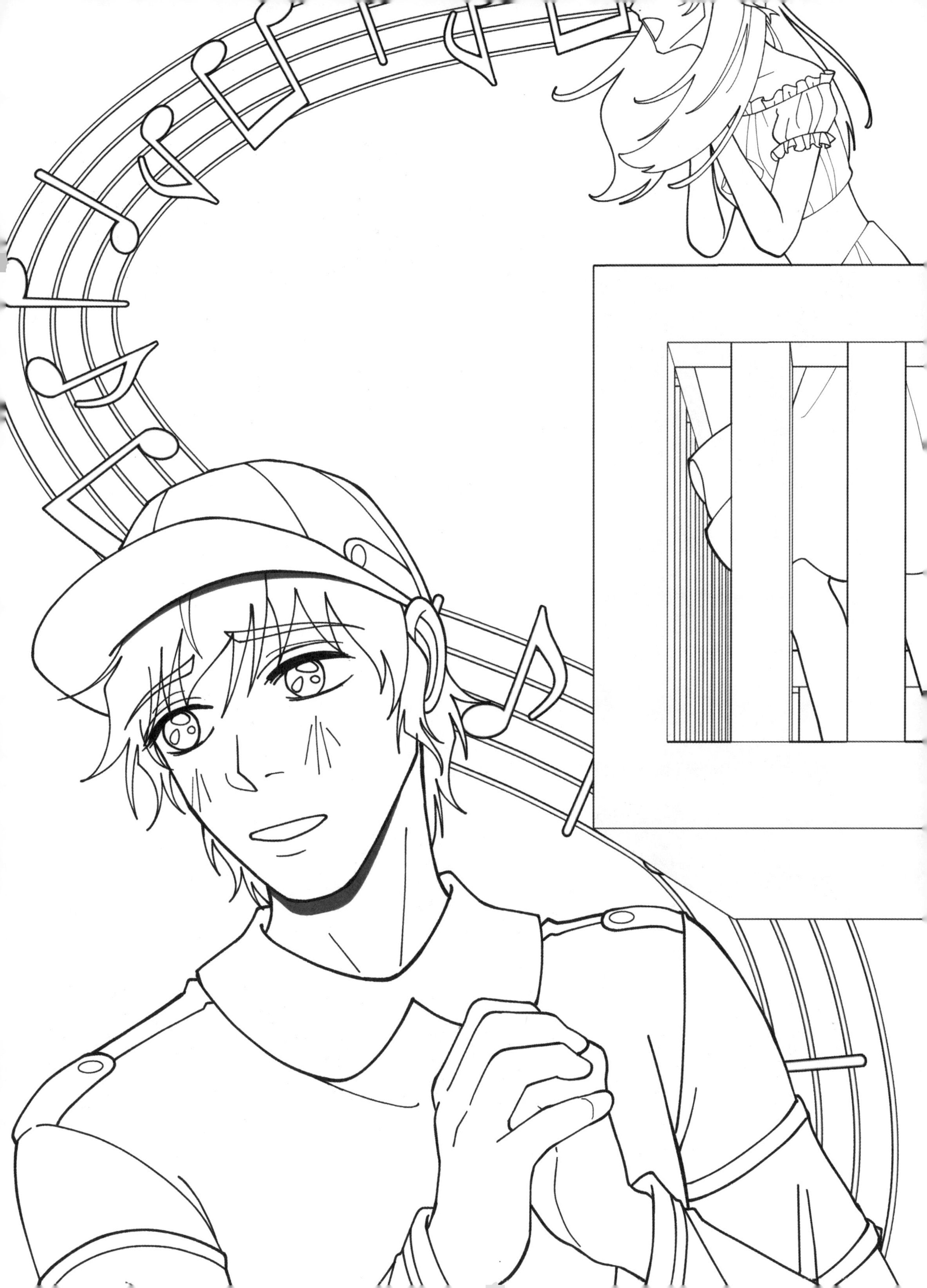

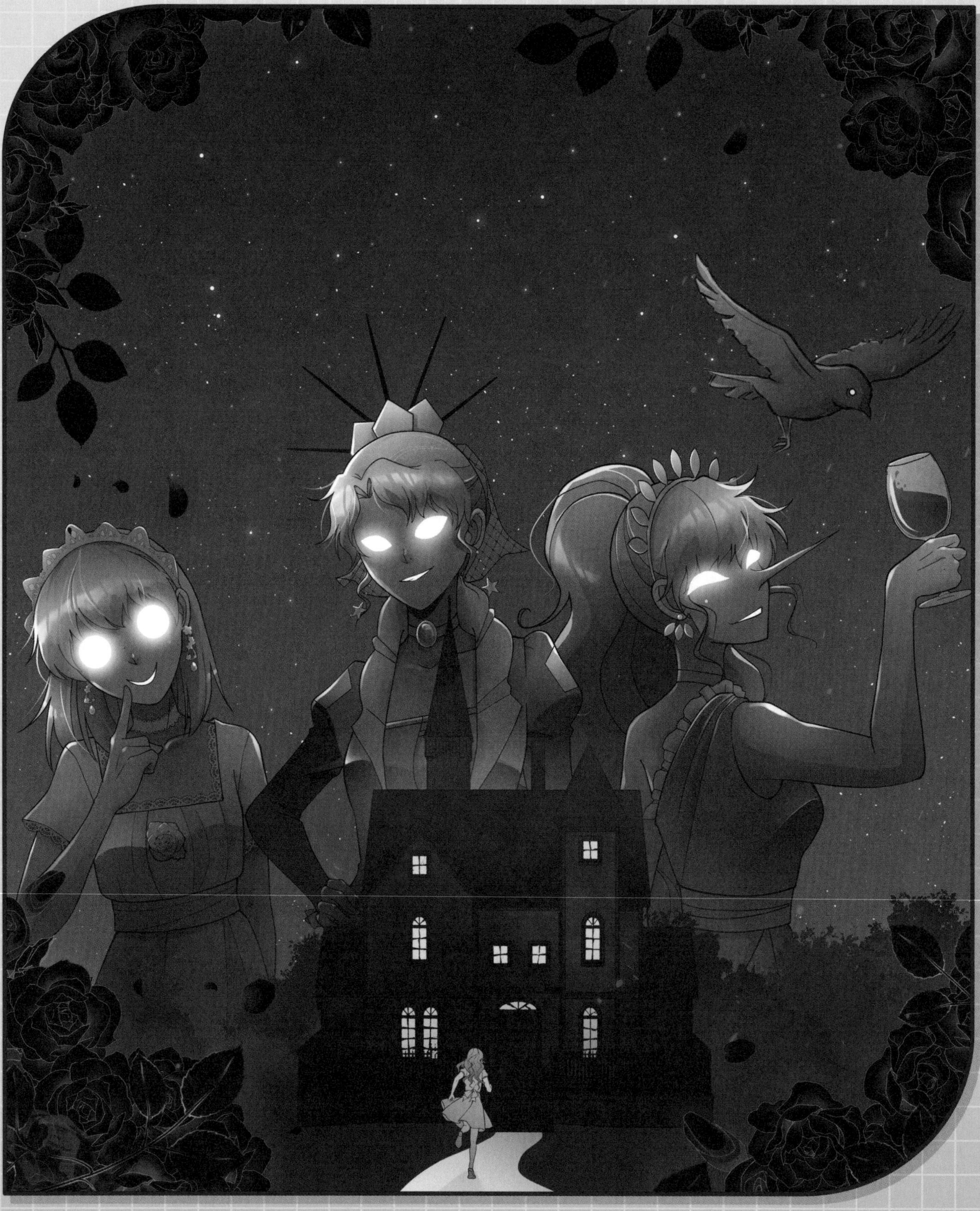

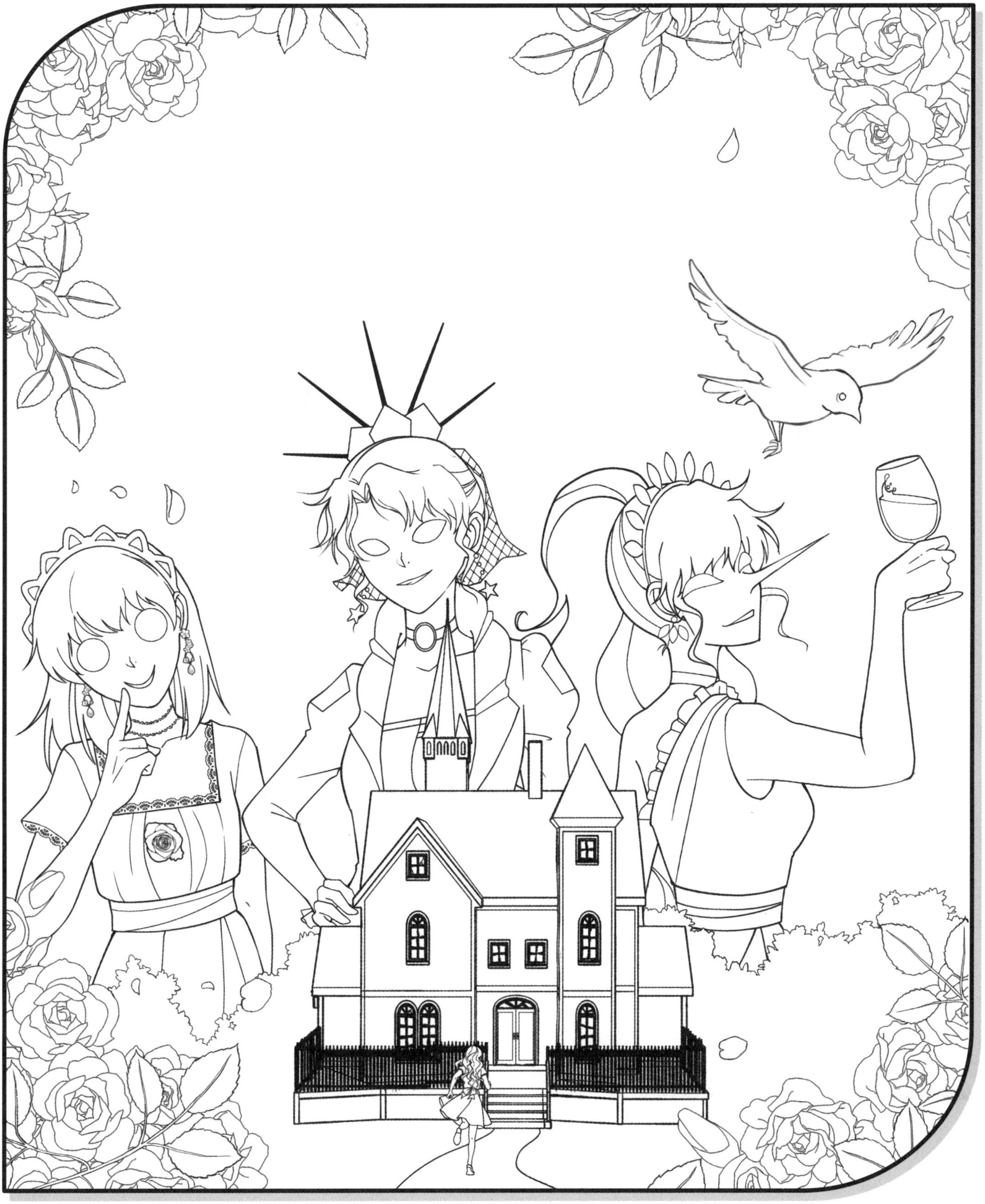

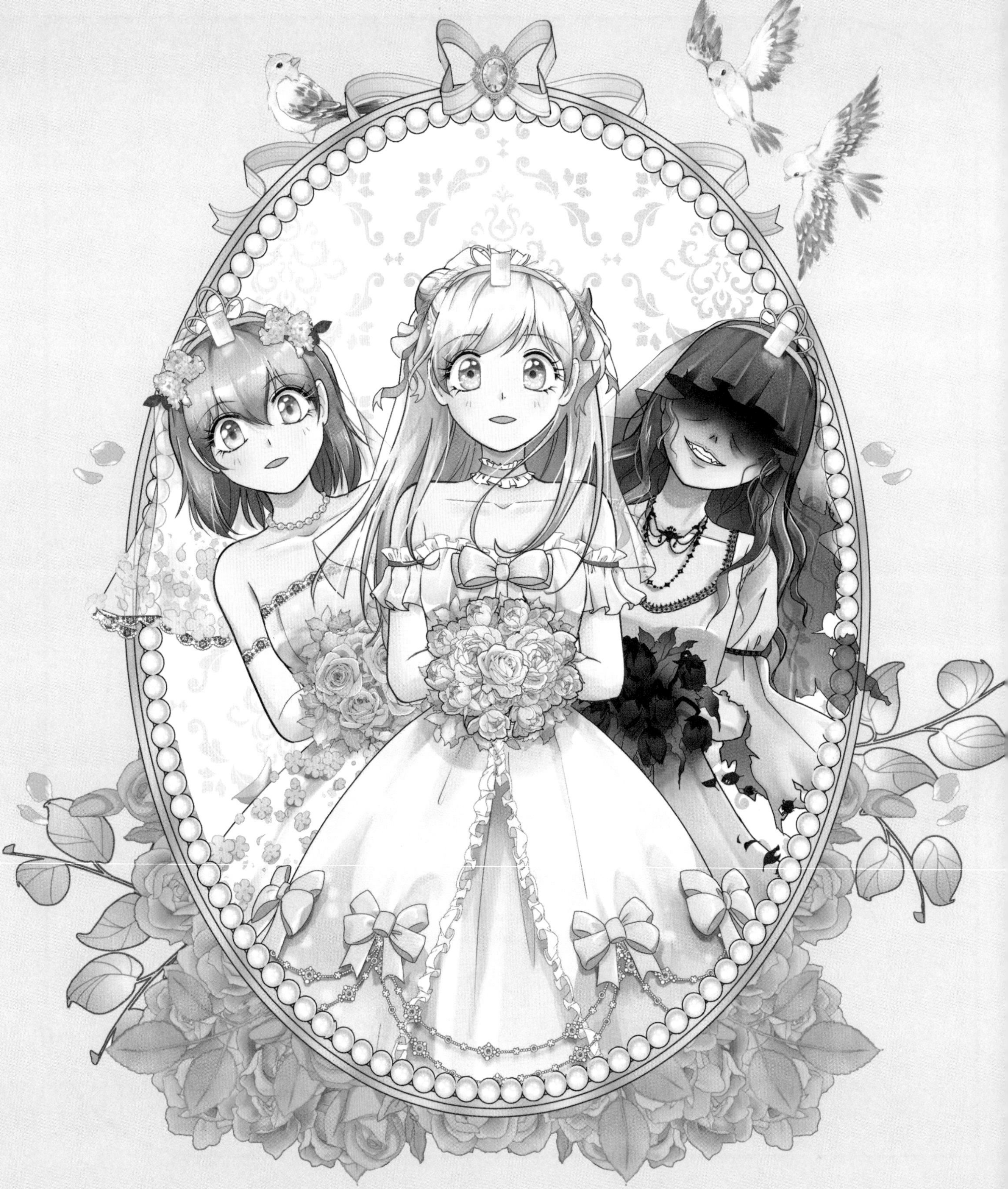

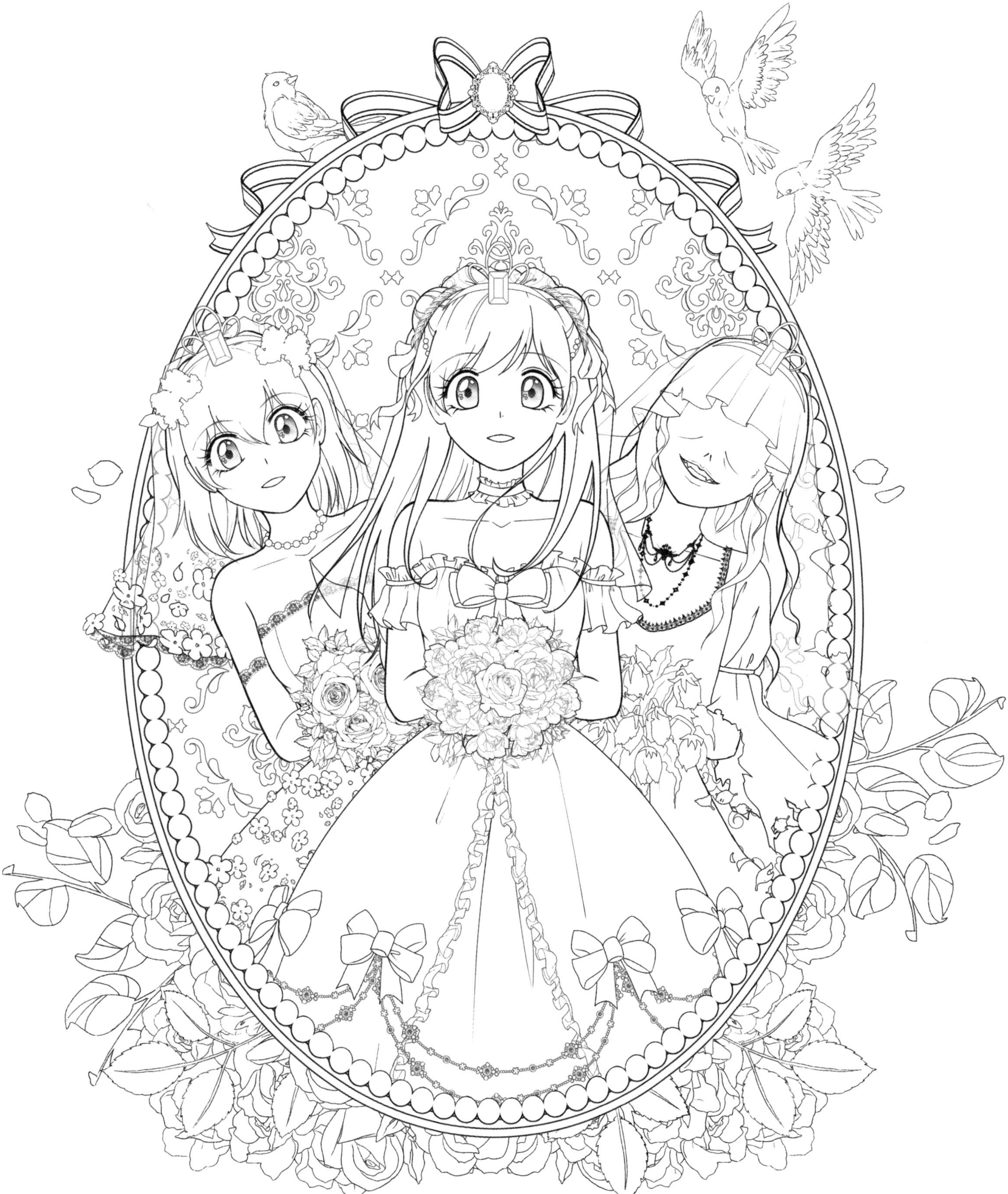

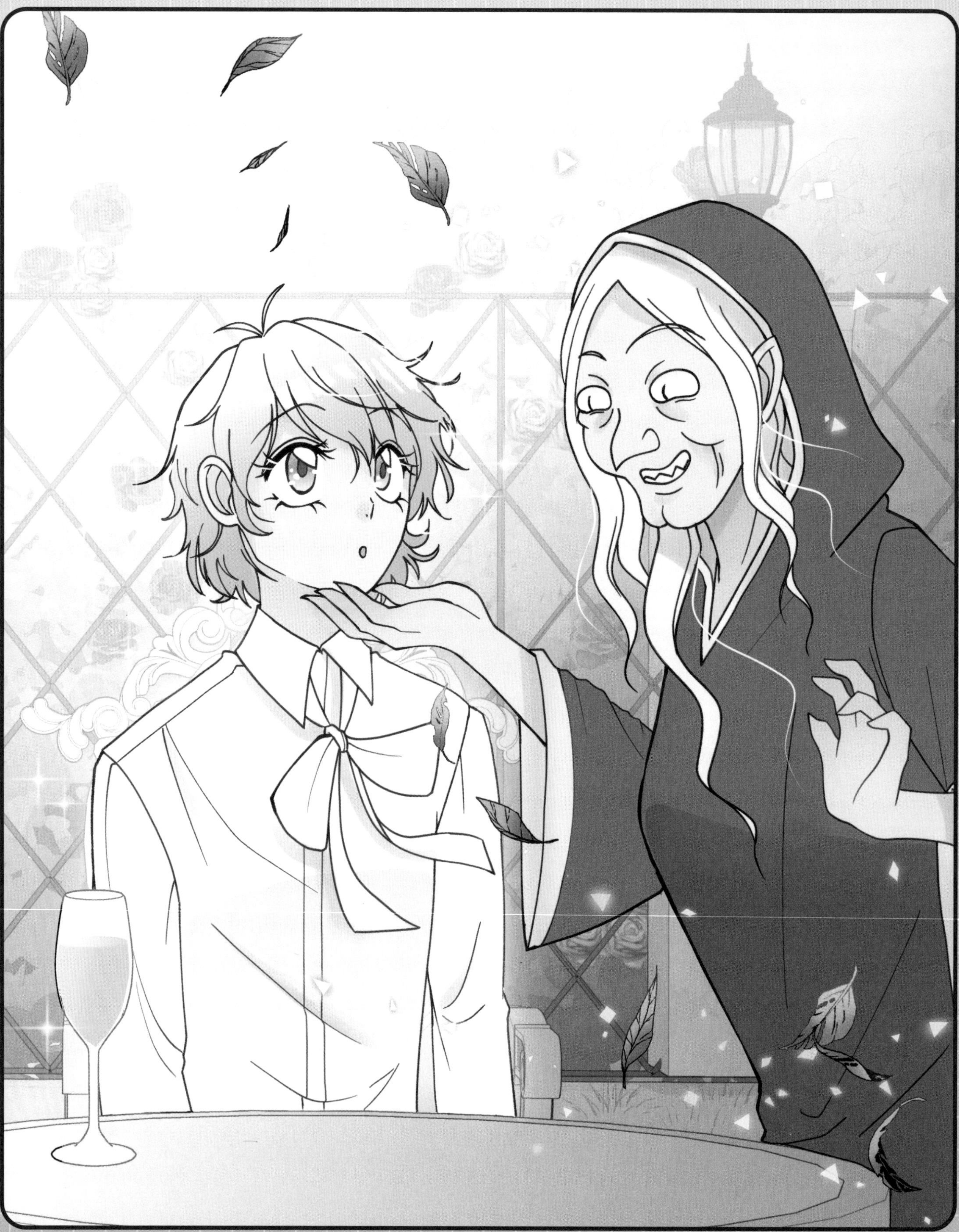

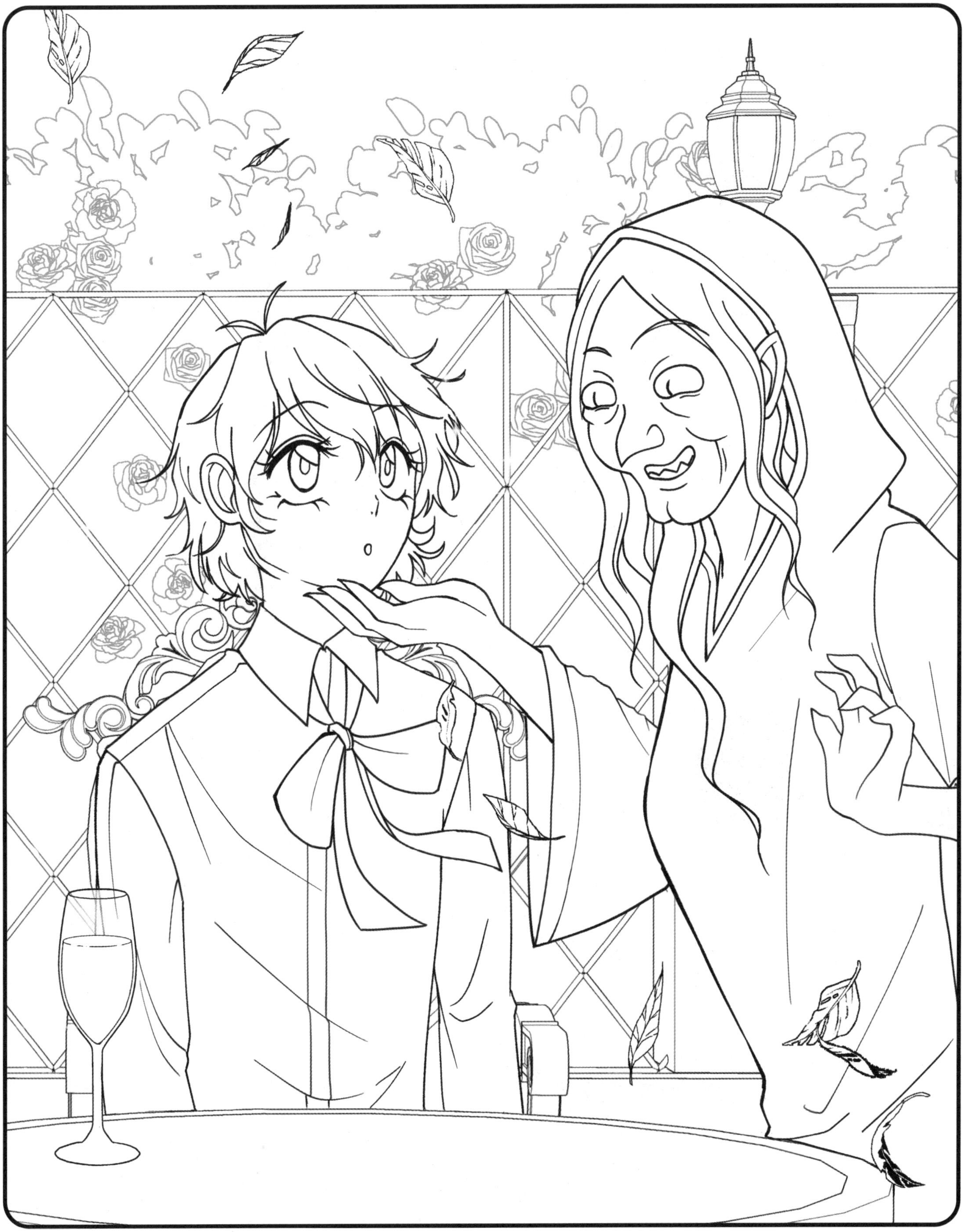

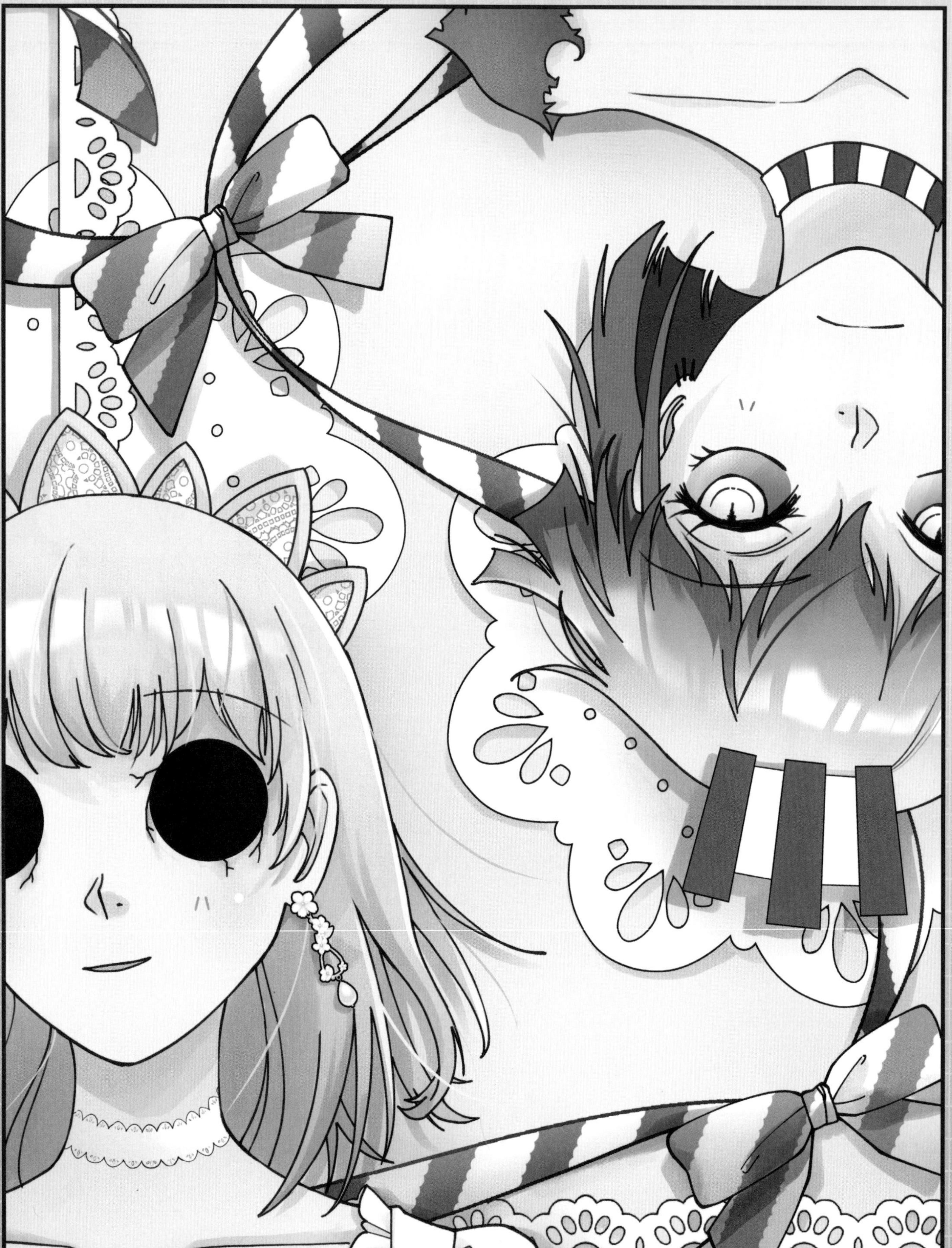

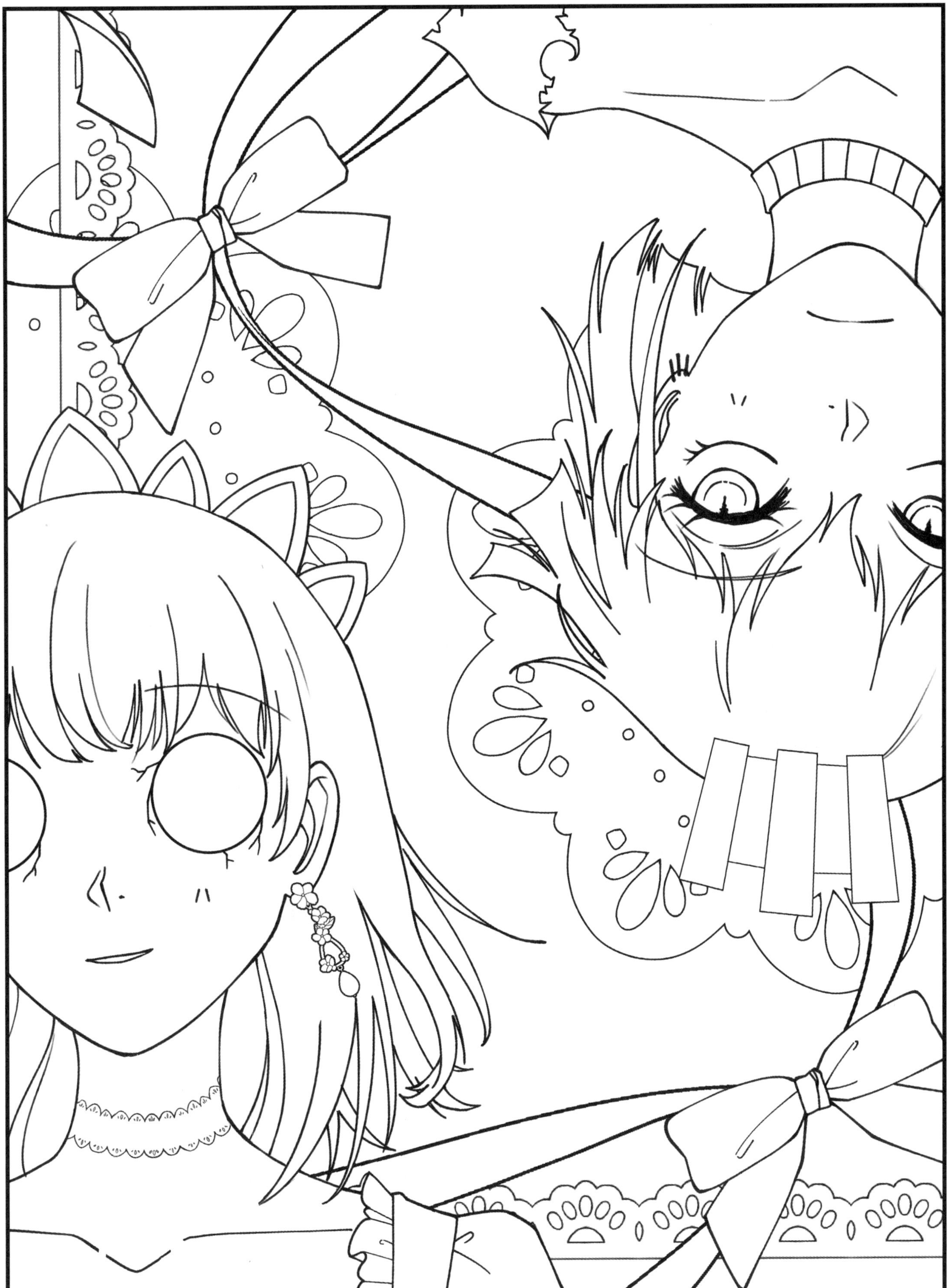

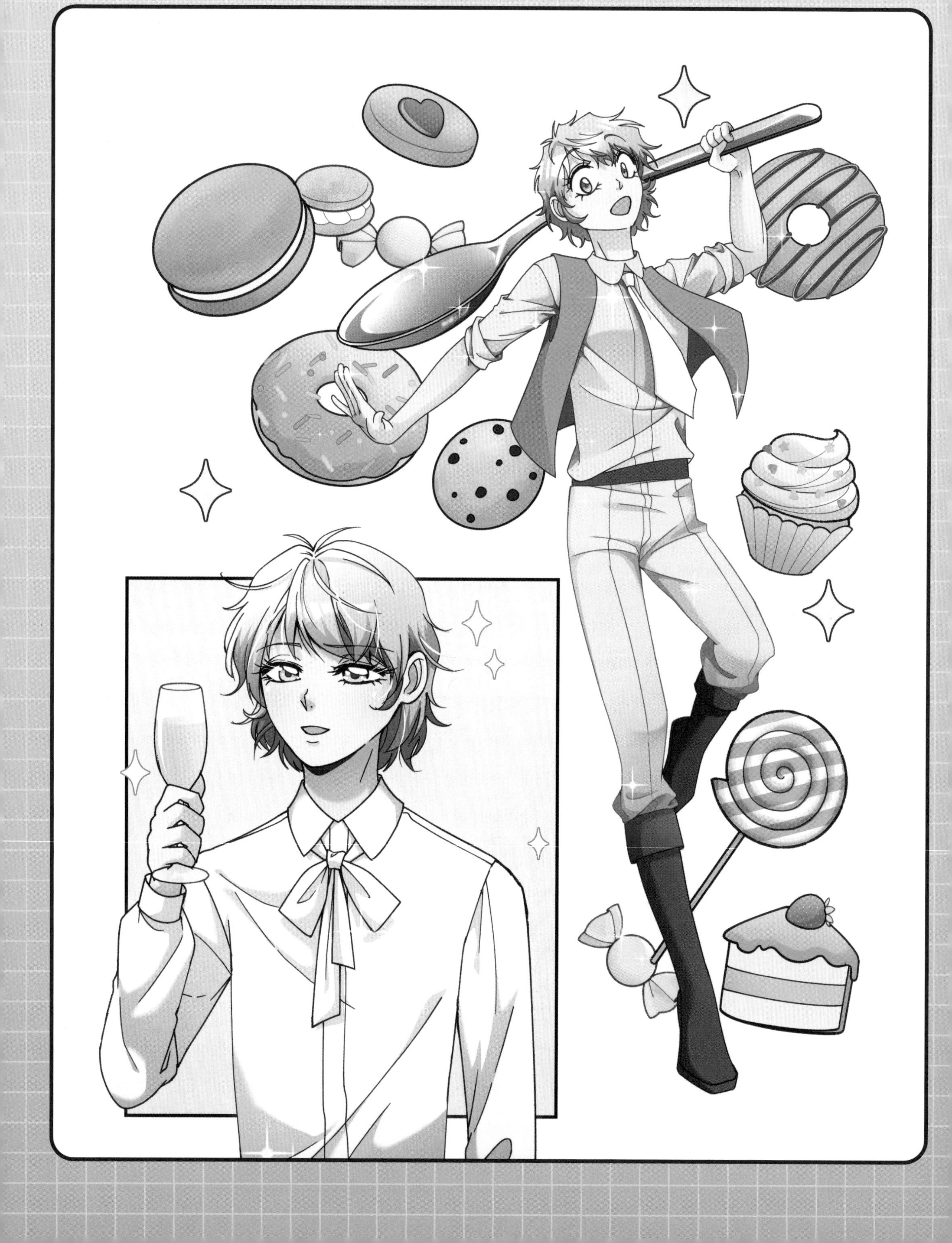

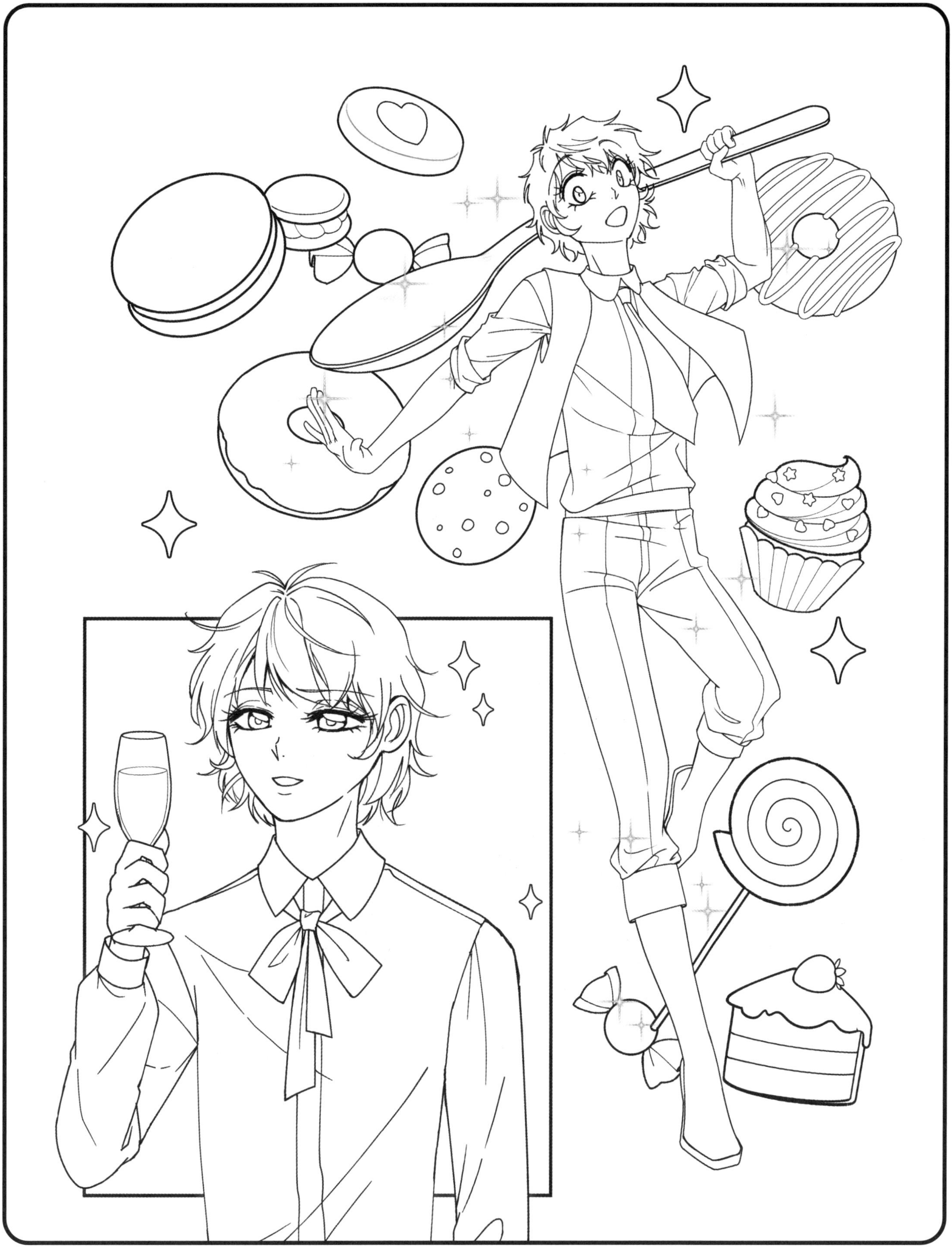

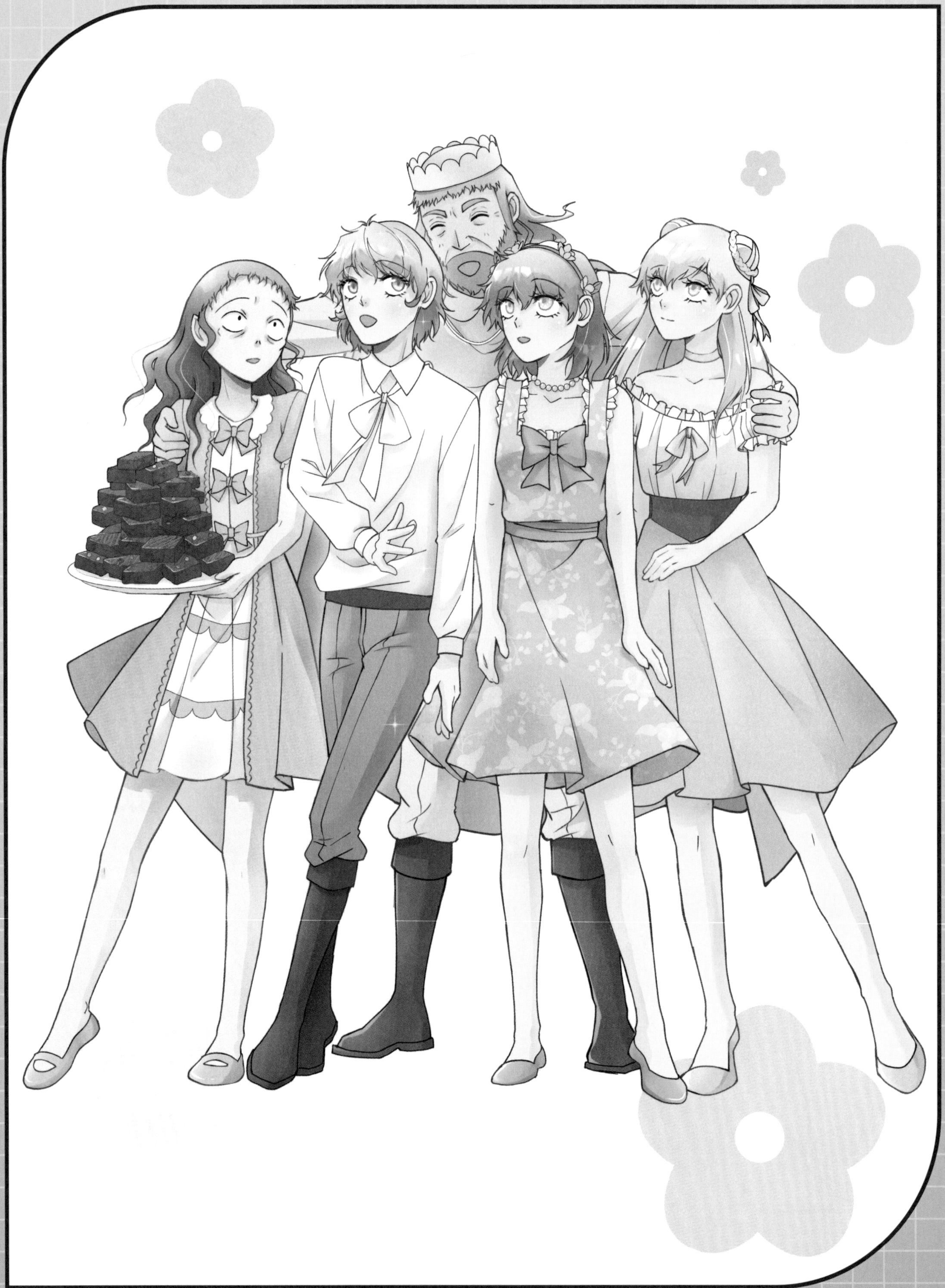

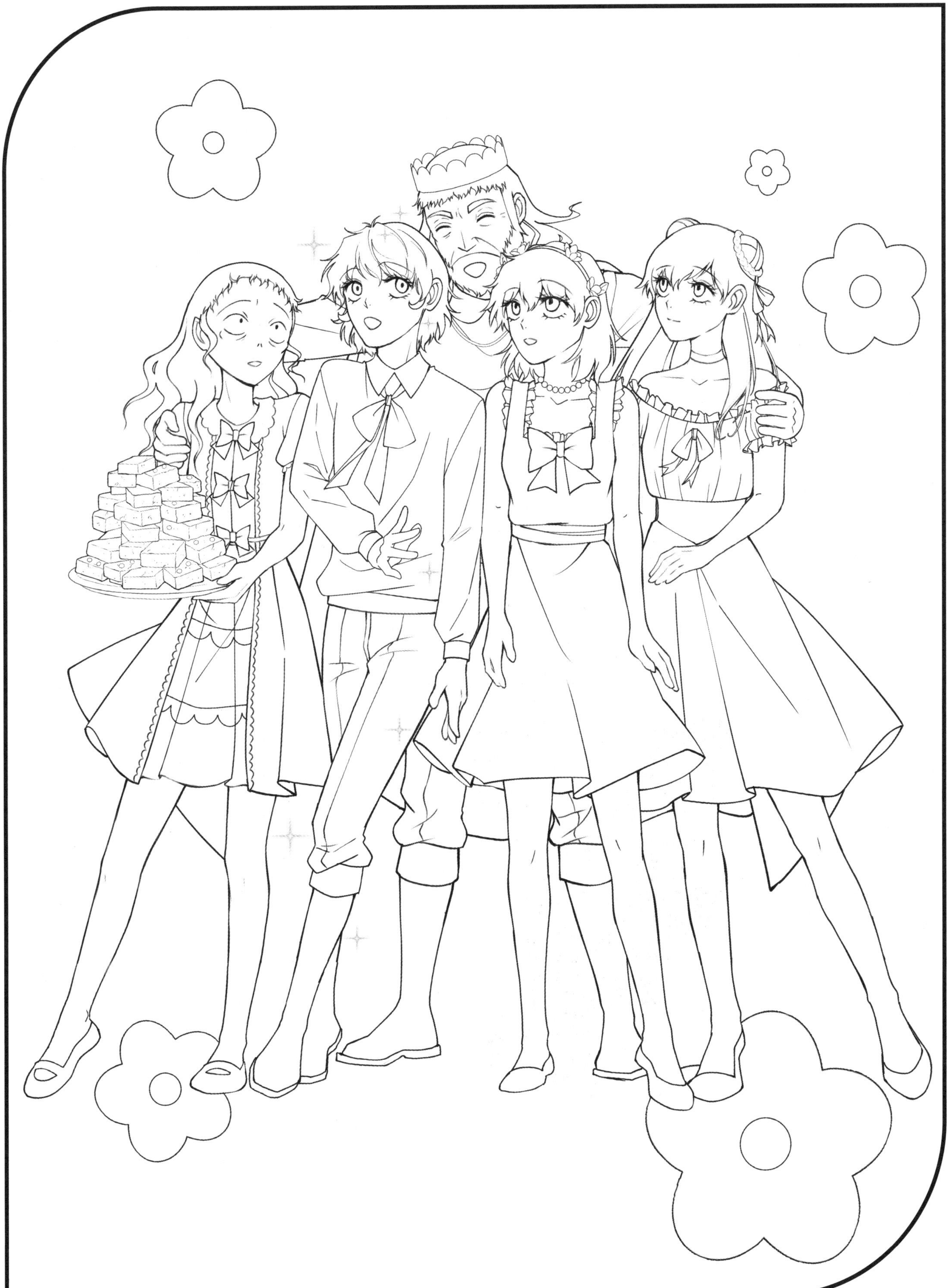

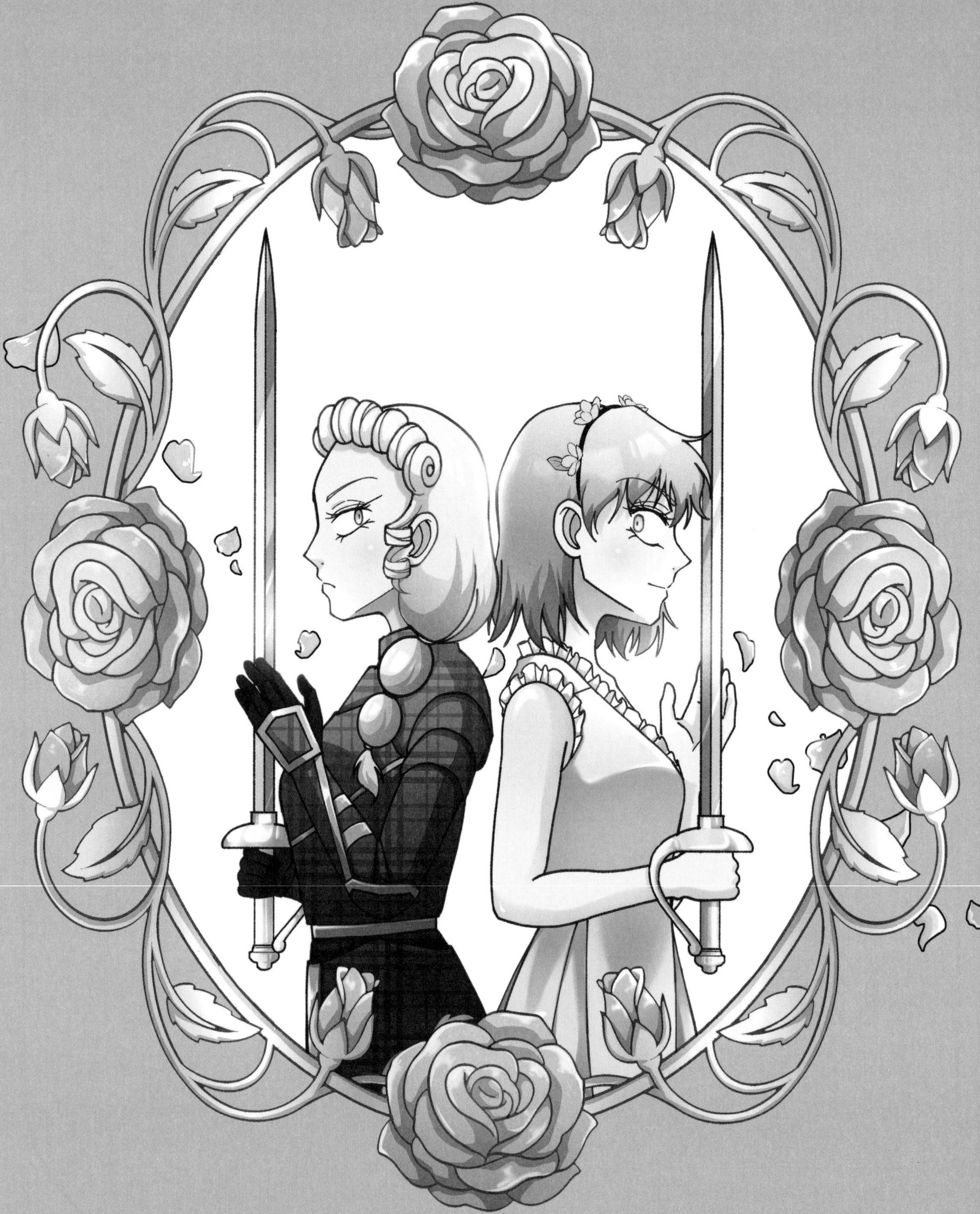

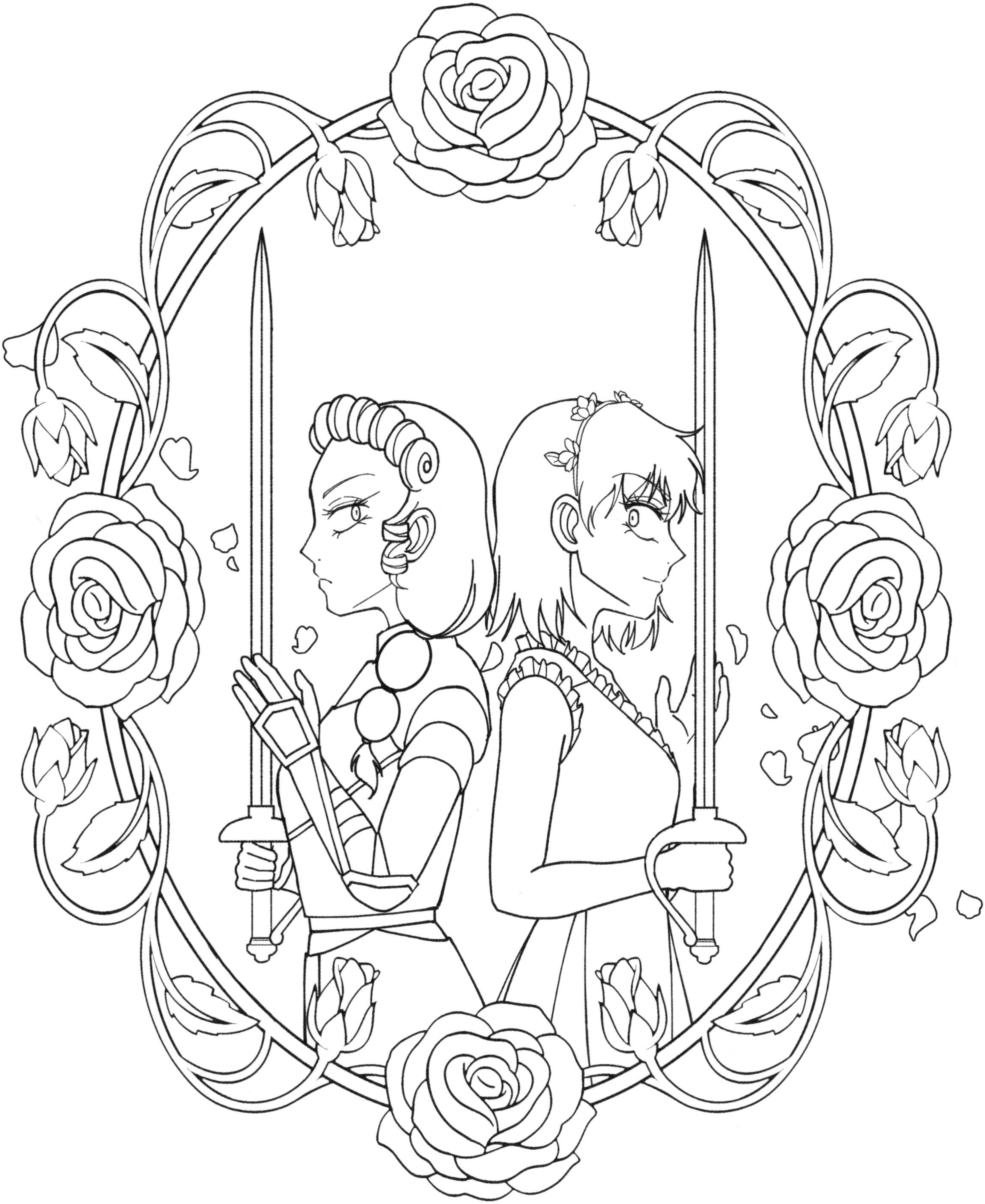

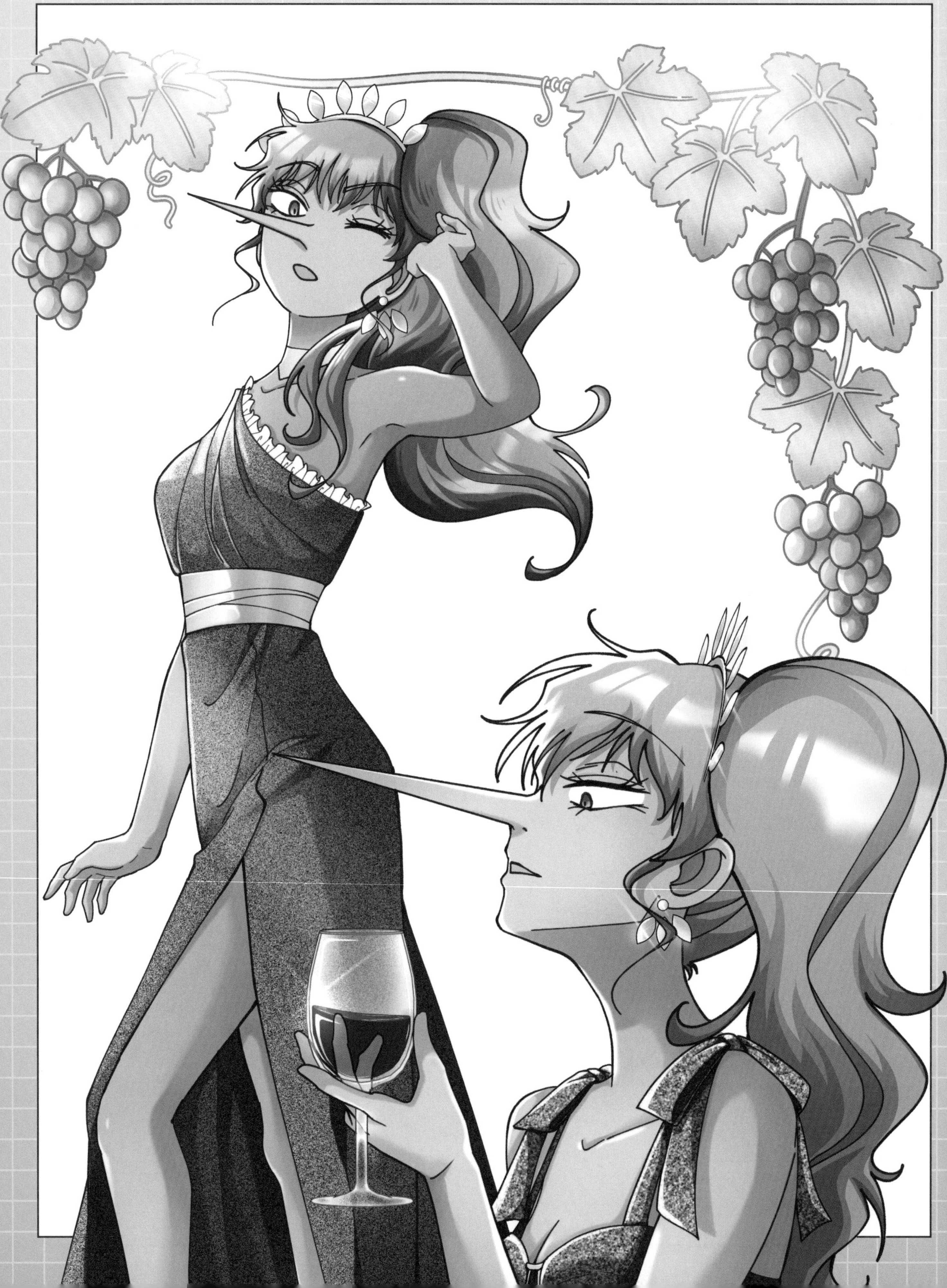

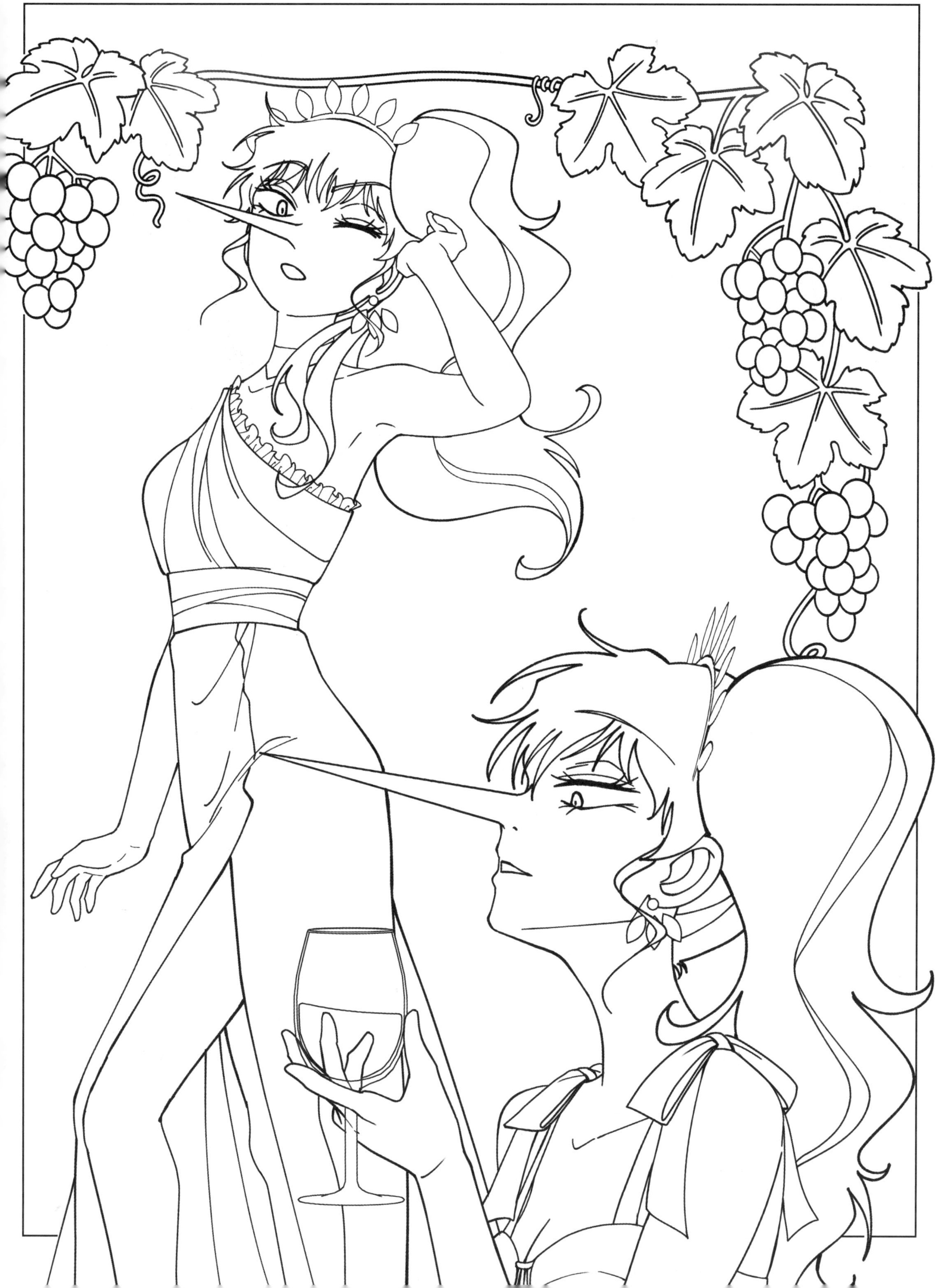

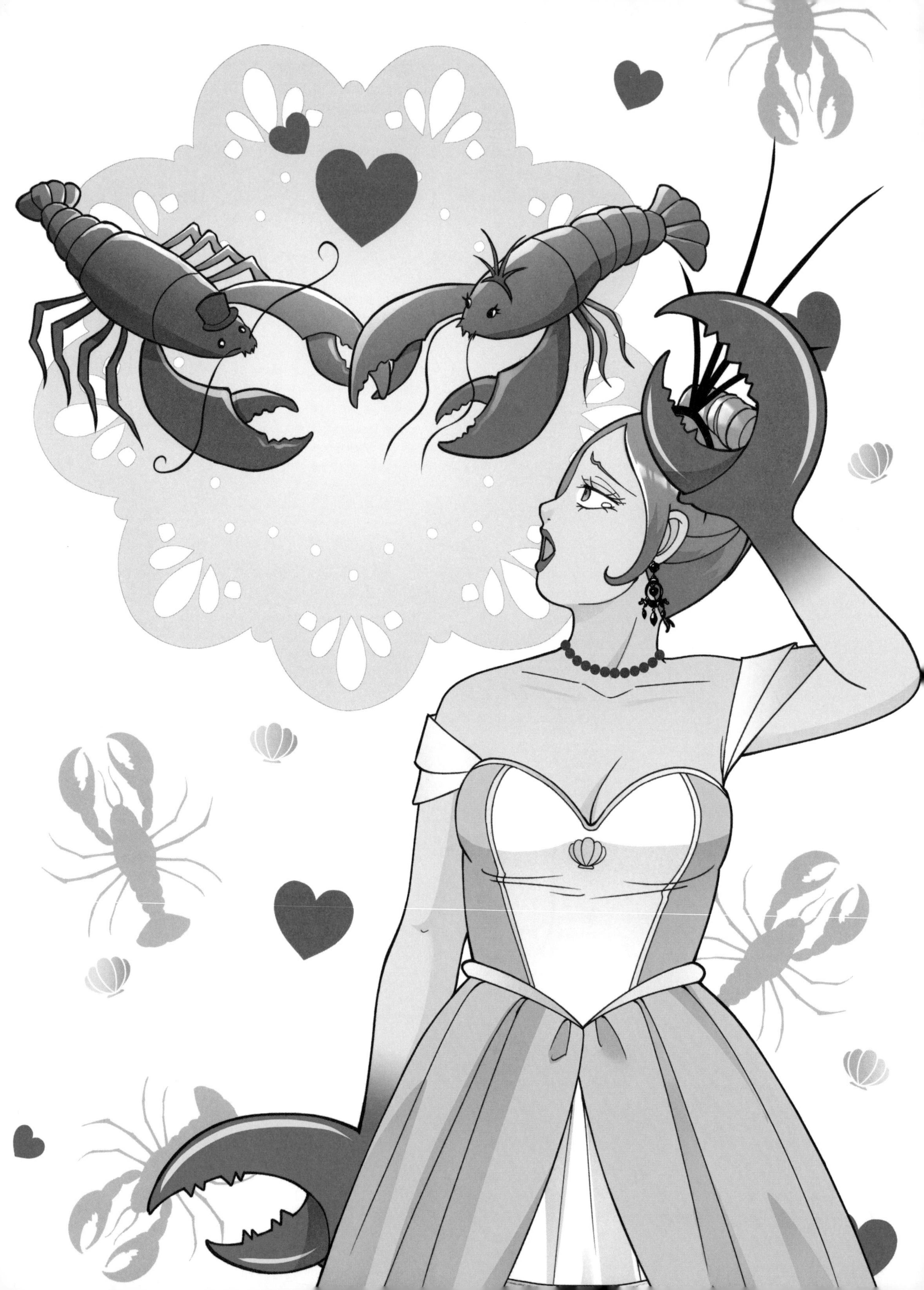

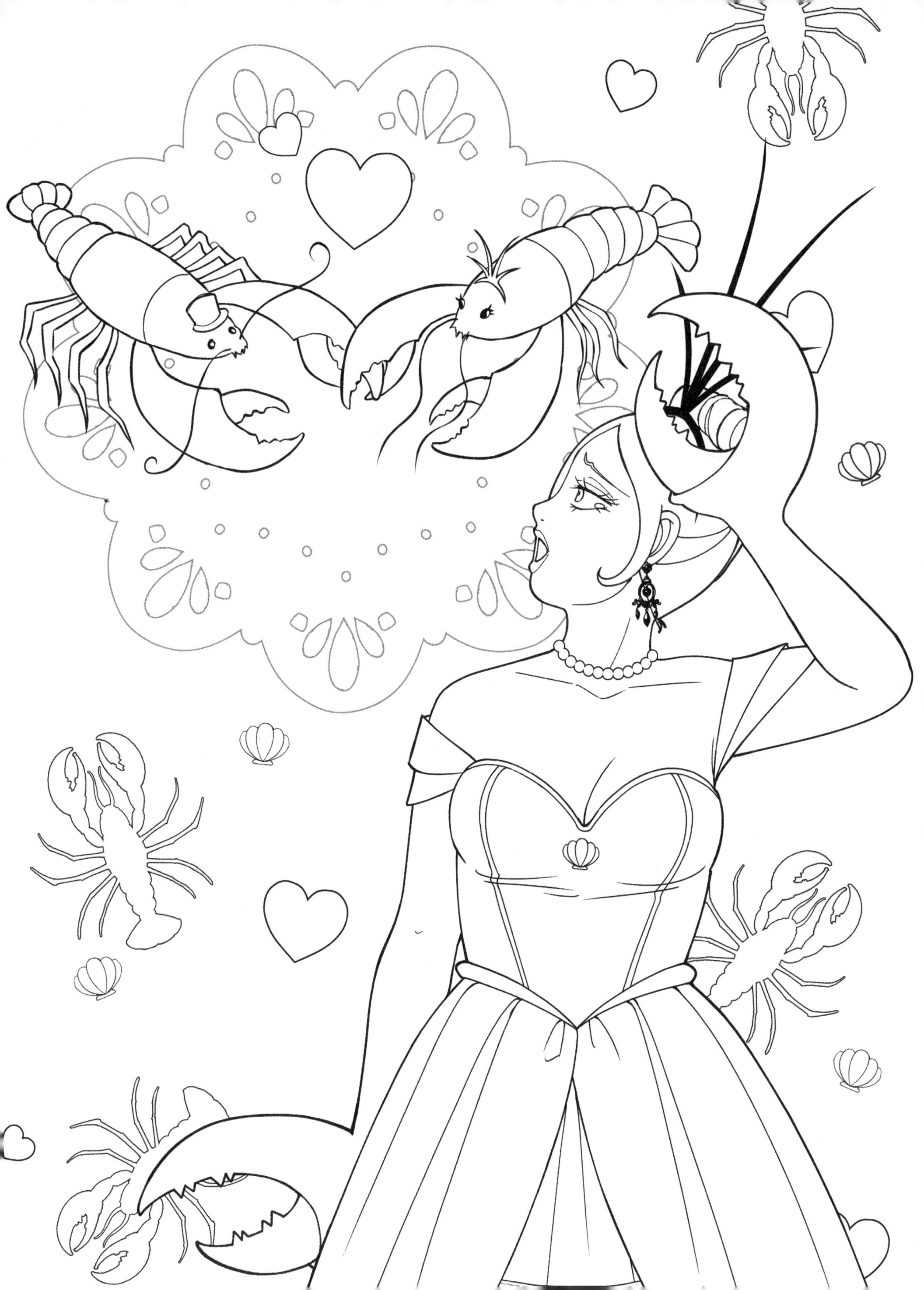

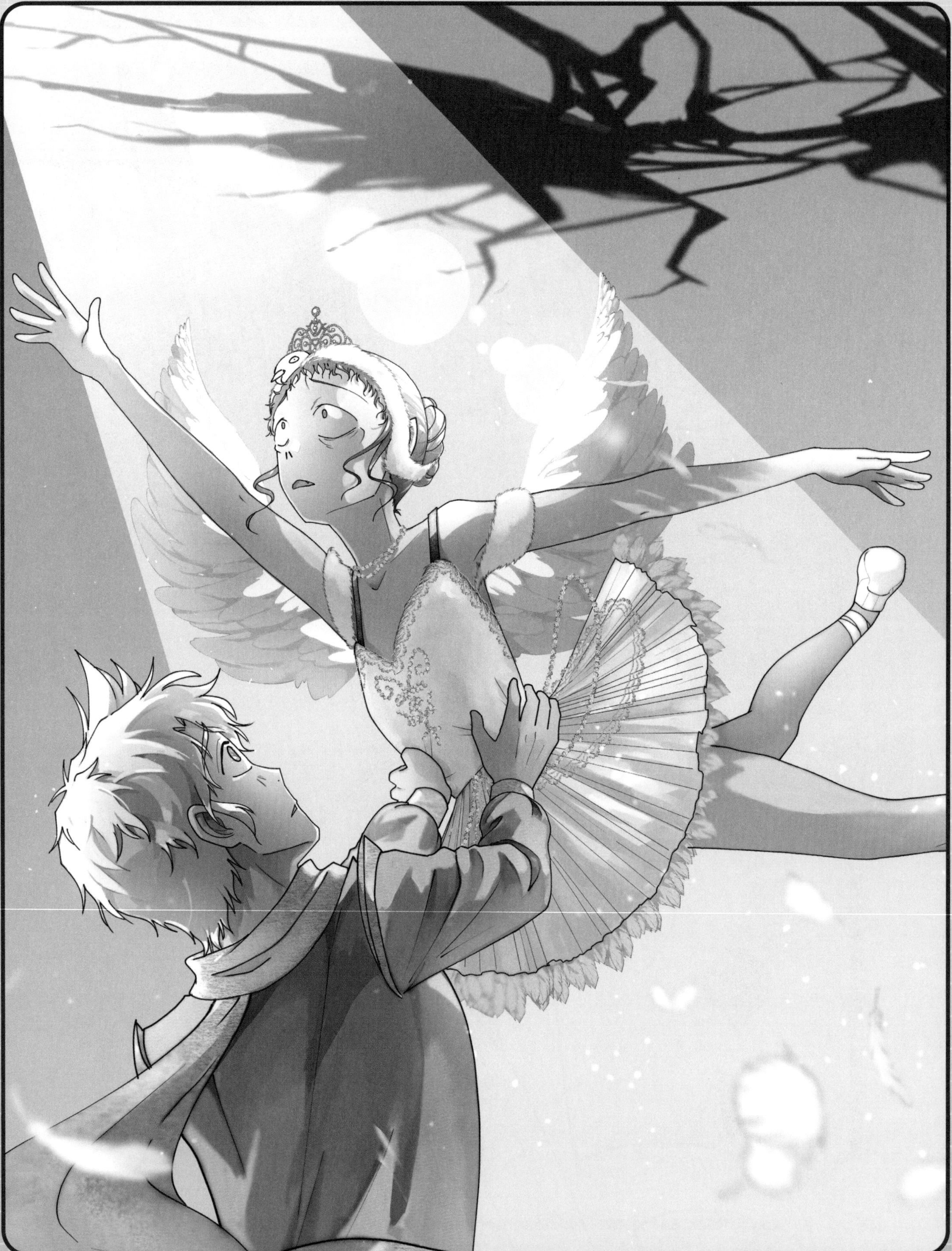

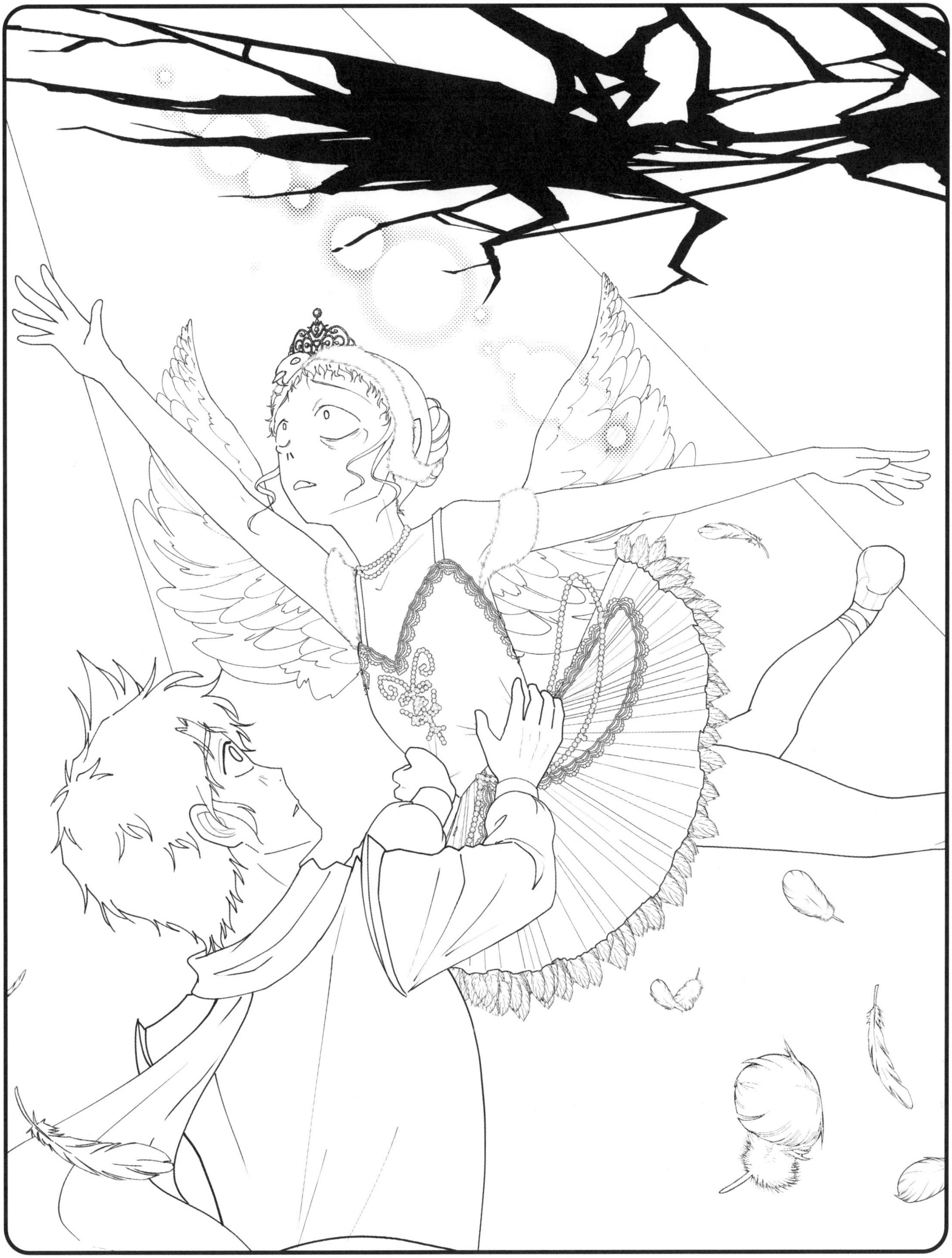

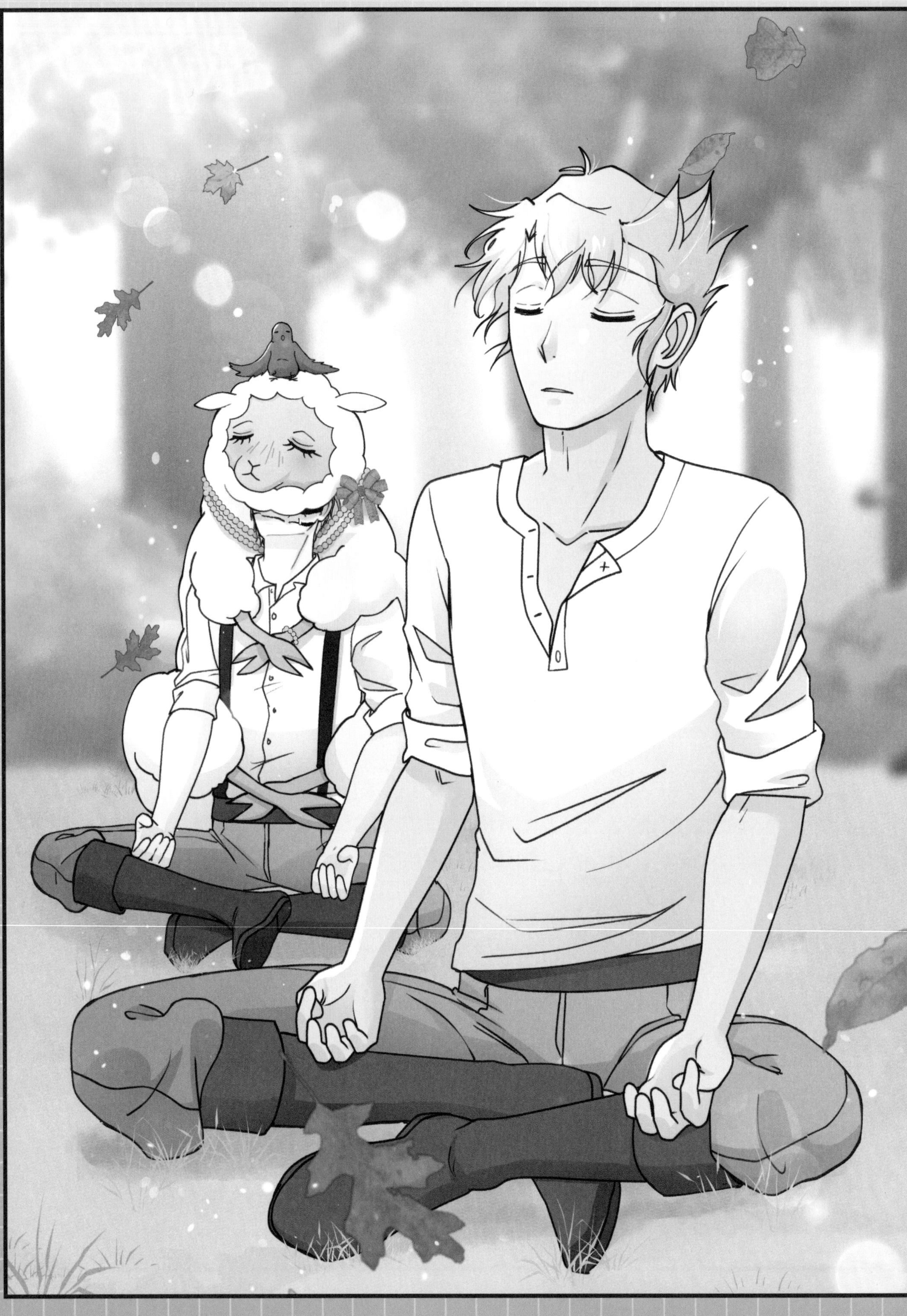

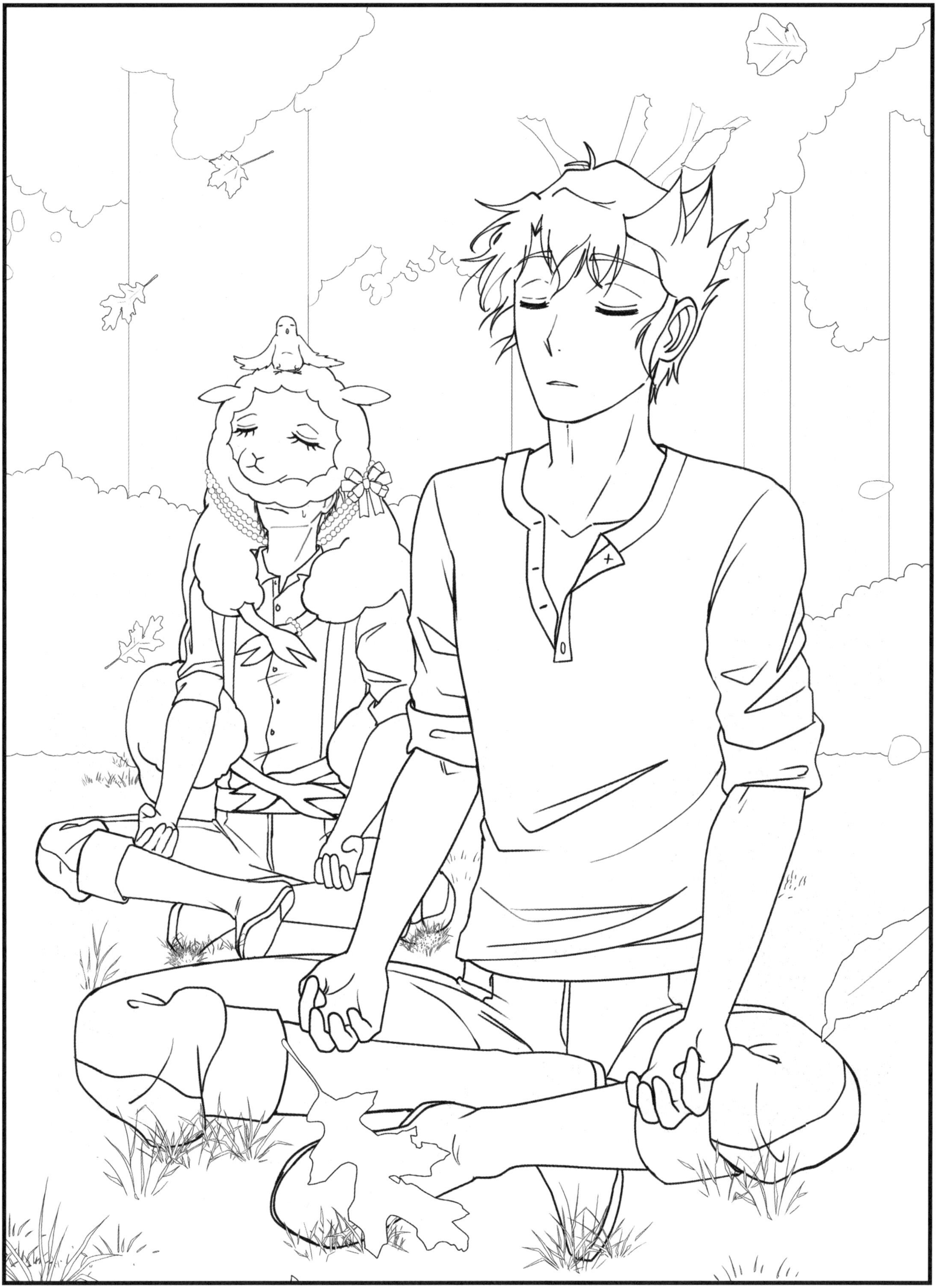

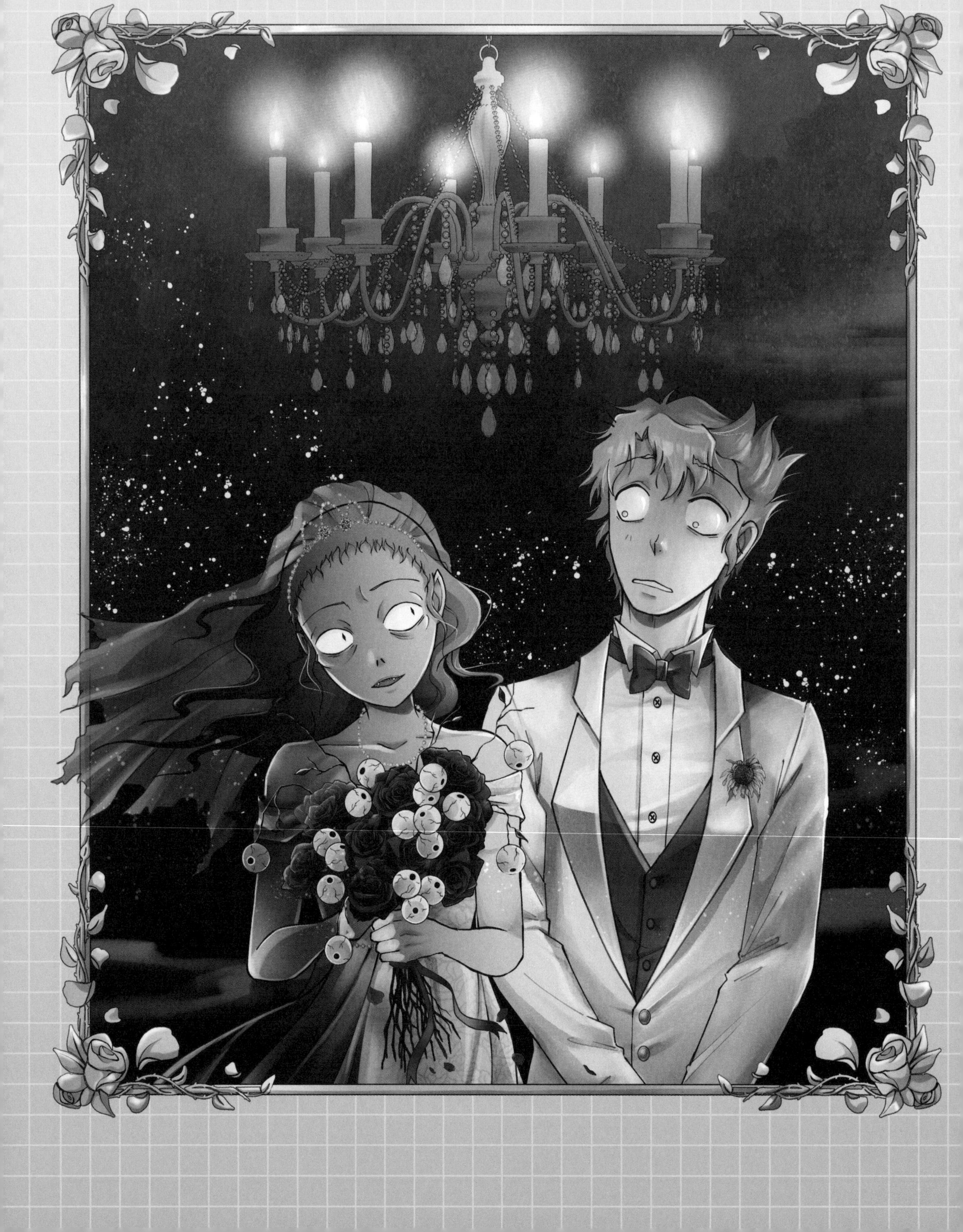

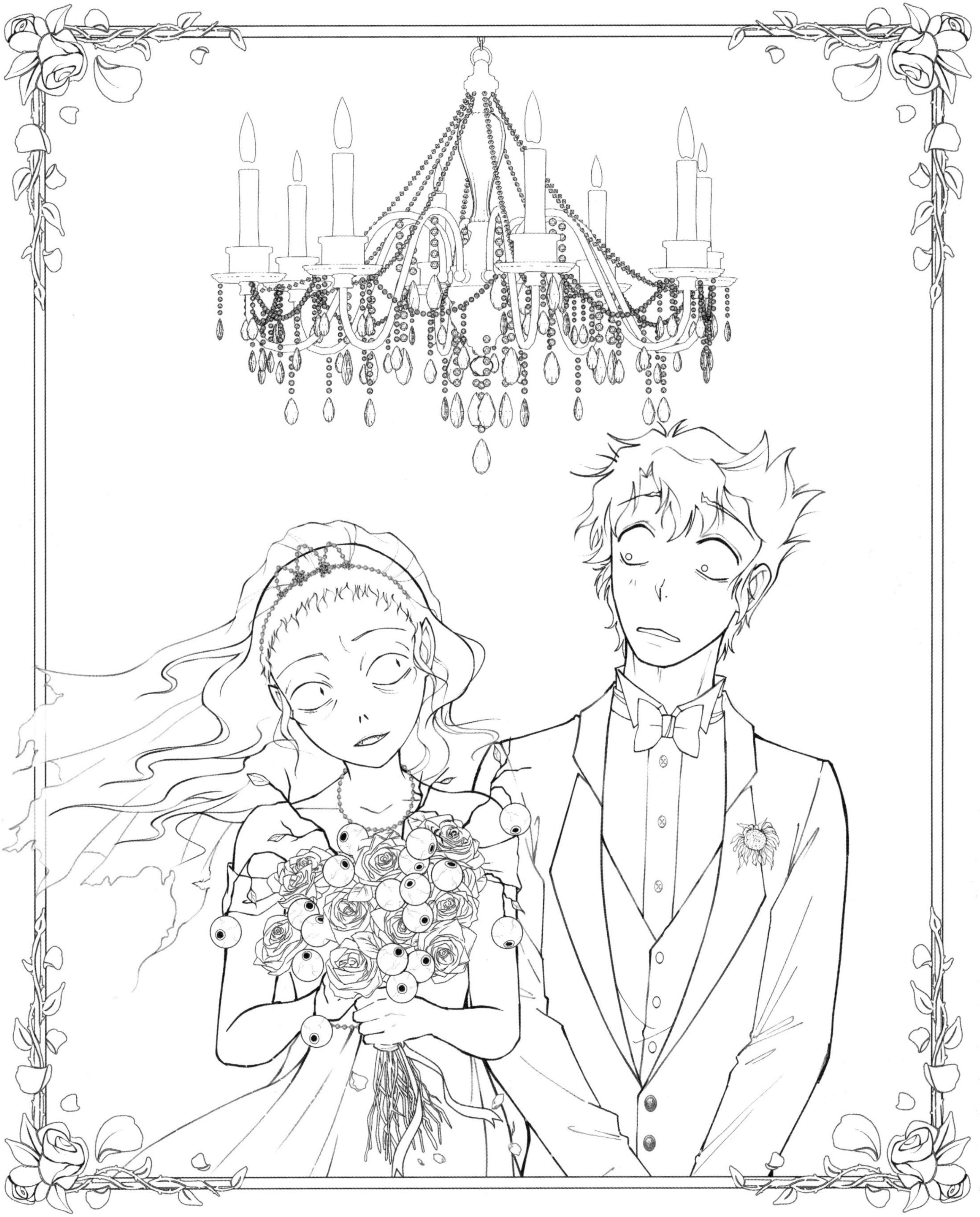

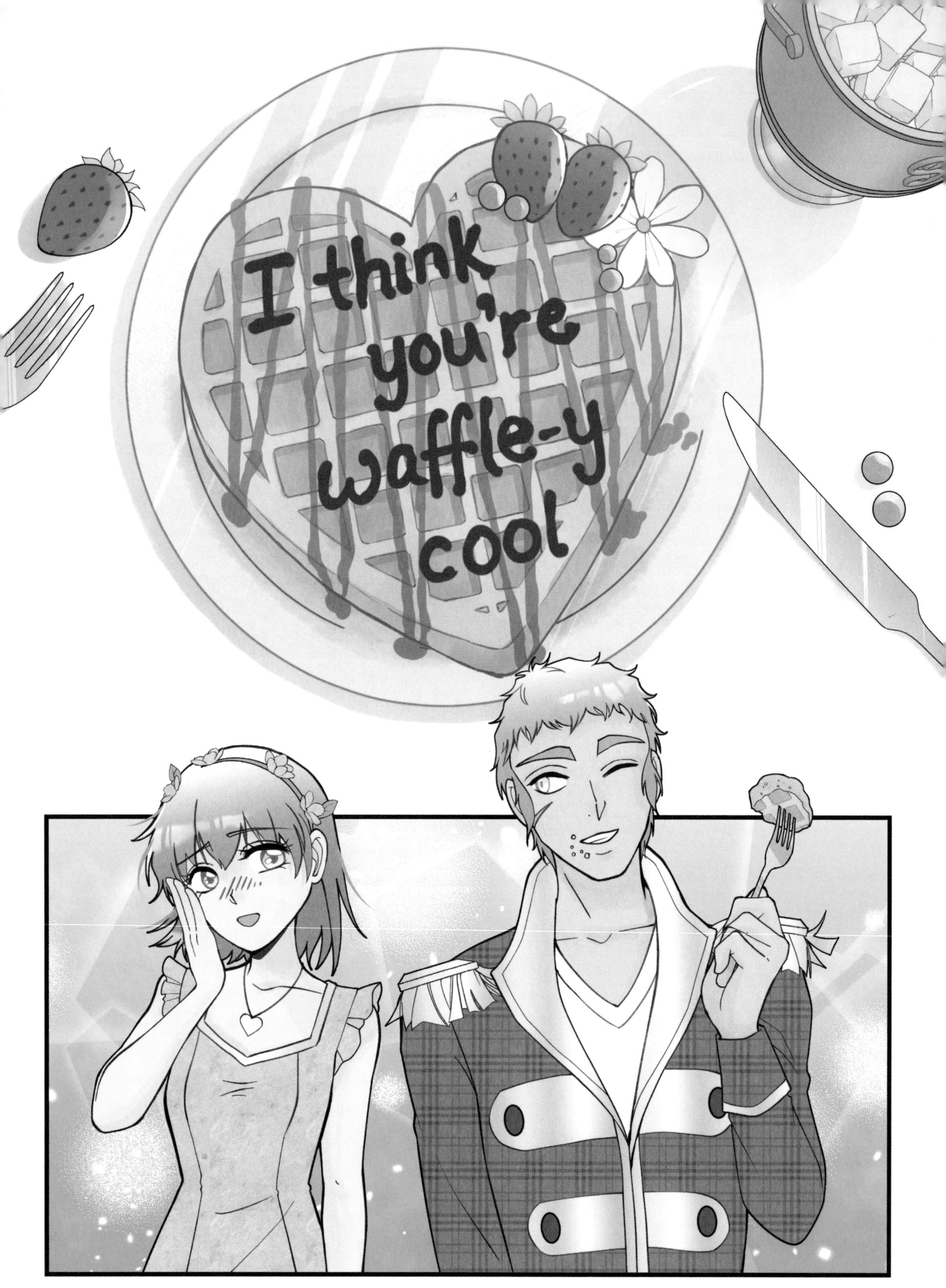
I think you're waffle-y cool

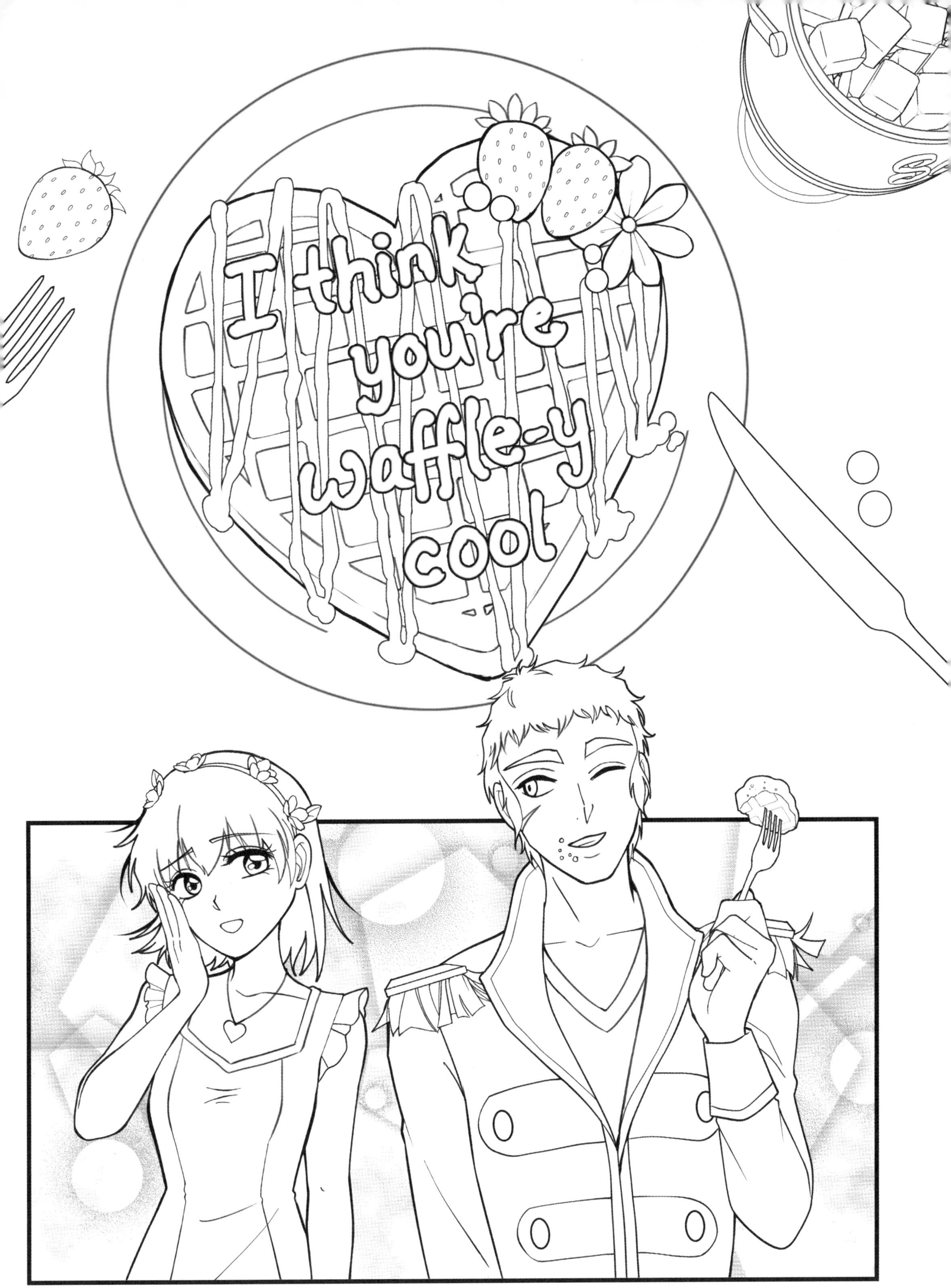
I think you're waffle-y cool

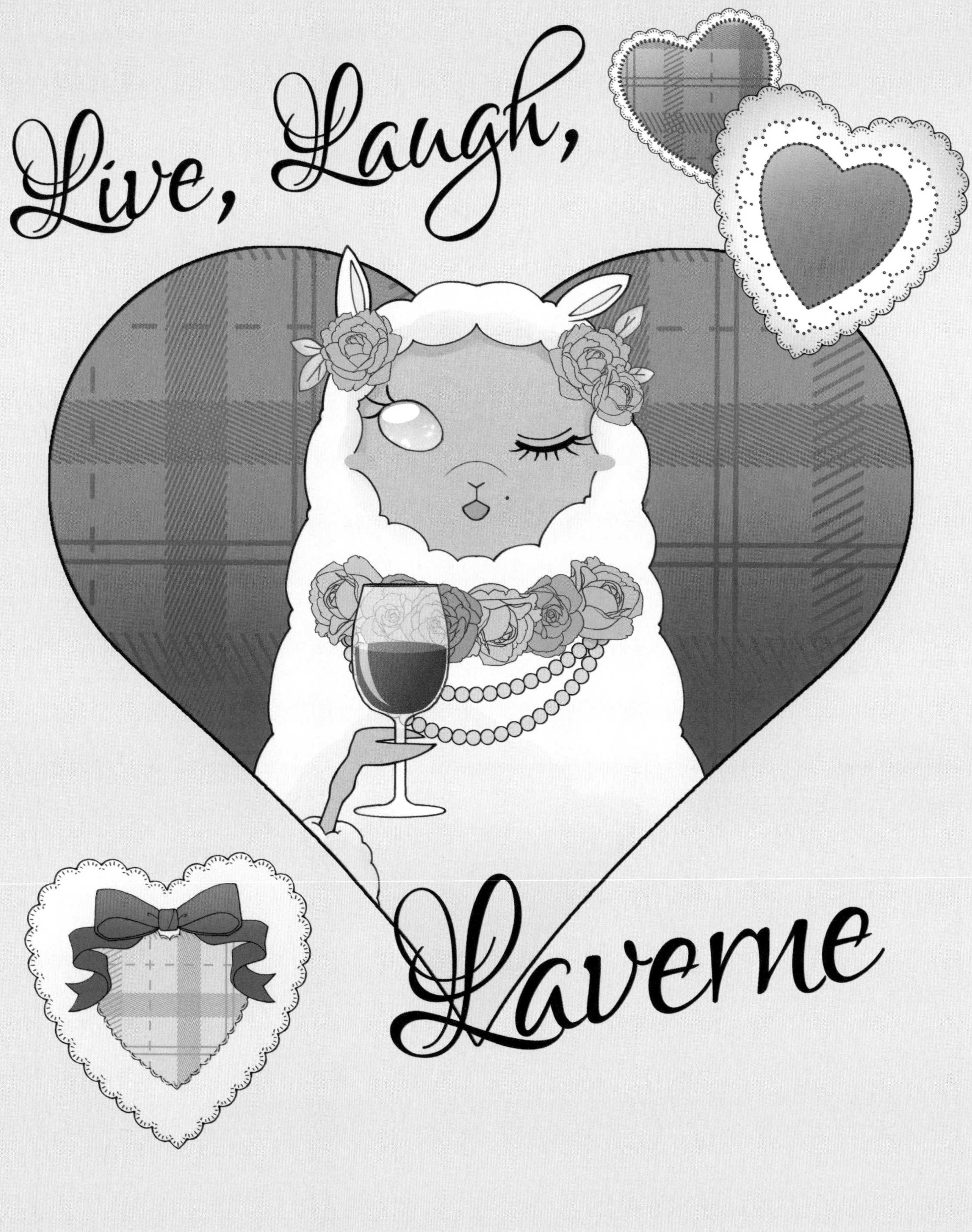
Live, Laugh,
Laverne

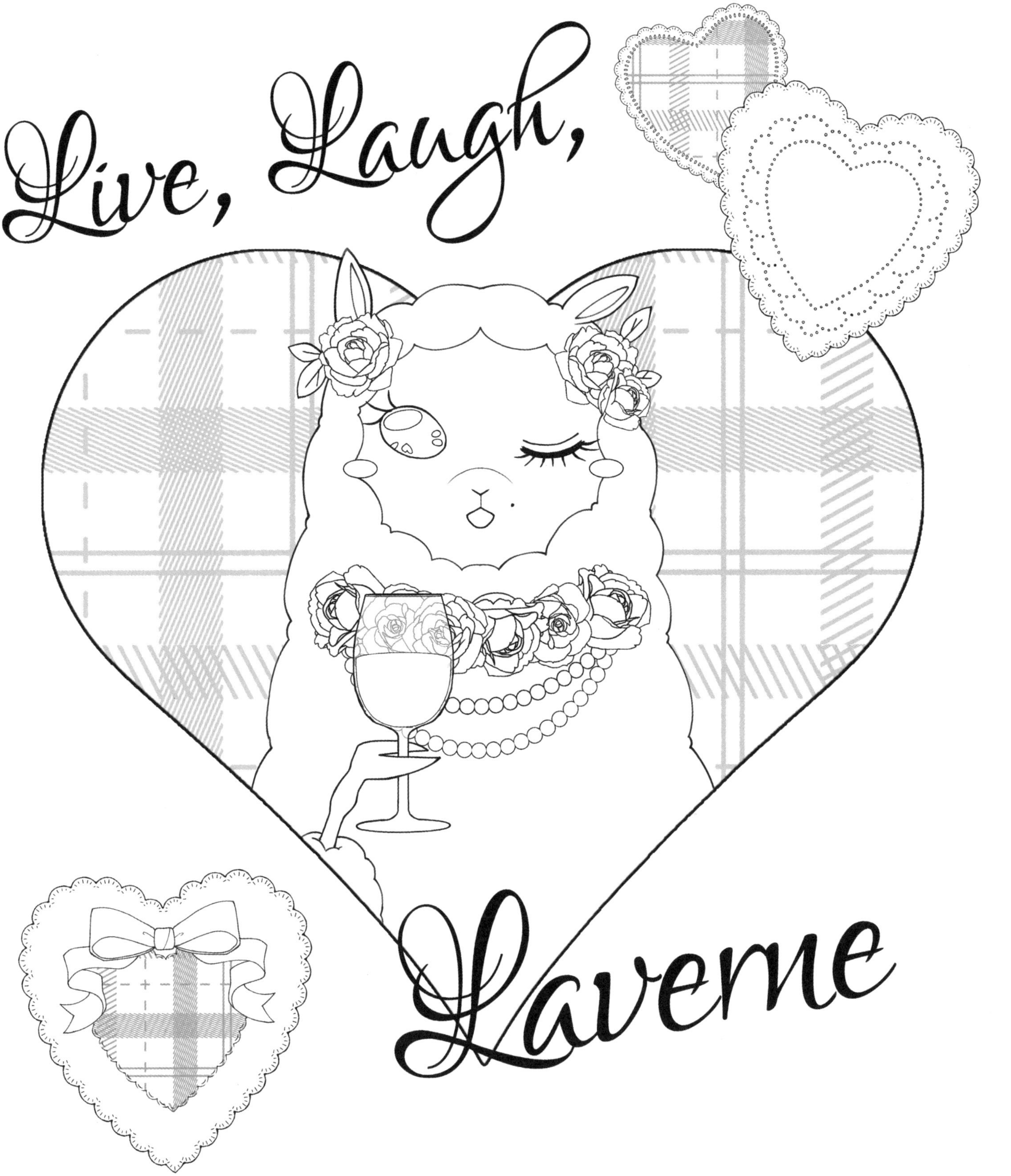
Live, Laugh,
Laveme

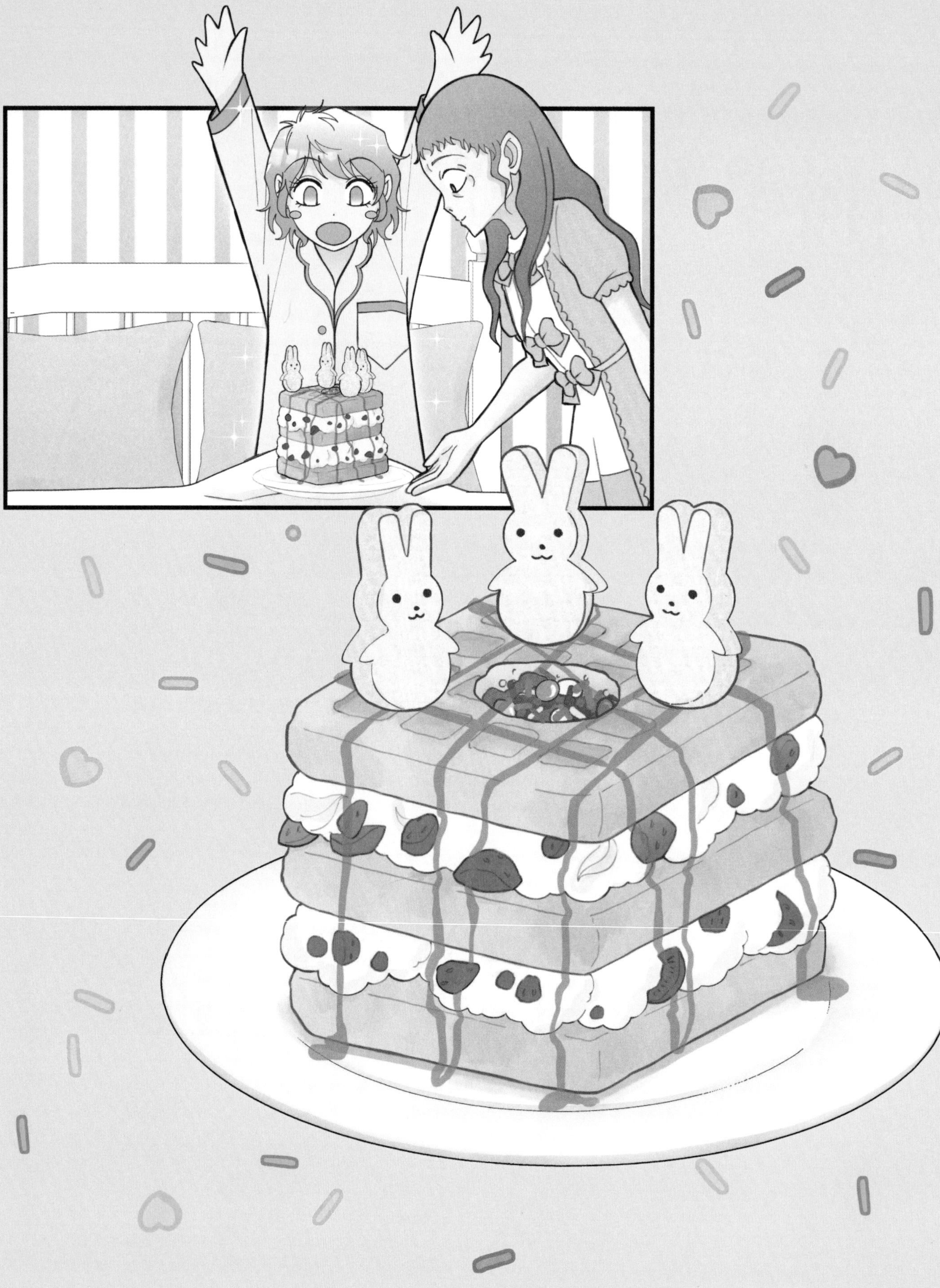

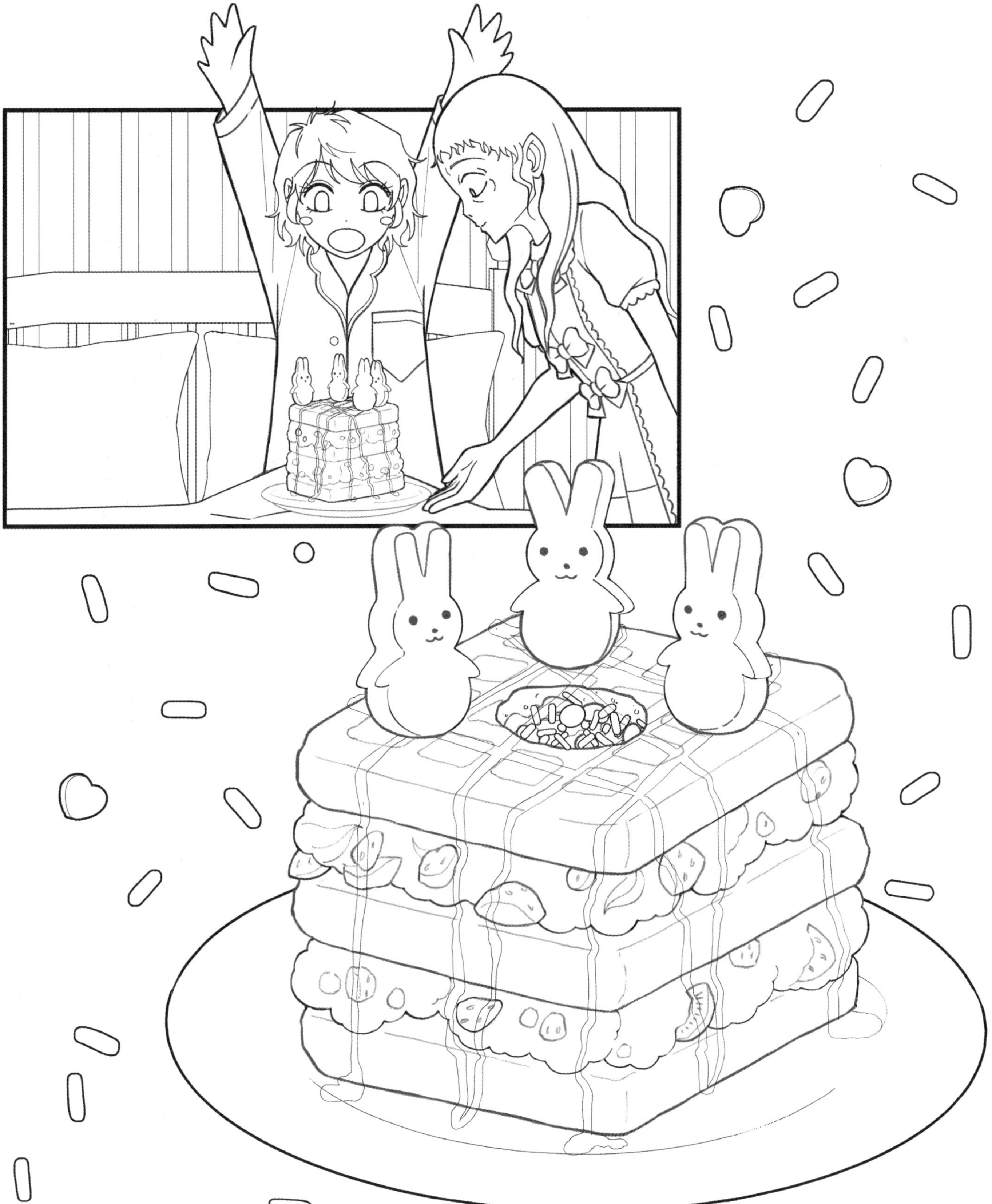

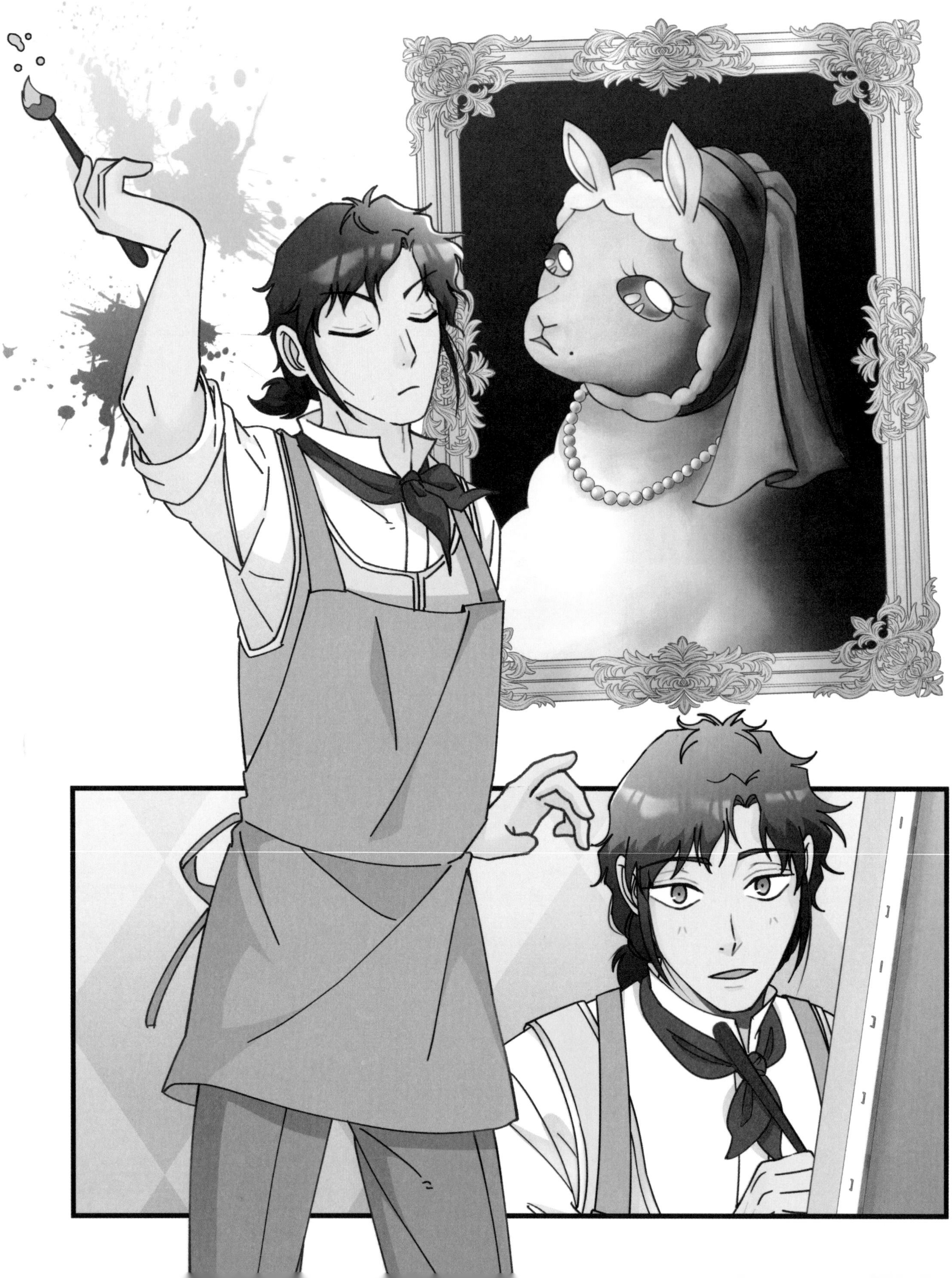

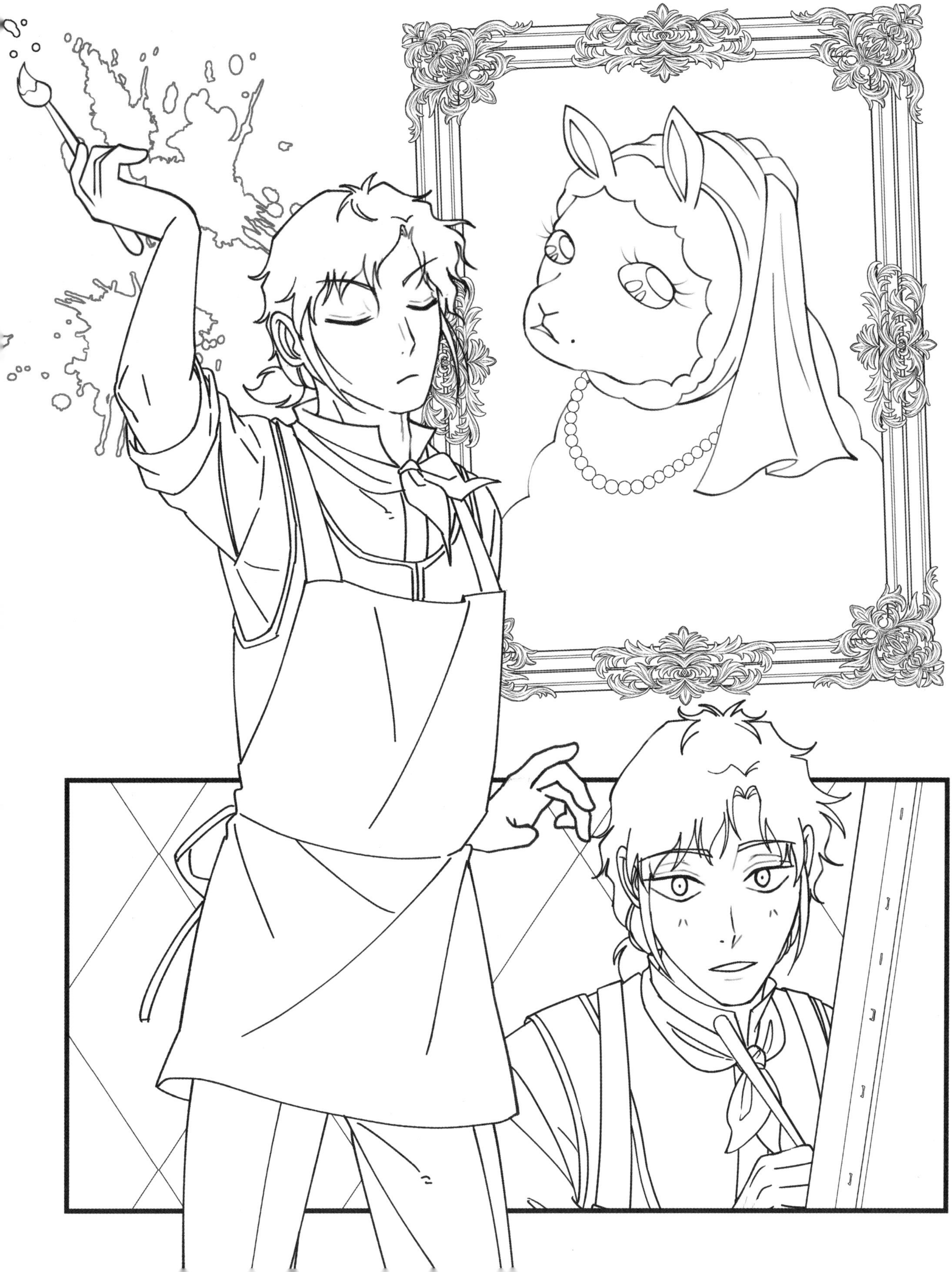

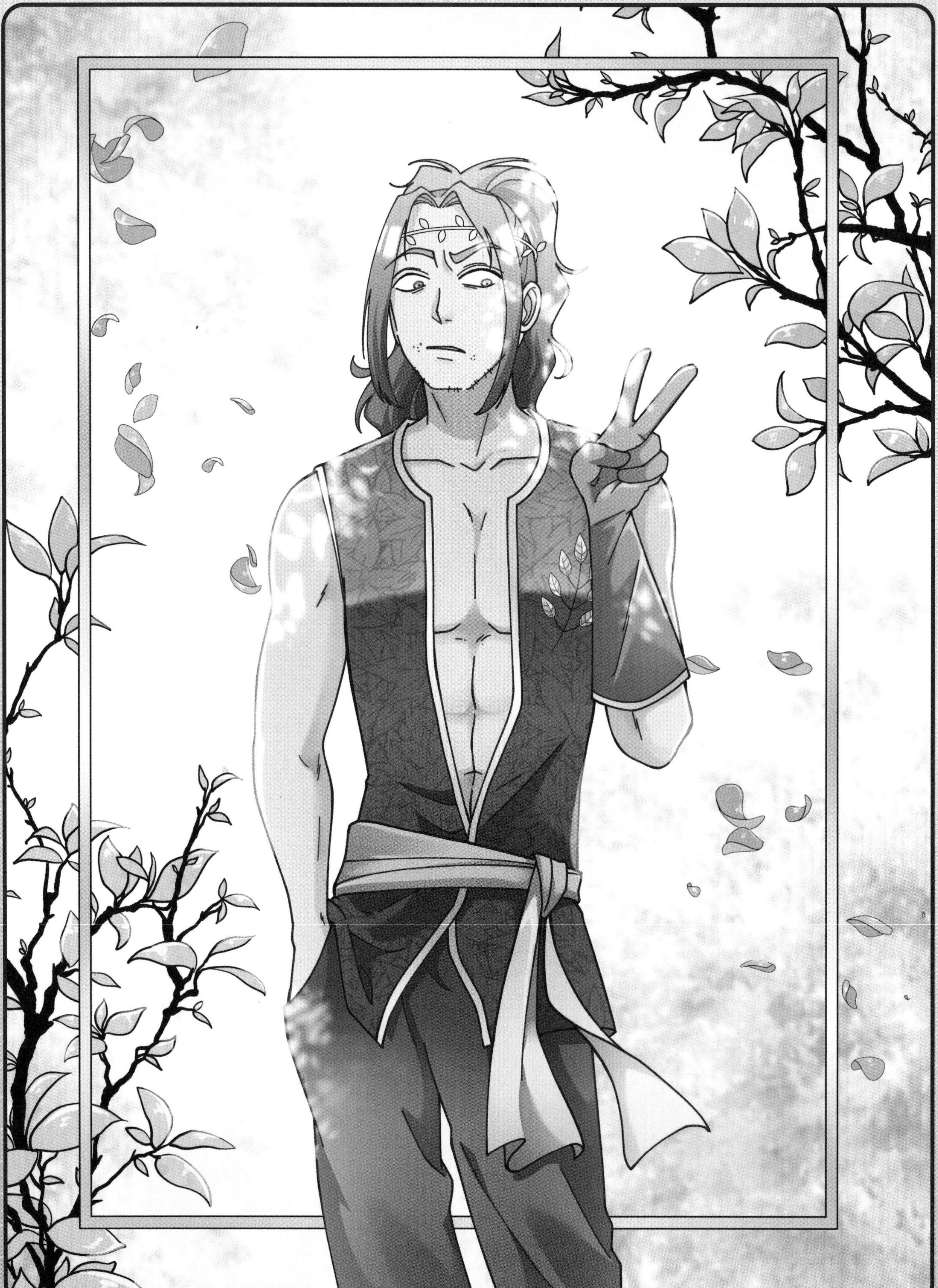

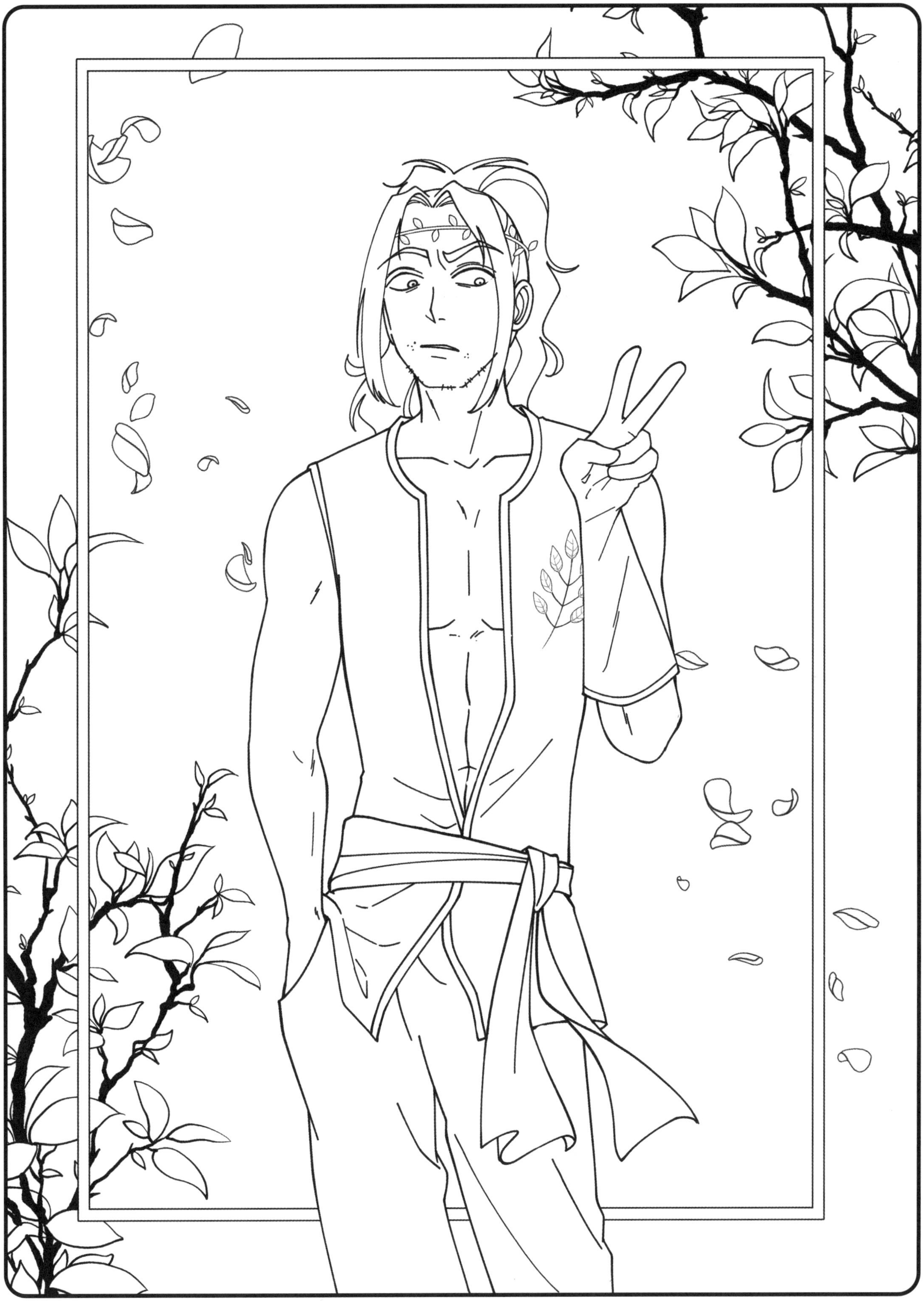

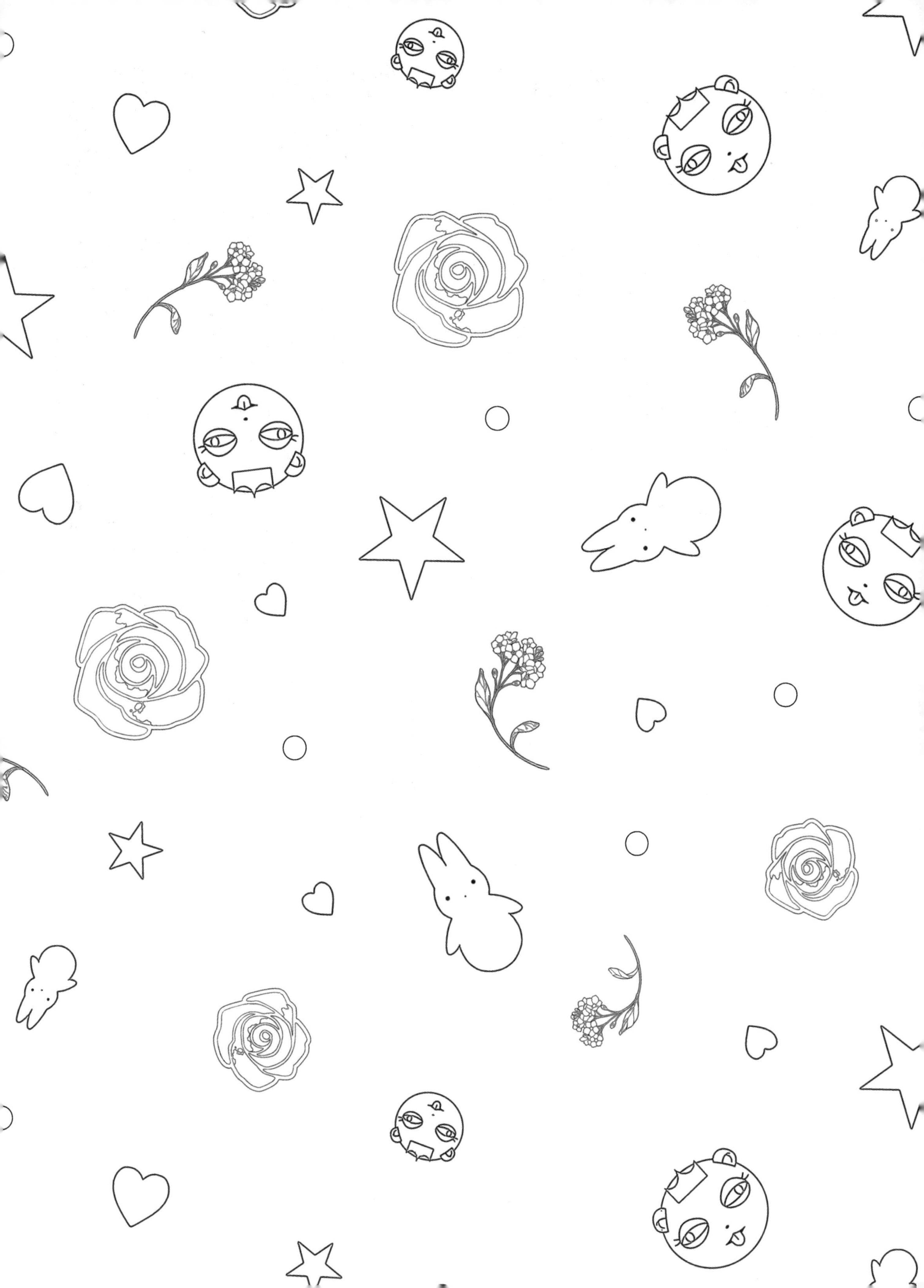

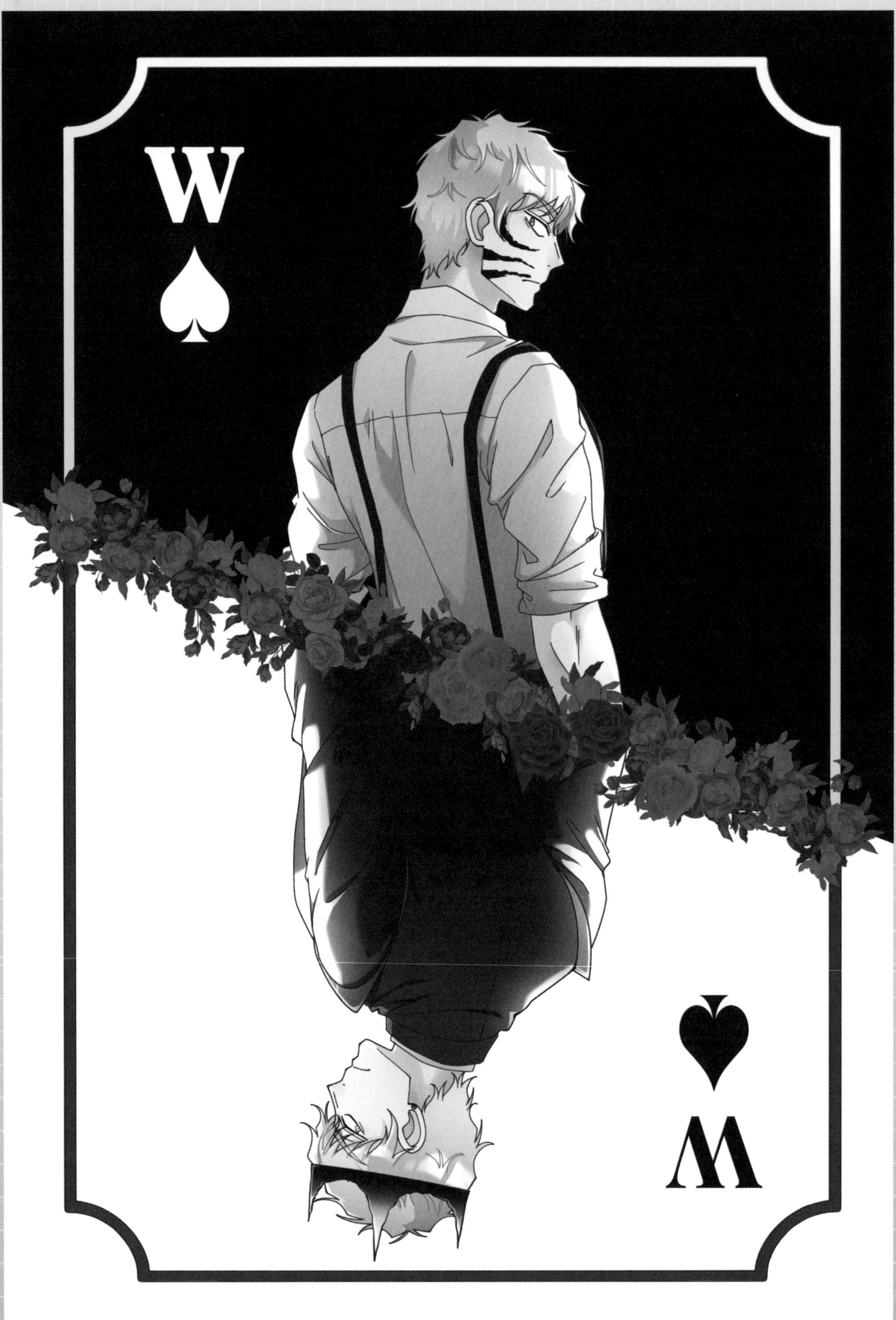
W
W

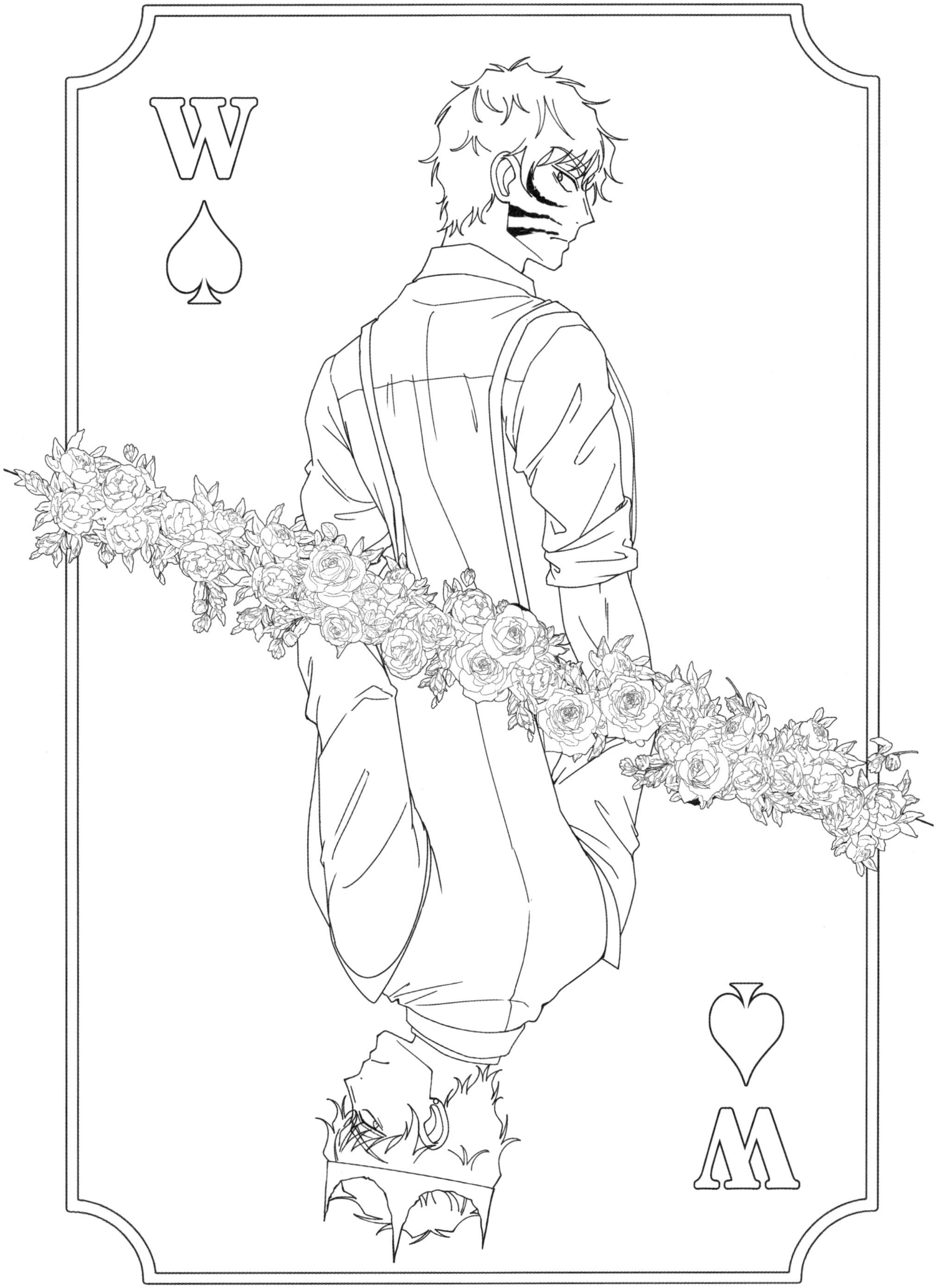
W

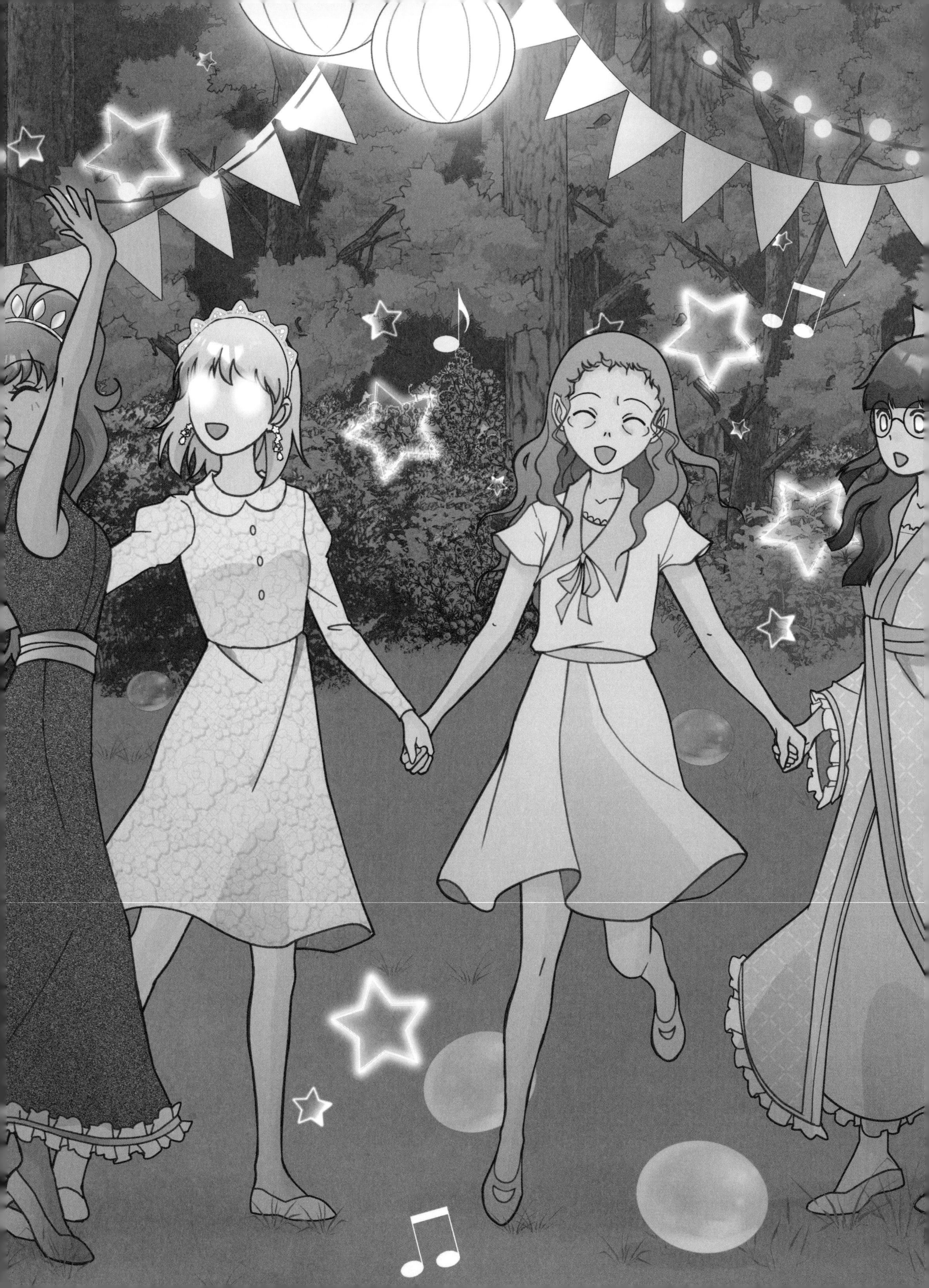

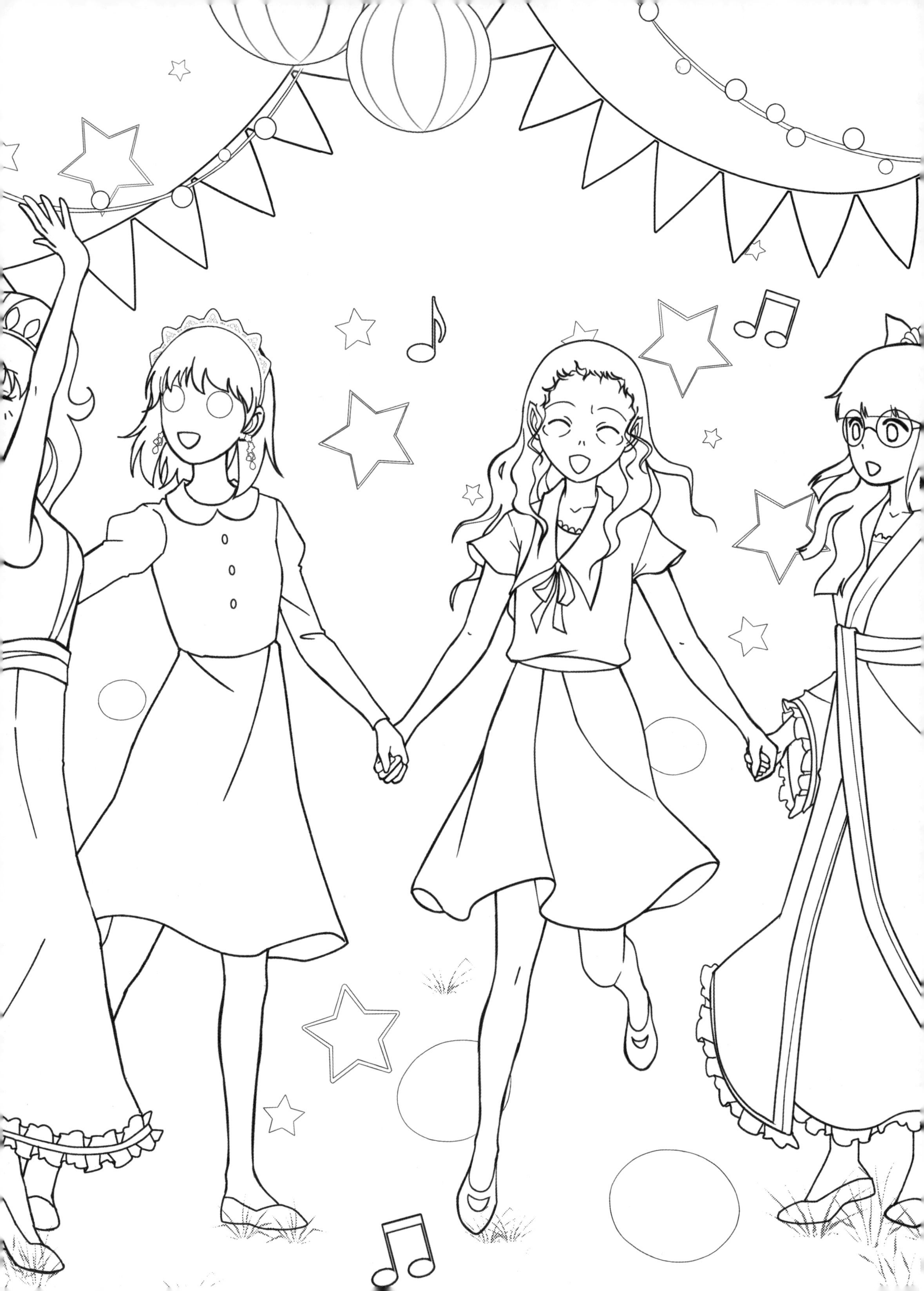

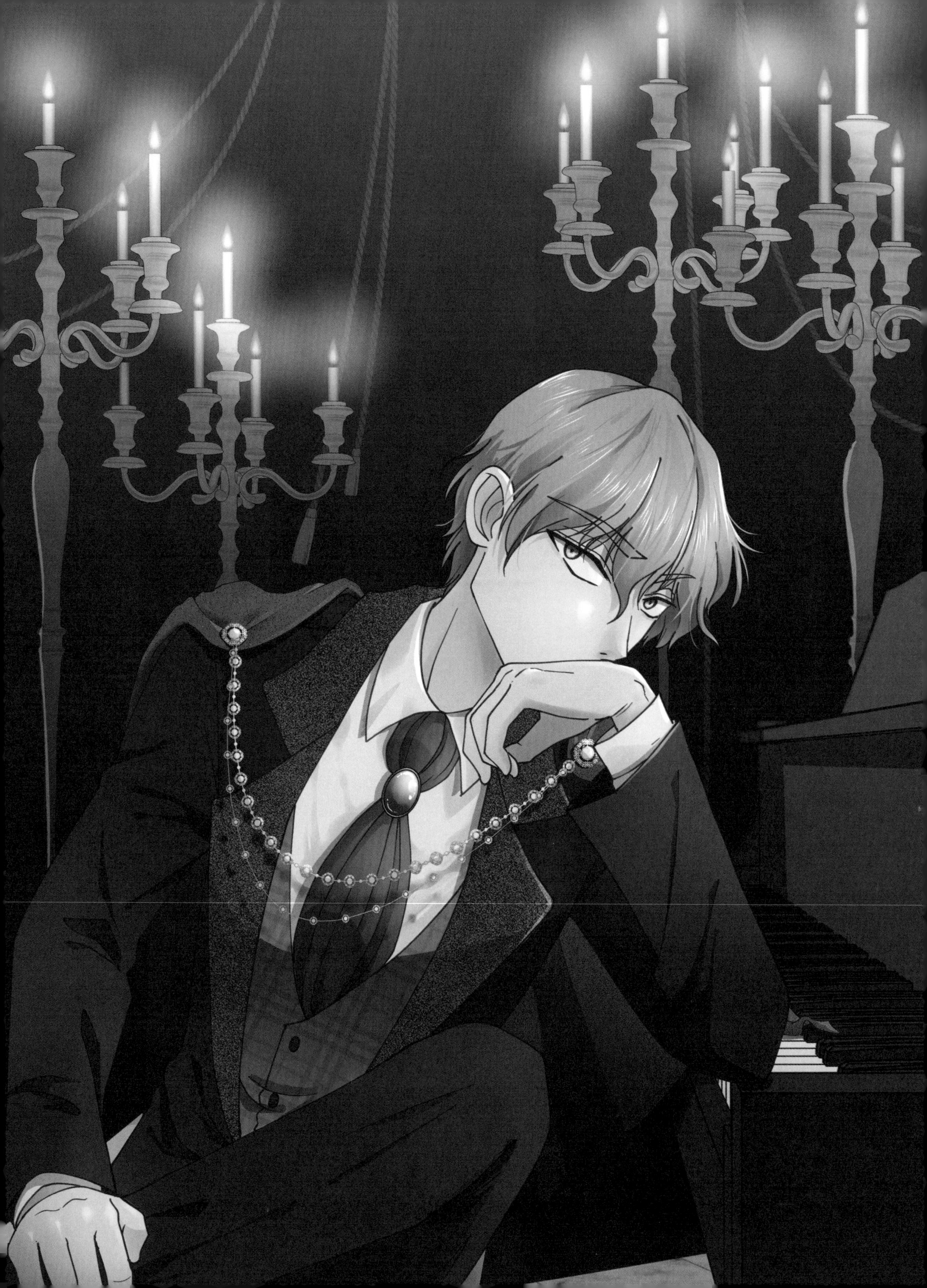

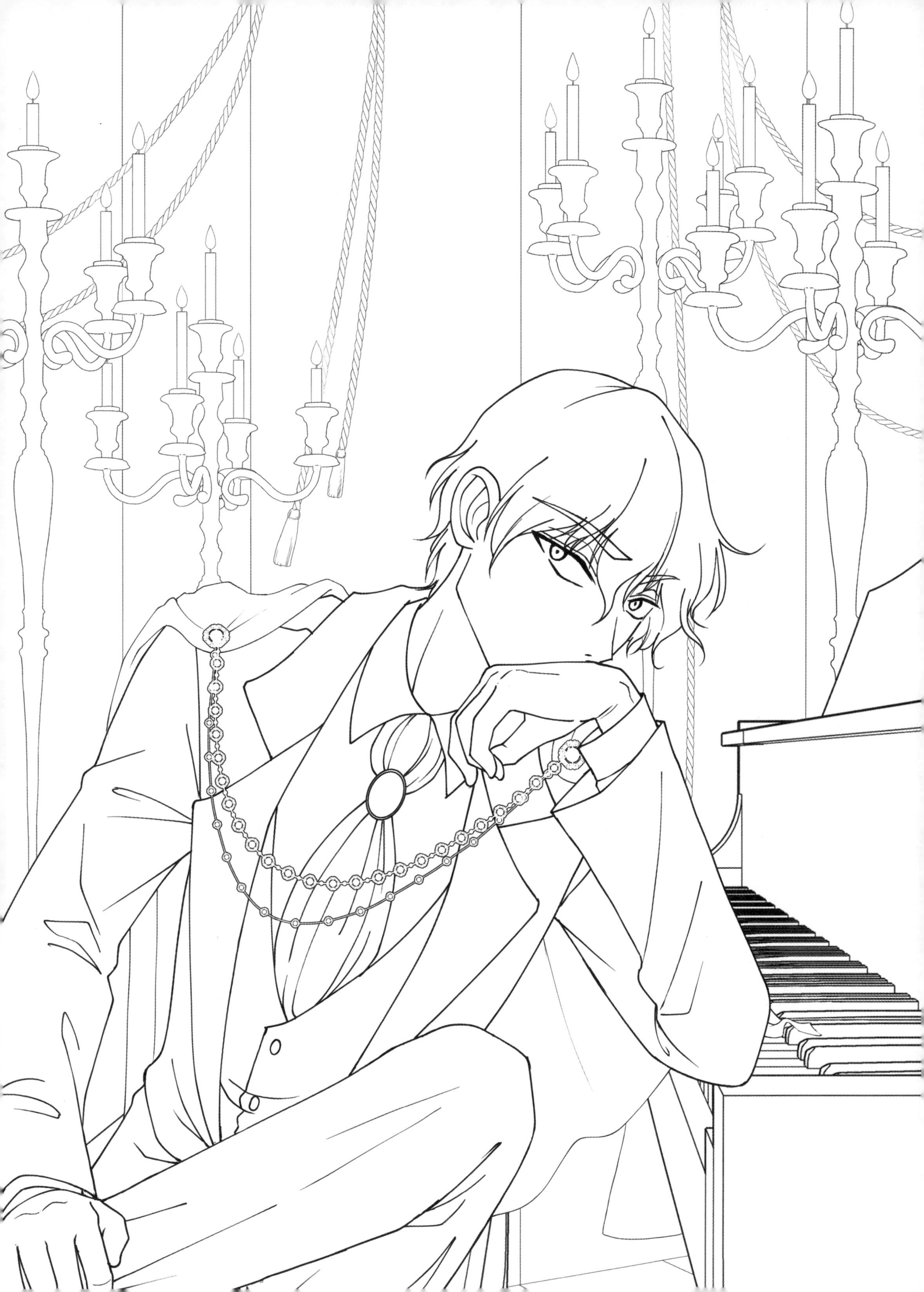

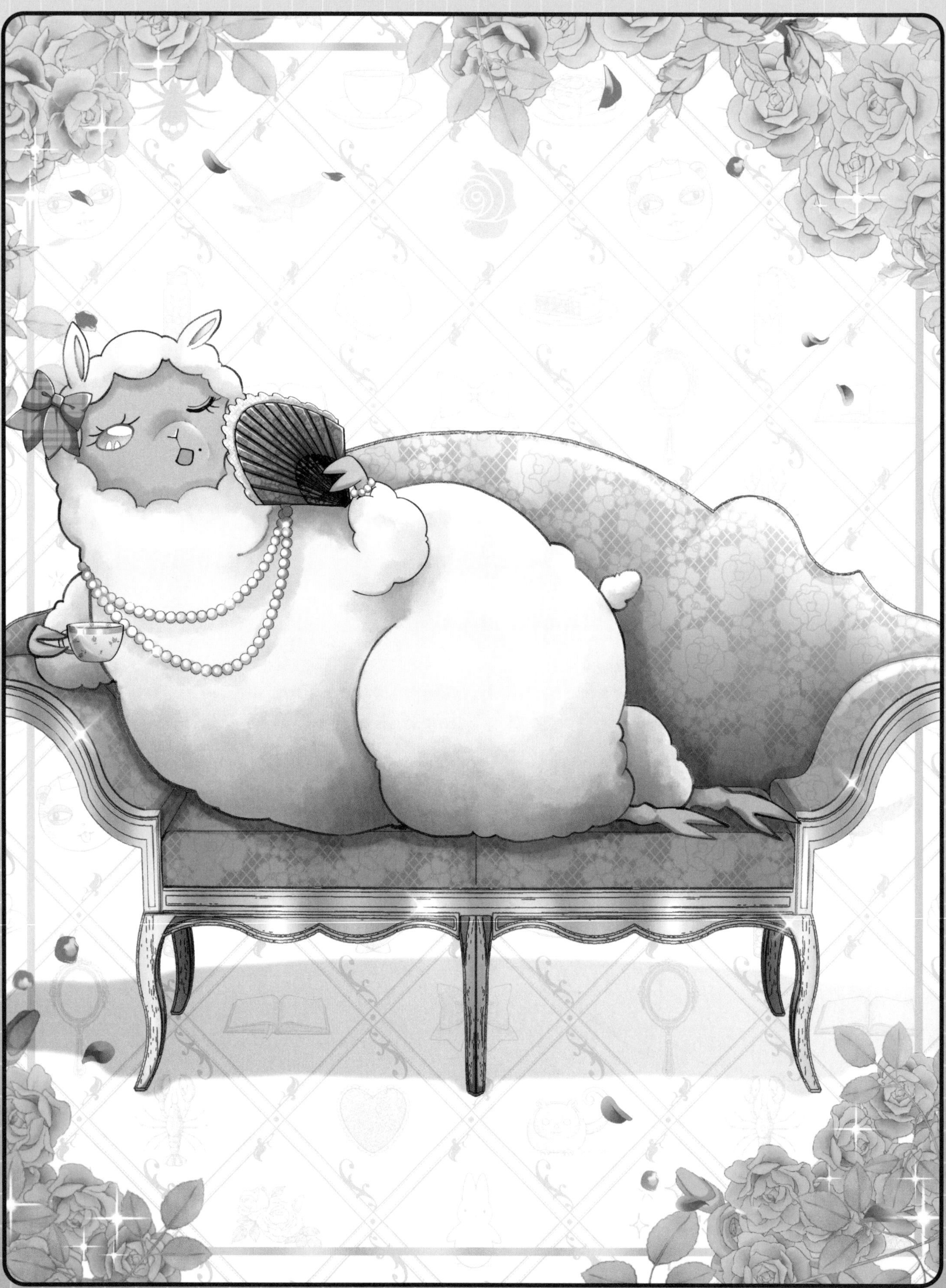

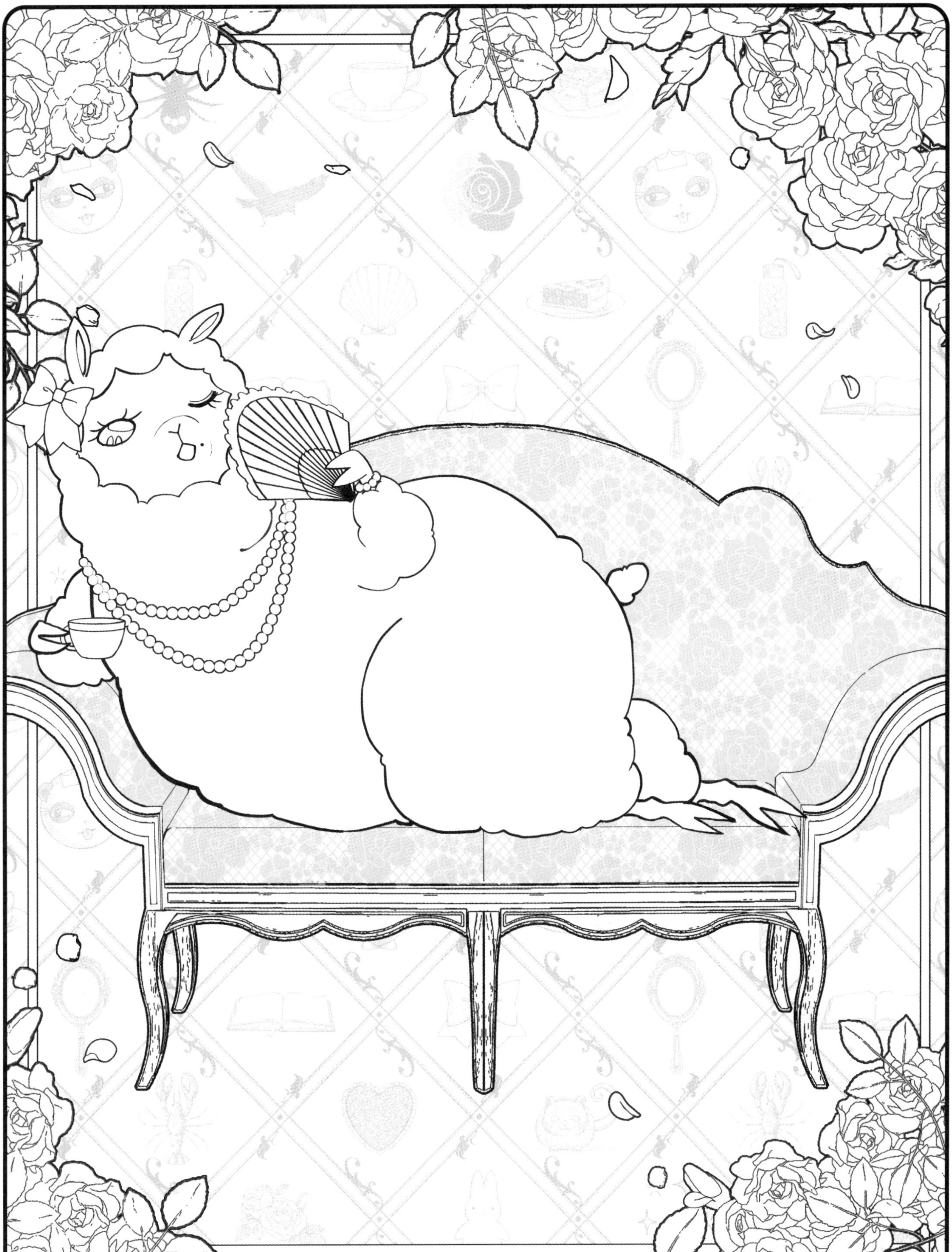

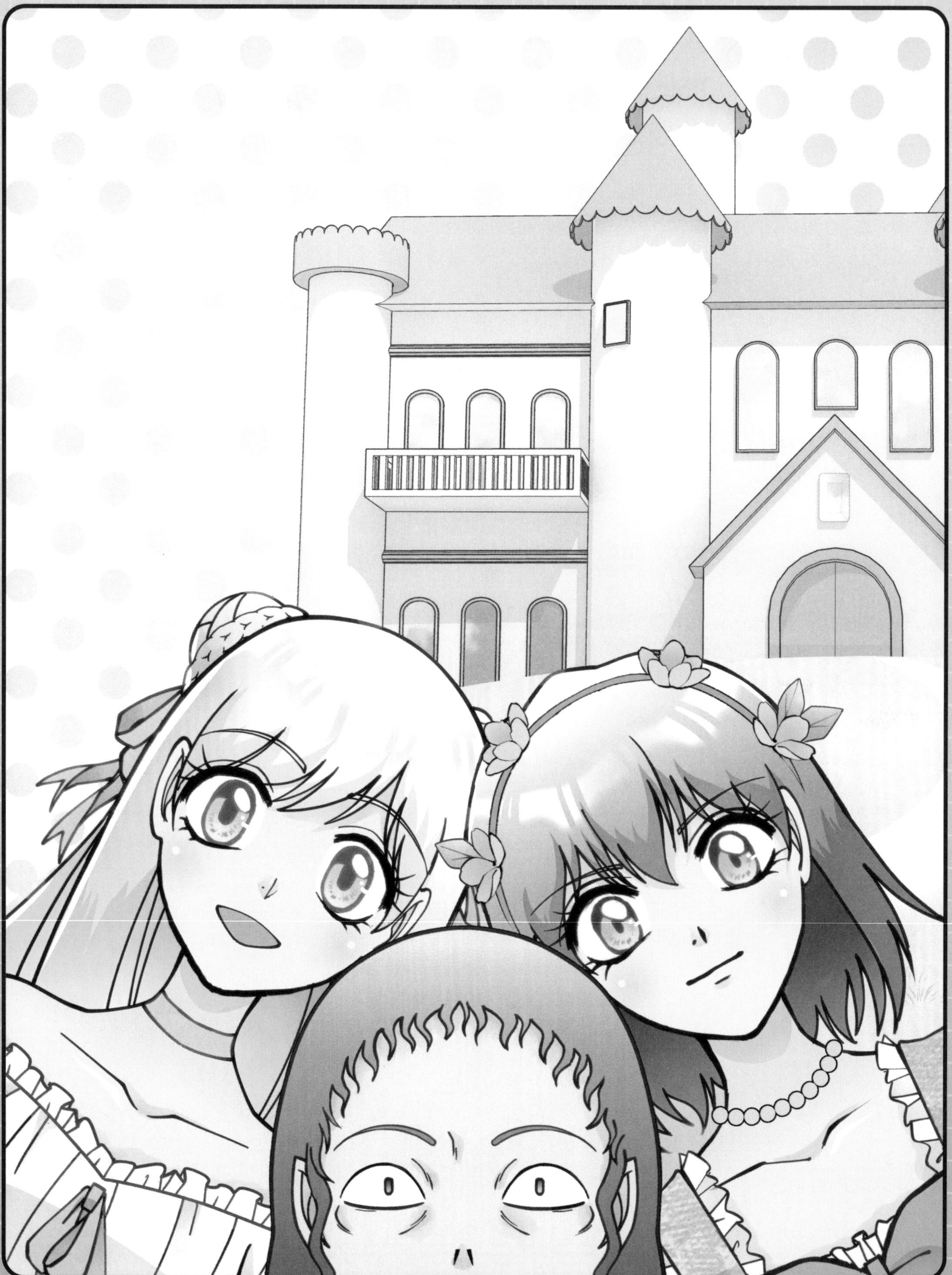

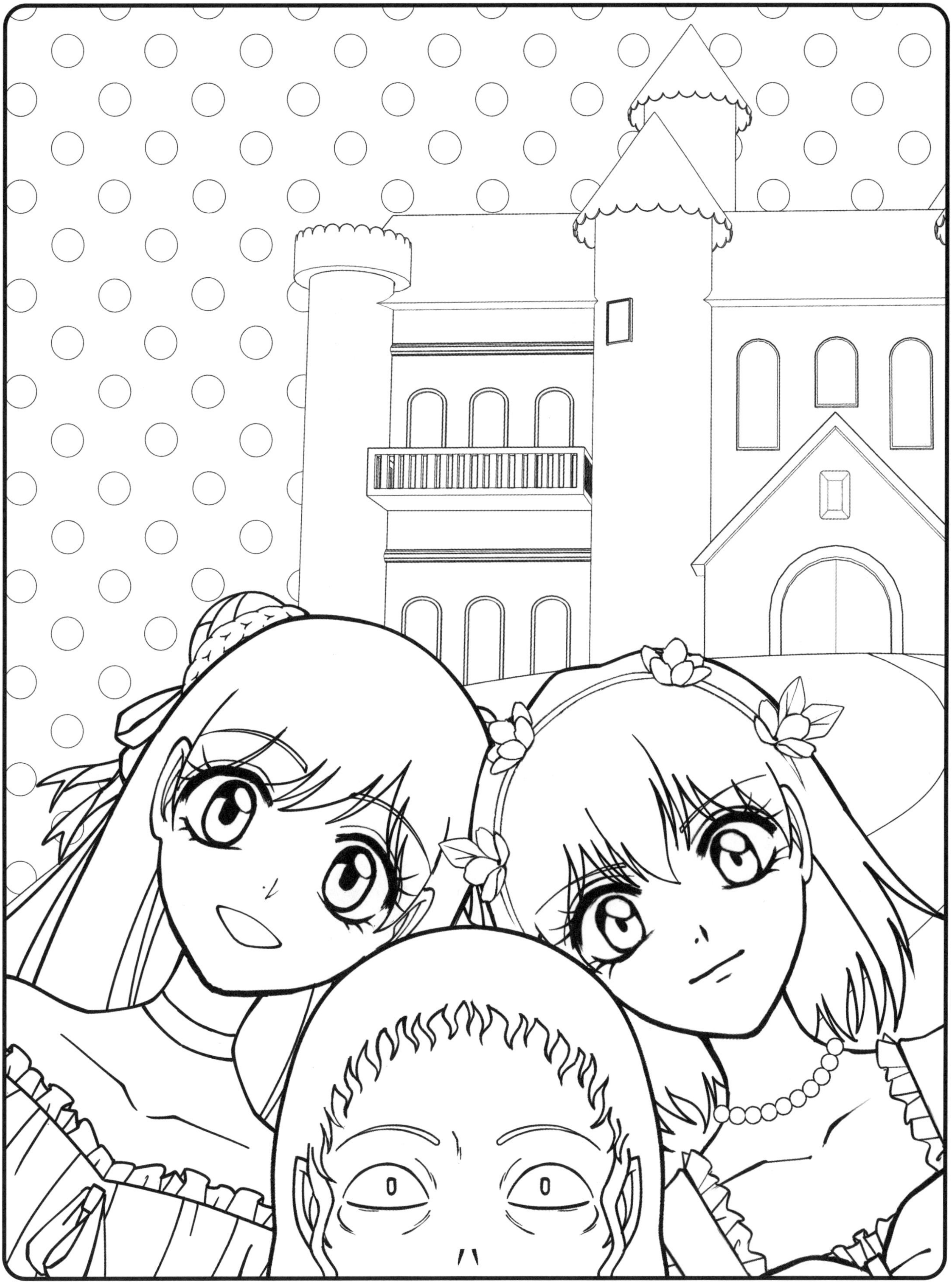

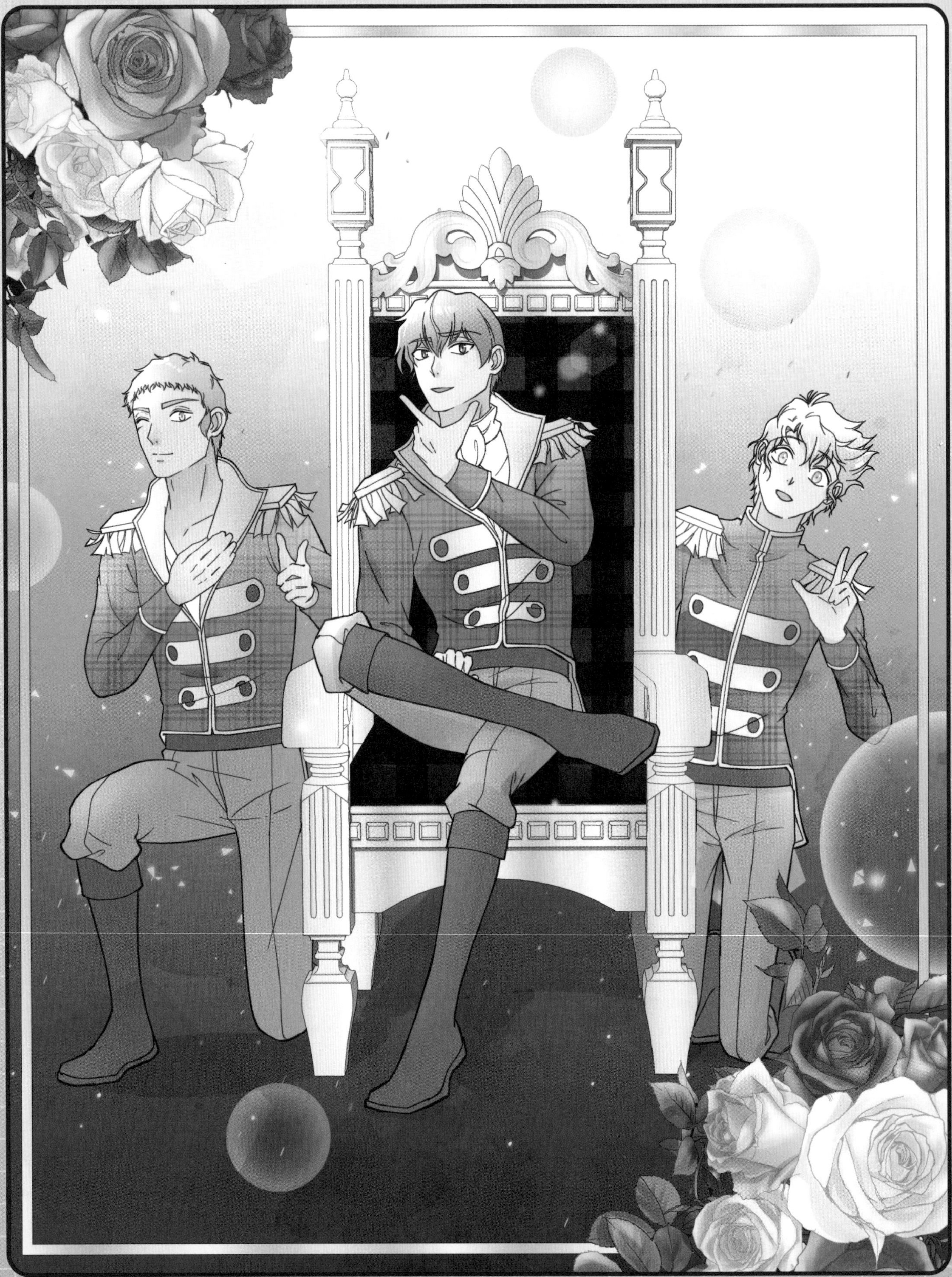

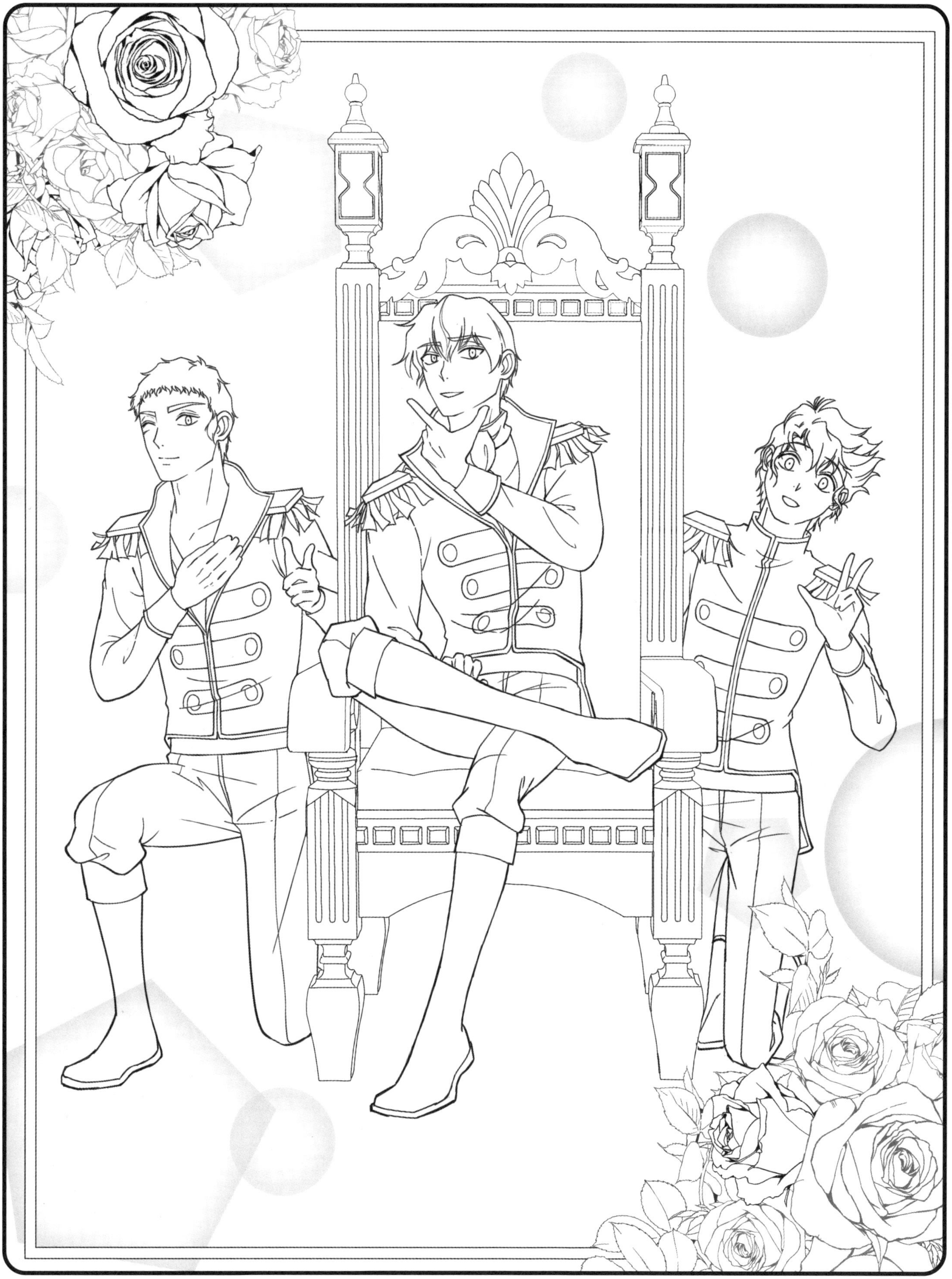

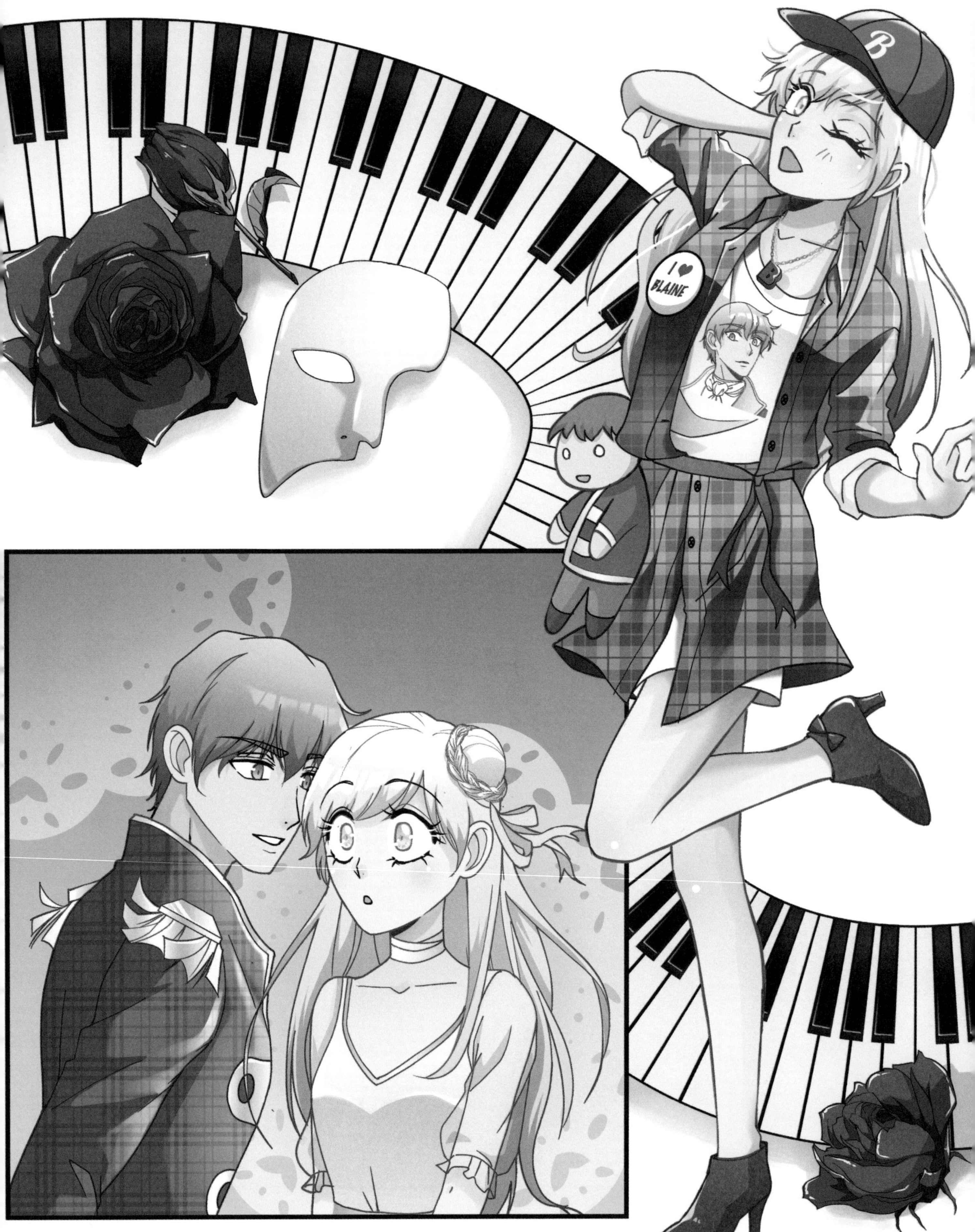
I ♥ BLAINE

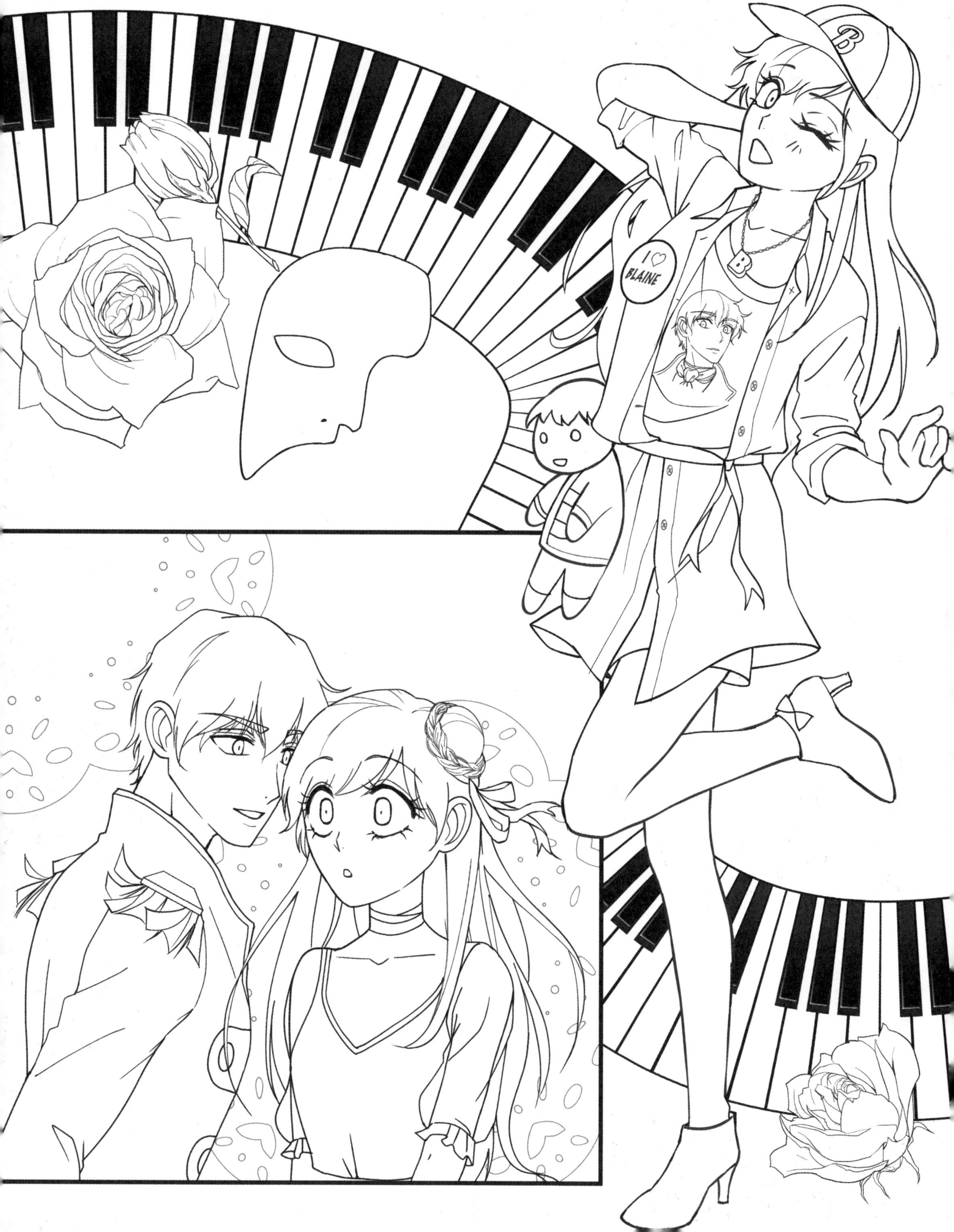
I ♡ BLAINE

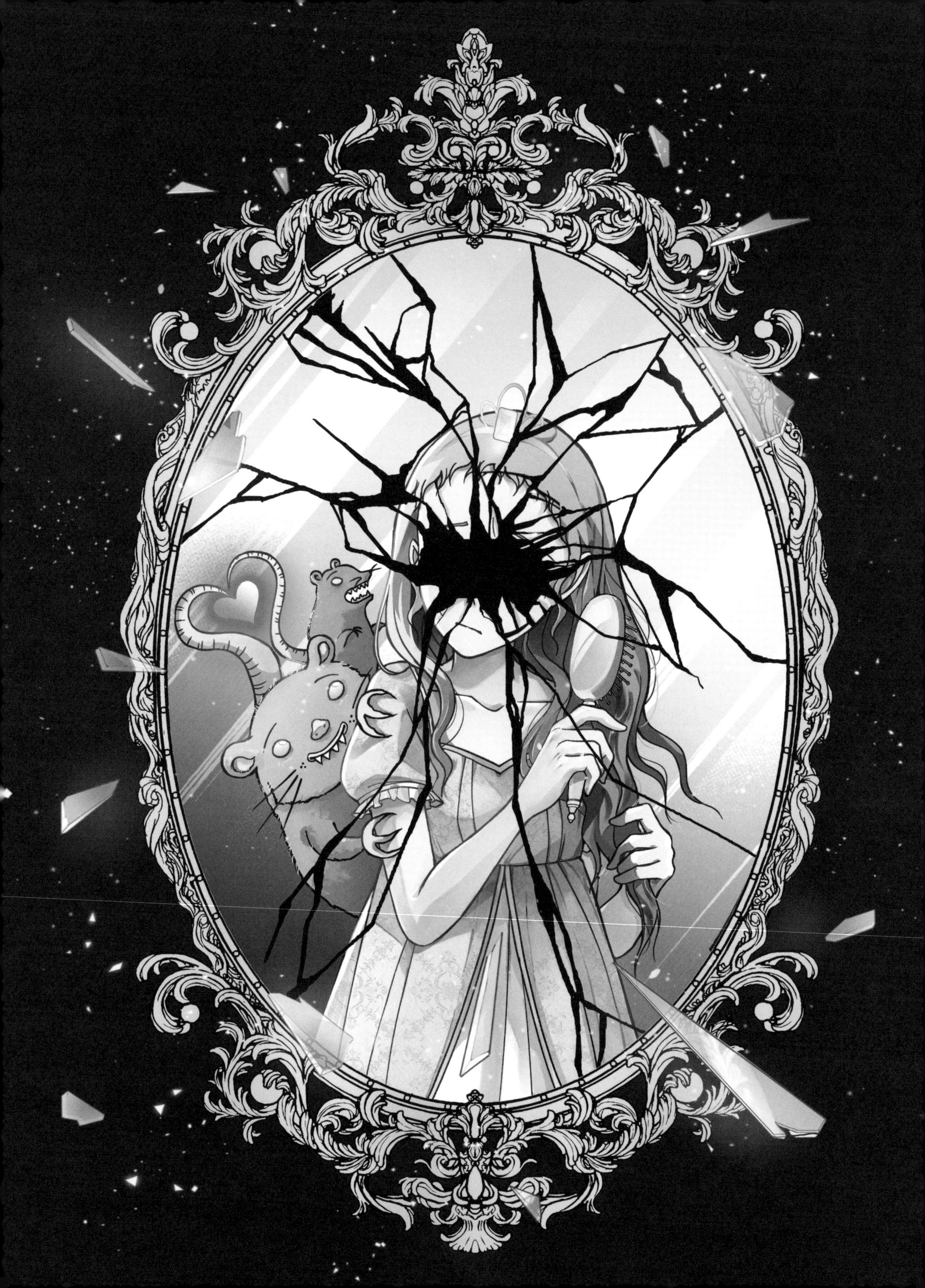

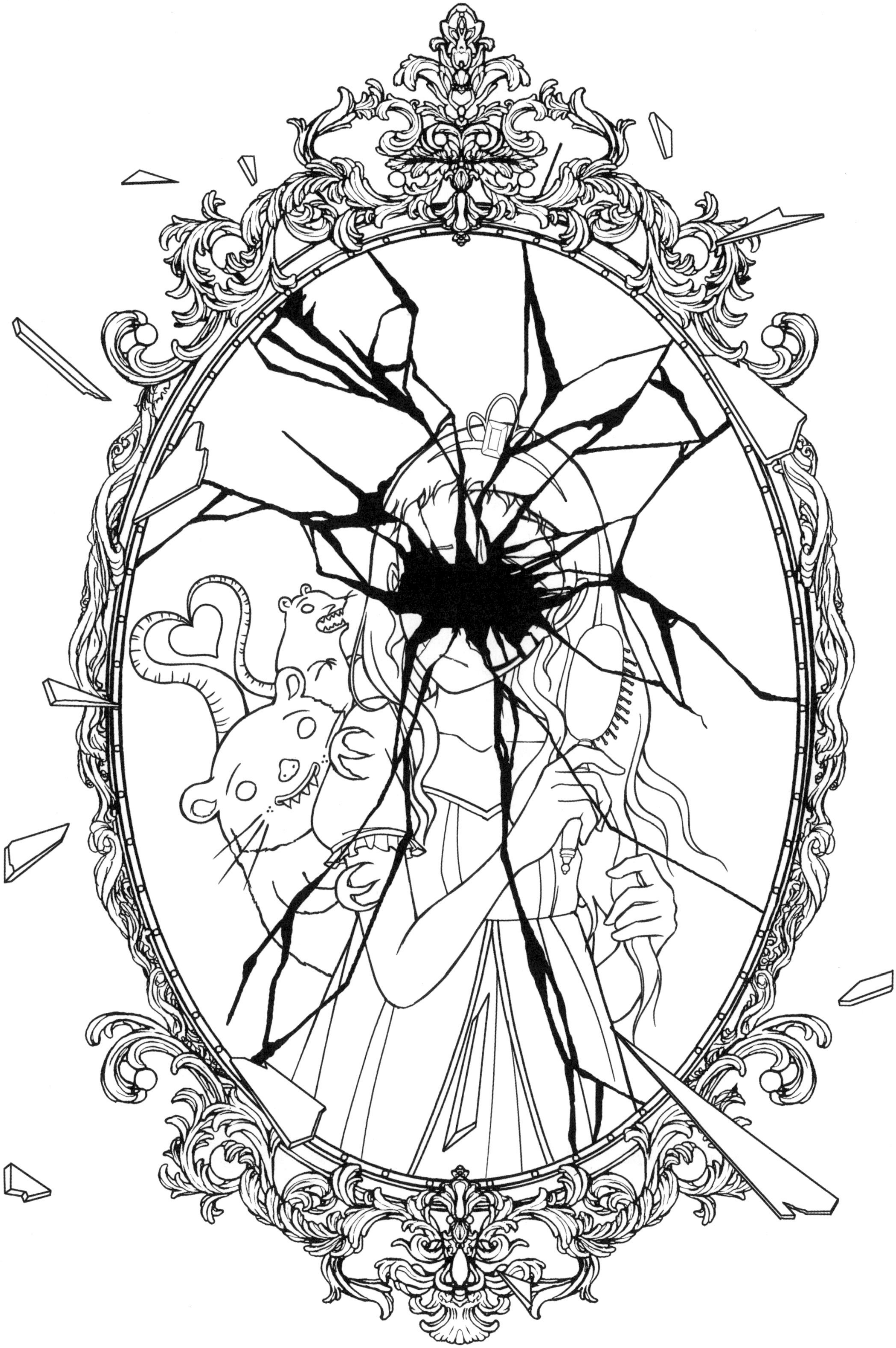

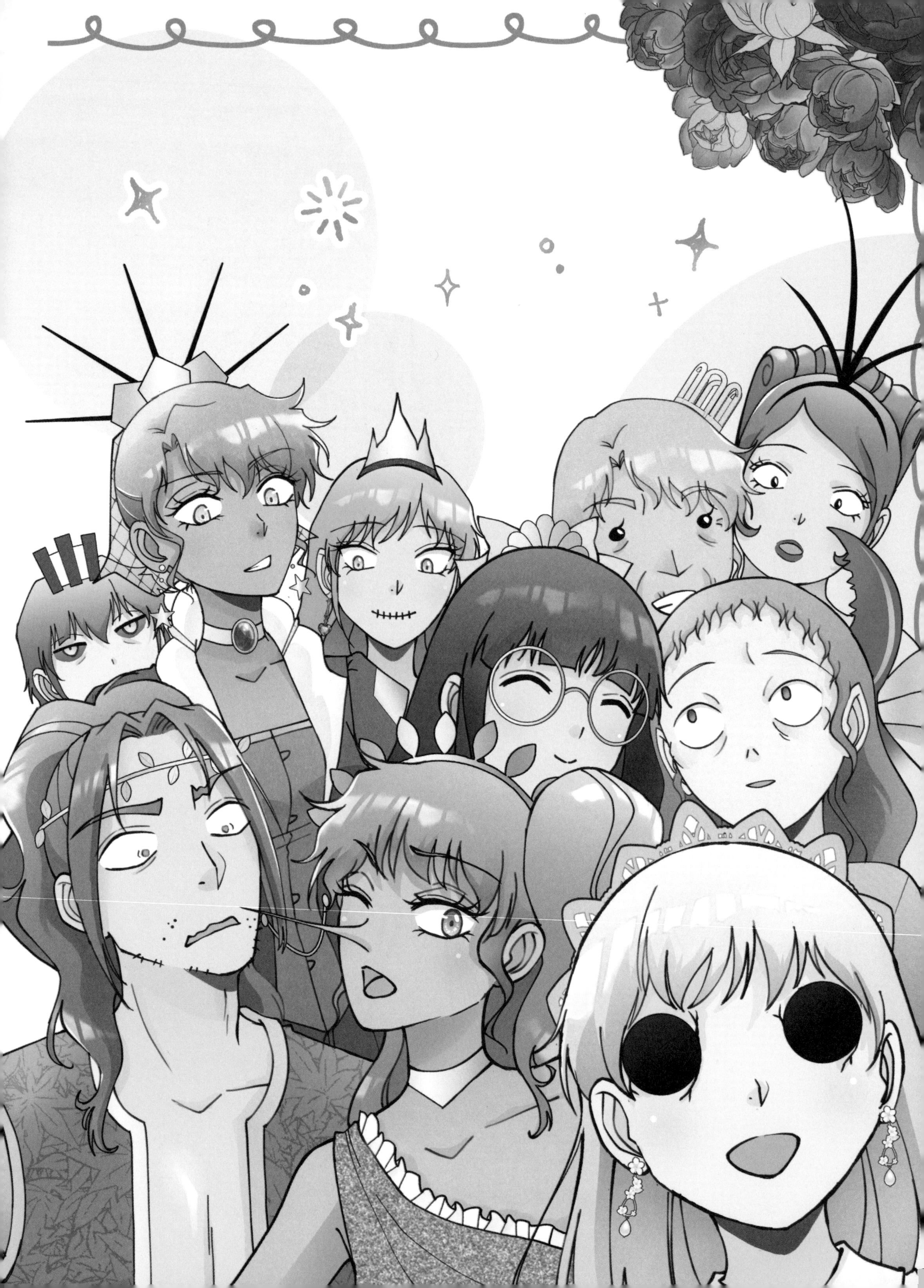

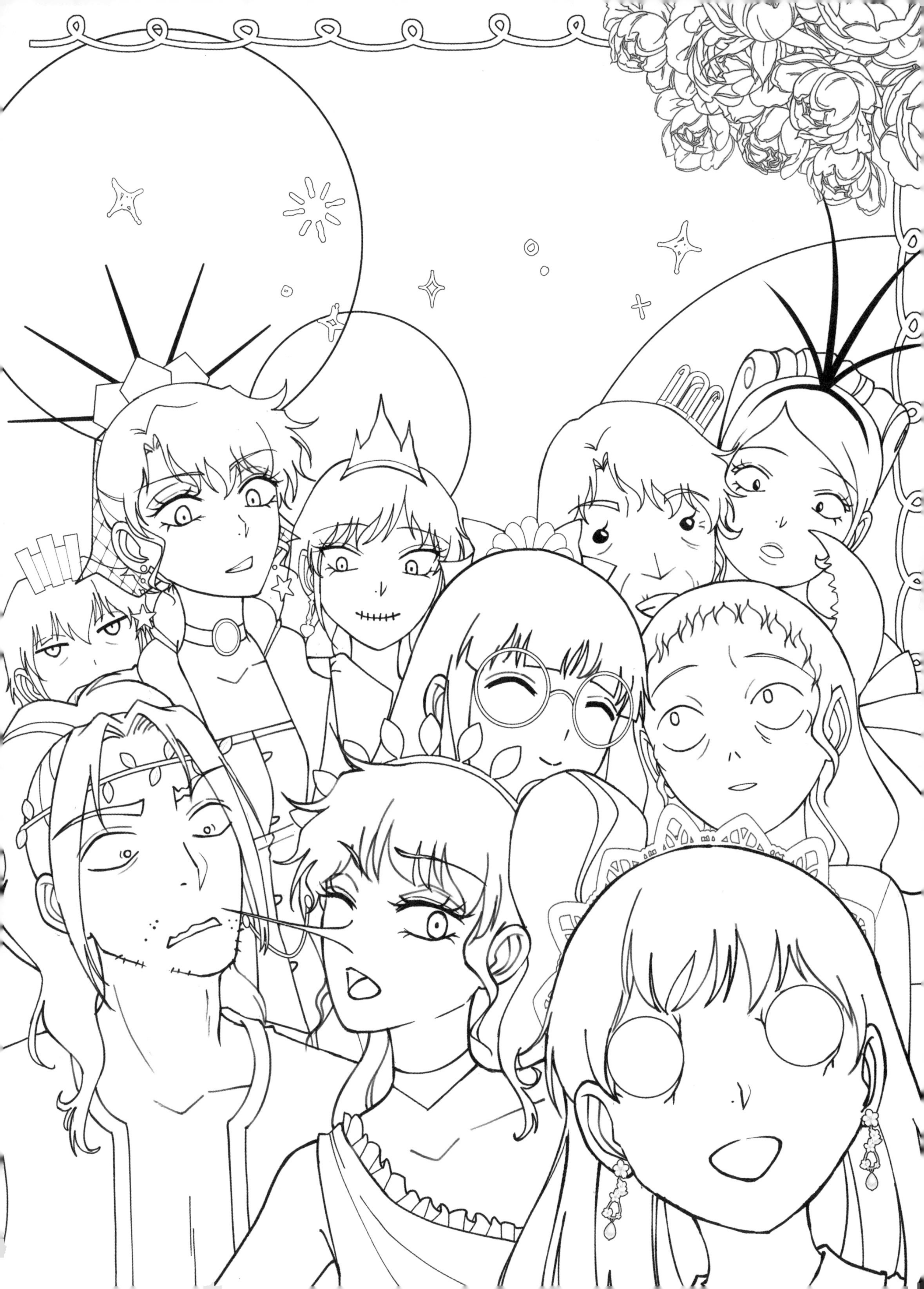

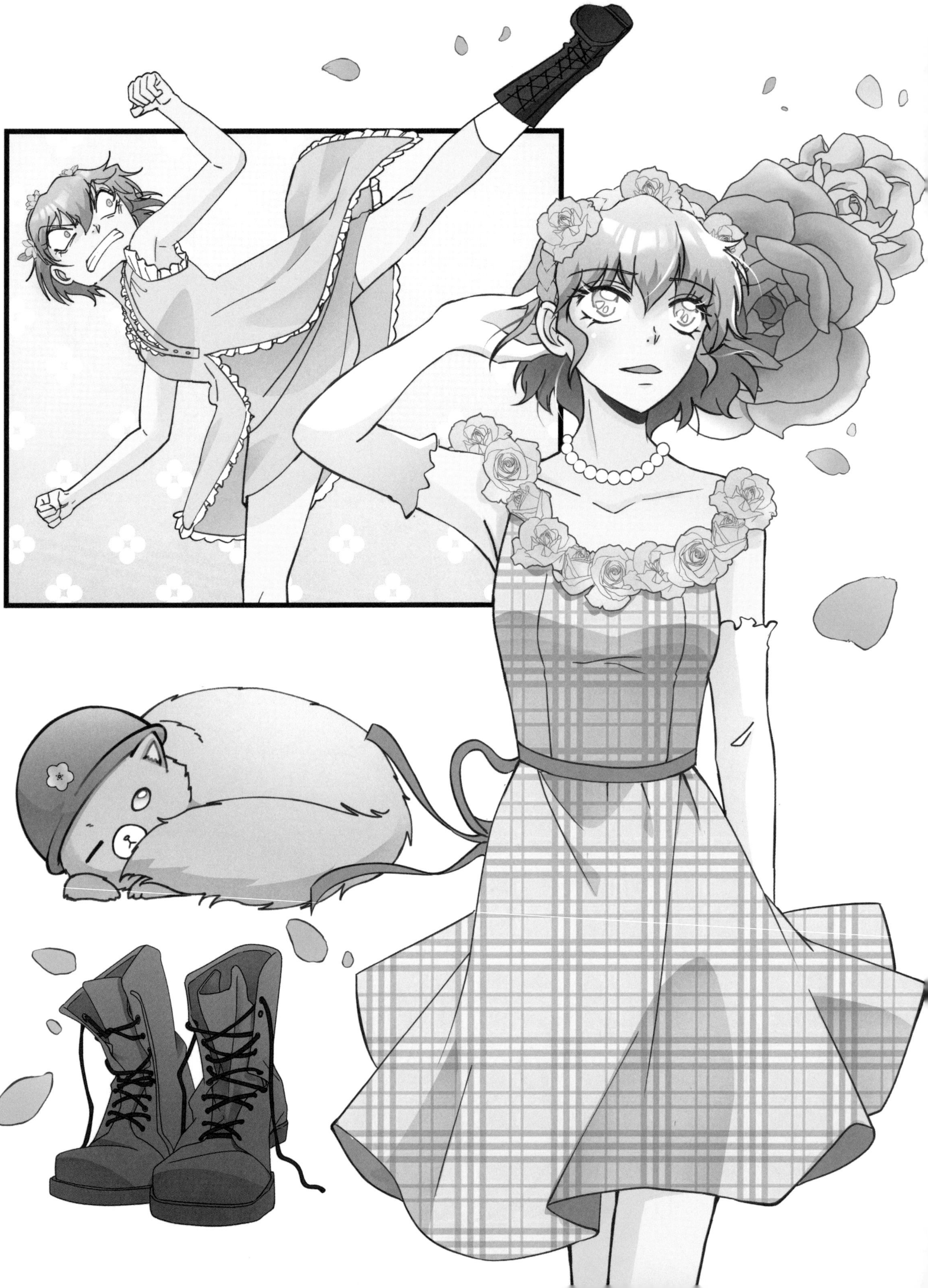

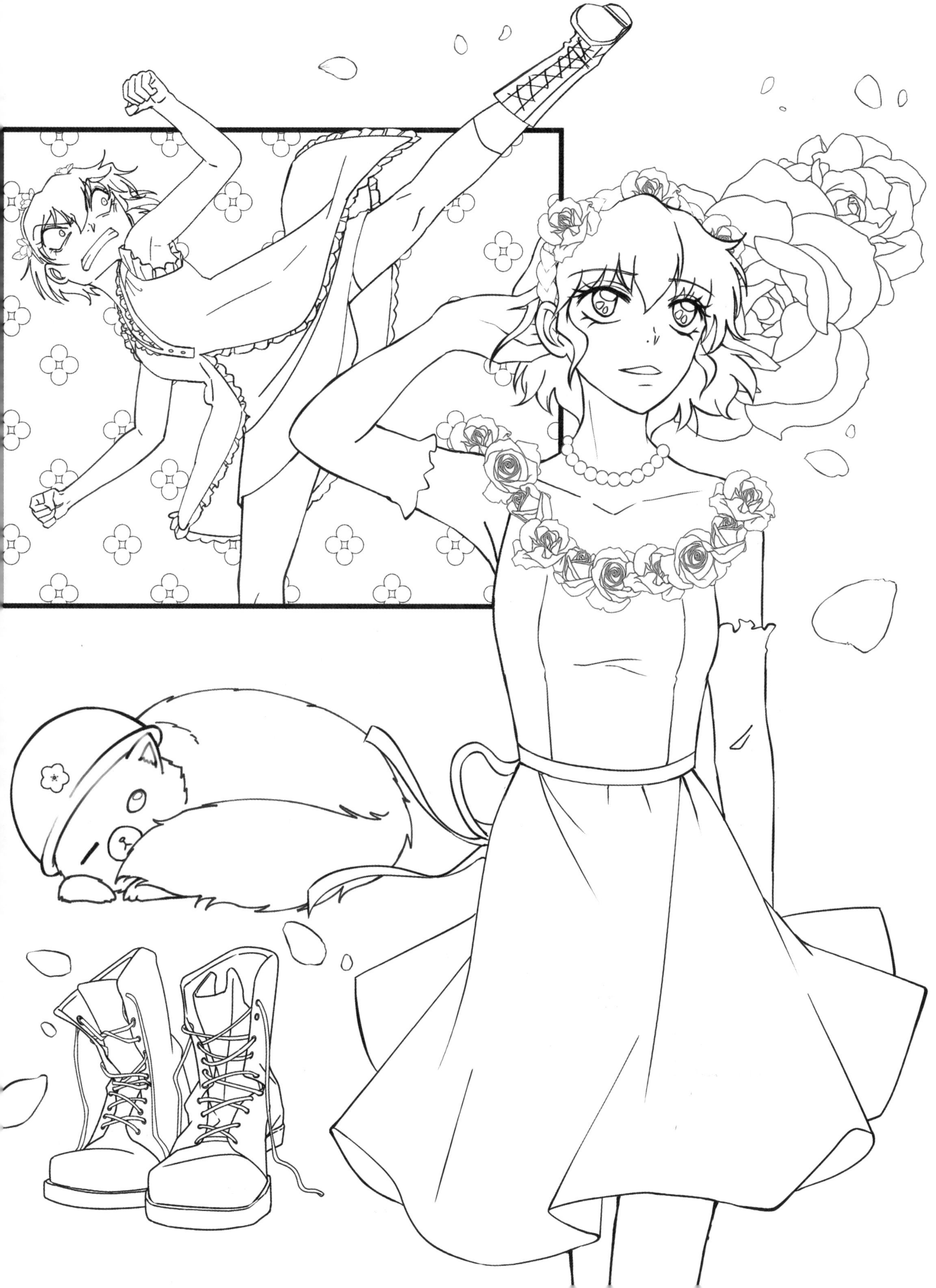

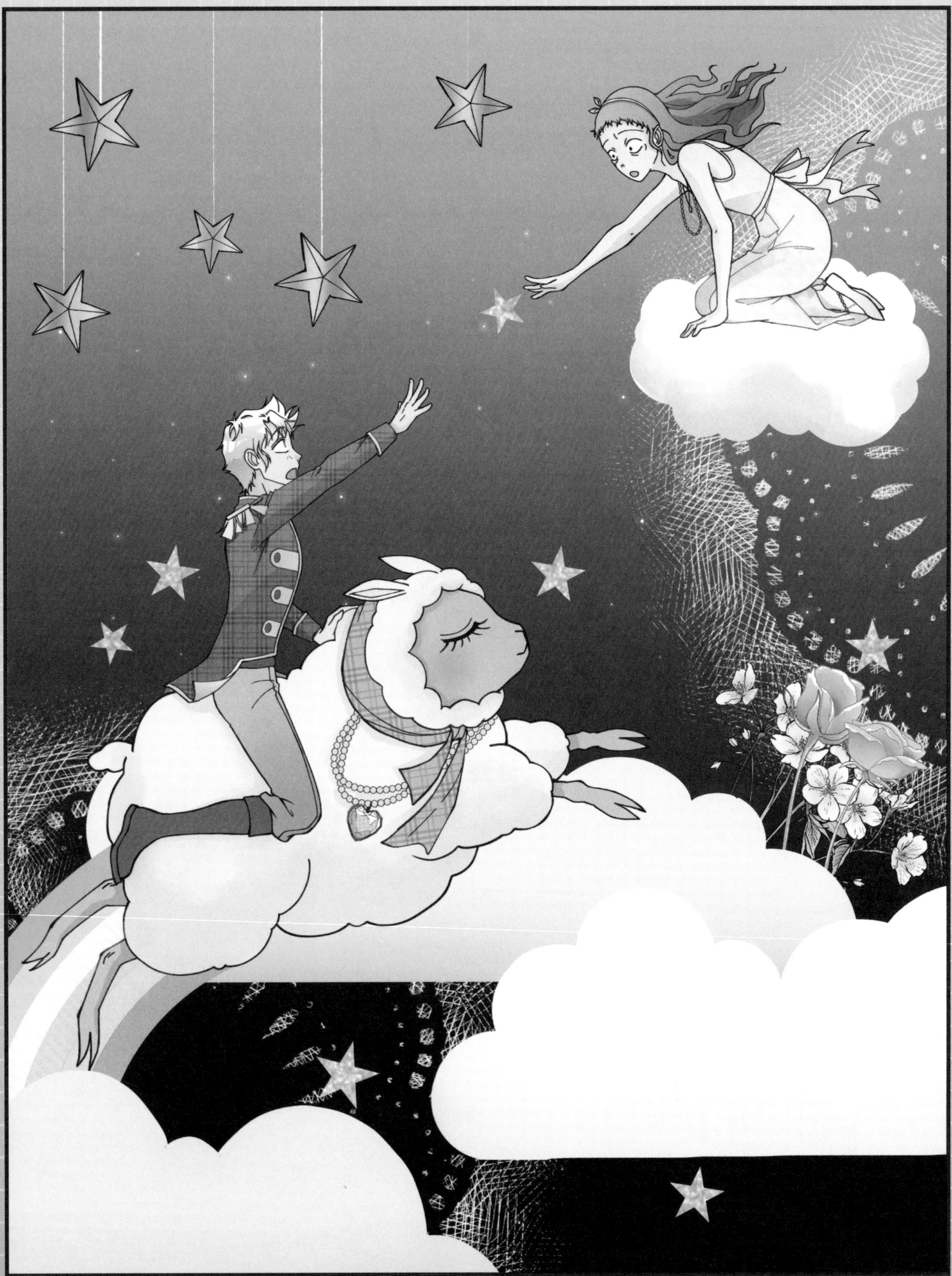

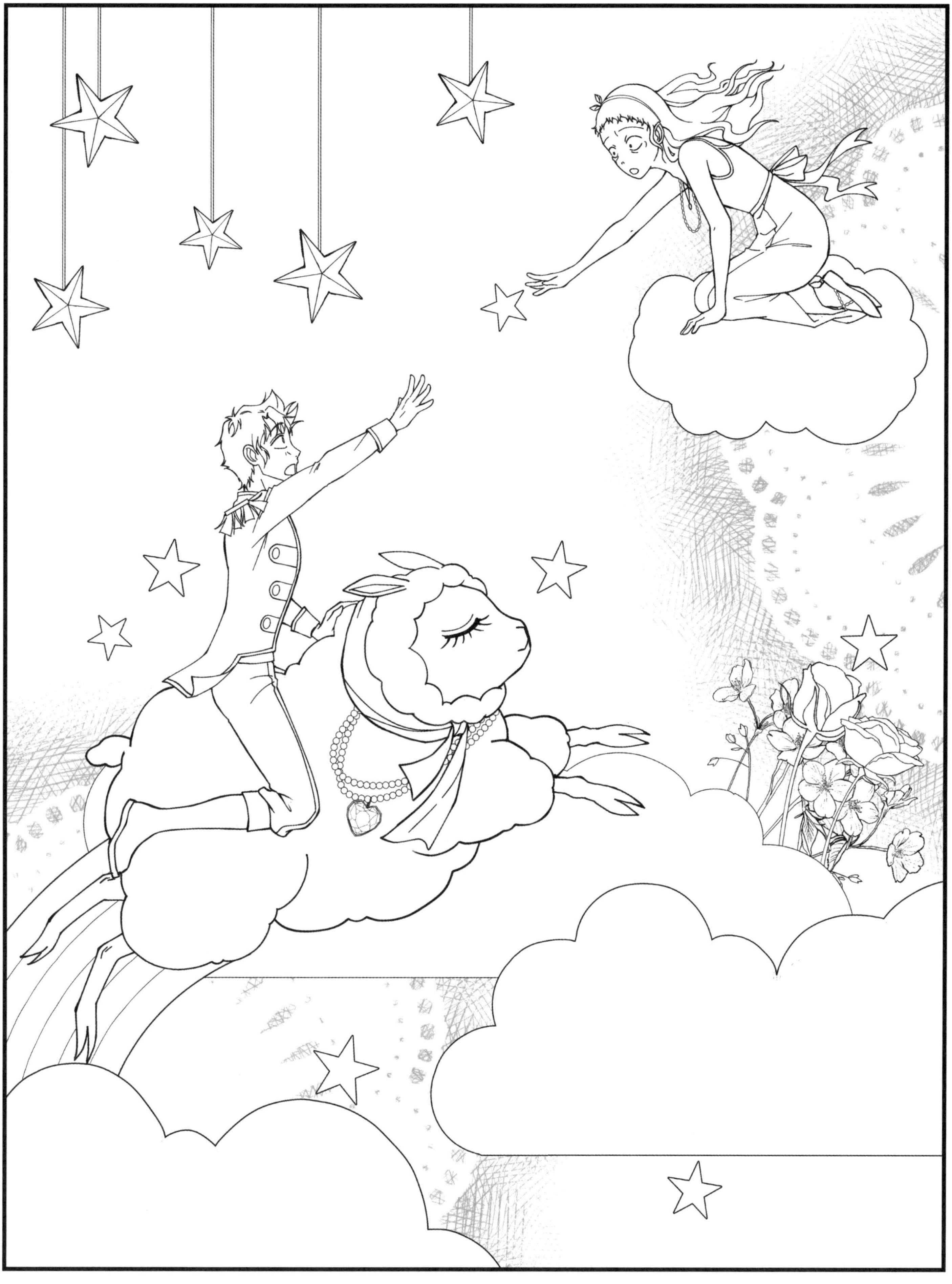

Quarto.com | WalterFoster.com

First Published in 2024 by Walter Foster Publishing, an imprint of The Quarto Group,
100 Cummings Center, Suite 265-D, Beverly, MA 01915, USA.
T (978) 282-9590 F (978) 283-2742

Walter Foster Publishing titles are also available at discount for retail, wholesale, promotional, and bulk purchase. For details, contact the Special Sales Manager by email at specialsales@quarto.com or by mail at The Quarto Group, Attn: Special Sales Manager, 100 Cummings Center, Suite 265-D, Beverly, MA 01915, USA.

10 9 8 7 6 5 4 3 2 1

ISBN: 978-0-7603-8975-1

Select line art: Gonzalo Garcia Rodriguez
WEBTOON Rights and Licensing Manager: Amanda Chen

Printed in USA

ABOUT THE CREATOR

LambCat is a small, omnivorous, and easily frightened creature who has burrowed deep into the Pacific Northwest to draw comics and make music.

For more from LambCat, check out:

patreon.com/iamlambcat

Instagram: @iamlambcat

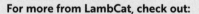